"Sign the contract, Laura, and let's get married," Jake urged.

"One thing, though," he added quietly.

"What's that?" Laura murmured, her heart leaping.

"We both know this isn't a love match. I don't want you to hope it will be. No emotional entanglements. If love becomes an issue, then the marriage will be dissolved."

He had said the words in a kindly voice, but Laura knew he meant them. Now he held out a pen. She took it and signed quickly. Then she stared up into his eyes.

She almost told him then. Almost said that she had already broken the contract. That she was desperately in love with him.

"Okay," she said instead, attempting a smile.

Jake folded the papers. "All right, Party of the Second Part." He smiled. "Are you ready to marry Party of the First Part?"

Dear Reader,

Welcome to Silhouette **Special Edition**...welcome to romance. This month we have six wonderful books to celebrate Valentine's Day just right!

Premiering this month is our newest promotion. THAT'S MY BABY! will alternate with THAT SPECIAL WOMAN! and will feature stories from some of your favorite authors. Marking this very special debut is *The Cowboy and His Baby* by Sherryl Woods. It's the third book of her heartwarming series AND BABY MAKES THREE.

Reader favorite Christine Rimmer returns to North Magdalene for another tale of THE JONES GANG in her book, *The Man, The Moon and The Marriage Vow*. The wonderful Joan Elliott Pickart continues her newest series, THE BABY BET, in Special Edition this month. *Friends, Lovers...and Babies!* is book two of the MacAllister family series. Also in February, Pamela Toth introduces the Buchanan Brothers in *Buchanan's Bride*— it's the first book in her series, BUCKLES & BRONCOS. Sharon De Vita's *Child of Midnight* is her first for Special Edition, a passionate story about a runaway boy, a caring woman and the renegade cop who loves them both. And finally, Kelly Jamison's *The Wedding Contract* is a marriage-of-convenience story not to be missed!

So join us for an unforgettable February! I hope you enjoy all these stories!

Sincerely,

Tara Gavin
Senior Editor

Please address questions and book requests to:
Silhouette Reader Service
U.S.: 3010 Walden Ave., P.O. Box 1325, Buffalo, NY 14269
Canadian: P.O. Box 609, Fort Erie, Ont. L2A 5X3

KELLY JAMISON

THE WEDDING CONTRACT

Published by Silhouette Books
America's Publisher of Contemporary Romance

For Daryl, for twenty-five great years.

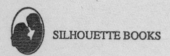 SILHOUETTE BOOKS

ISBN 0-373-24014-7

THE WEDDING CONTRACT

Copyright © 1996 by Linda Buechting

Printed in U.S.A.

Books by Kelly Jamison

Silhouette Special Edition

The Wedding Contract #1014

Silhouette Desire

Echoes from the Heart #579
Hearts in Hiding #626
Heartless #760
Will #798
The Daddy Factor #885
Forsaken Father #930

KELLY JAMISON

grew up in a small town and often makes rural communities the settings for her books. After her college graduation, she worked for a newspaper that was so tiny it didn't even have its own camera. Whenever a staff member needed to take a picture, he'd borrow a camera from the woman next door.

Kelly is a rabid chocoholic and pizza addict who also paints in watercolors and rides her bike. She has also written as Kelly Adams.

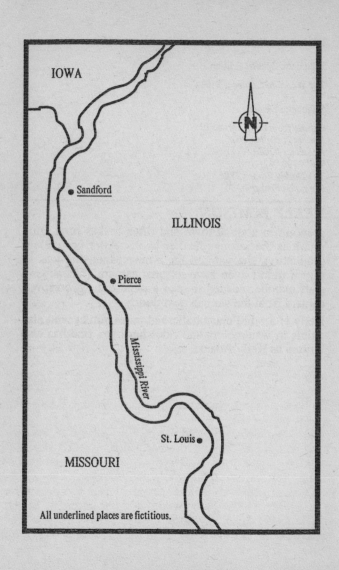

IOWA

ILLINOIS

● Sandford

● Pierce

Mississippi River

St. Louis ●

MISSOURI

All underlined places are fictitious.

Chapter One

He could tell that the red-haired woman across the room wasn't enjoying the party any more than he was. He caught a glimpse of her searching furtively for an escape avenue—at least it looked like escape she was seeking if her frown was any indication—before a large woman in an equally large flowered print dress accosted her, effectively blocking his view of the long red hair and the frown.

Jake McClennon wasn't in the mood for a party. Especially not a party that wasn't really a party. This one was a fund-raiser, thinly disguised as a celebration of the town's historic past.

He would have preferred to prop his feet up on the nearest chair and pop the tab on a cold soda. But Jake couldn't do either of those things. The first, because there wasn't a chair sturdy enough in the whole mausoleum of a house that wouldn't crumble under the weight of two shoes, and the second because the party served only champagne punch, and he didn't drink anymore. He supposed he could get a bottle of mineral water if he asked the circulating waiter, but the nervous, tuxedoed boy looked as if he'd been forbidden to speak.

So Jake leaned against a shadowed wall, partially obscured by a large predatory-looking plant, and sipped the paper cup of water he'd purloined from the bathroom.

He wouldn't have been here if he hadn't agreed in a moment of weakness to join the Historic Home Preservation Committee of Sandford, Illinois. He had nothing against historic homes—actually he made his living restoring them. What he didn't like was committees. Or fund-raisers.

While he was making lists of things he didn't like, he might as well add the splinter he'd lodged in his thumb that morning. Preoccupied and harried, he'd grabbed a two-by-four and let it slide through his hands, thereby acquiring the splinter. He wouldn't have been so careless if his mind hadn't been on his financial books. He had to find time to work on them soon or the IRS would send a less-than-polite inquiry about his next quarterly tax payment.

He wondered if the redhead worried about taxes.

He had her in his line of sight again when two women in their late sixties stopped in front of him, blocking his view.

"I *heard* she was back in town," one of them said. "I just didn't believe it."

She was pointing, and Jake followed her accusing finger to the redhead. The only other woman in that vicinity was the flower-garden dress, and Jake would bet that no one worried about *her* being back in town.

"Why?" the other woman asked. "What did she do?"

Jake found himself straining to hear the answer.

The first woman shook her head. "She was wild, that girl. They threw her in jail once. Oh, yes, I remember that well. Her father wouldn't post bail, so she stayed at the juvenile detention home. And of course she 'had' to get married. She was quite the scandal."

"I don't remember that."

"Oh, it was a long time ago," the first woman said. "She's probably in her late twenties now."

"I wonder why she came back?"

"That child had no shame. From what I hear she's going to cause just as much a ruckus this time. She's got a child from some man who died recently. They say the son's mother doesn't want that woman raising her grandchild. The girl's parents are dead now, so I guess she thought she'd bring her problems back where they started." The woman turned to her companion, and Jake saw her raise her brows in skepticism. "Of course she may have changed by now."

"Even so, a lot of people will remember. I wouldn't want to come back here to live with *her* past," her friend said. "A pity, too. She's such a pretty girl."

So the redhead had more to worry about than taxes, Jake mused as the two gossipers moved on. He abruptly remembered his mother dragging him to see a little theater production of *The Music Man*. He'd been a kid who'd thought plays, especially plays with singing, were worse than even the most diabolical vegetable a parent could force on a child. The one thing about the play that stood out in his mind was a song about the hero's interest in women who had made mistakes in their lives.

Jake hadn't really understood the song, but he'd sensed there was something to it, and he'd asked his mother about it later. His mother, to her credit, had sat him down and given him a straight explanation. The mistakes the women in the song made, his mother had said, were the kind that involved choosing the wrong man and the wrong time and, most of all, the wrong person to find out about it. She told him that he already knew about sex, but this was about what rules there were when it came to sex. Some women broke the old cardinal rule, the rule that said a woman did not have sex with a man until they were married. And she certainly didn't have a baby out of wedlock. The woman usually ended up paying for that lesson, his mother had said, even in this day and age. She wanted him to remember that, because when he got older she didn't want him making any woman pay for something that was half his fault.

He'd always remembered what she'd said, but it wasn't until he was older that he understood it. And, now, he still sometimes saw a woman pay the price. It had happened to his own brother John and his wife.

But Jake had no romantic interest in a woman who'd paid her dues. In fact he had no long-term romantic interest in any woman. After the death of his wife he'd found himself unable to feel anything for any other woman. That realization plus his grief had nearly driven him insane. The bottom of a beer bottle had provided temporary relief until the solution became more painful than the problem—now he stuck to soda.

He lived alone, working long hours, making his life as simple and uncluttered as possible. So he really had no interest in the pretty redhead, not even as he watched her dodge a group of men who looked intent on preening before her like peacocks. The redhead escaped them by smiling and gliding quietly around them into another room.

Laura Halstead resisted the urge to press her cold glass of champagne punch against her forehead. She was beginning to wish Alison hadn't invited her to this party. But she could never refuse Ali much of anything, not even when they were in school together and Ali would insist on restyling Laura's hair or wiping off some of the heavy makeup she had applied.

This was more than hair and makeup, though. This was having to endure the whispers of women her mother's age who remembered her as an adolescent and the not-so-subtle approaches of men who had only heard the rumors and wanted to check them out in person.

This wasn't even Ali's house. Huge, cold monster of a house that it was, it belonged to the chairman of the Historic Home Preservation Committee, a woman who had flinched visibly when Ali had suggested a week ago, with Laura in tow, that Laura should attend the fund-raiser.

"Laura bought the old Connally house and she's going to open a shop here," Ali had persisted in her quiet but firm way. "She'll be a valuable addition to the group."

Laura had seen in the woman's face that she was all but biting her tongue to keep from asking just what kind of shop Laura planned to open.

But in the end she had accepted Laura's forty dollars and handed over a dinner ticket. It had taken all of Ali's convincing to make Laura believe that this party would be good for her future business.

"So this is where you're hiding," a voice said, making Laura jump before she recognized Ali.

"I'm in danger of inciting mob action in there," Laura said, nodding toward the other room.

Ali laughed. "They'll get over it. Trust me. As soon as they see how successful your shop becomes, your money will be as moral as theirs."

Laura grinned. Ali never pulled any punches.

"So what do you think?" Laura teased her. "Should I go back out there and start putting silverware in my purse? Or maybe I should unbutton my blouse to the waist. I'm sure that's what they all expect."

"The ladies would faint, and the men would drool themselves to death, not that they're not doing that already," Ali said dryly. "What I want you to do is go back out there and introduce yourself to Jake McClennon. He's the one I told you about who restores old houses. He'd do a great job on your place."

"Ali," Laura protested gently, "I'm not in the mood to meet any more men tonight."

"This one's different."

"Aren't they all?" Laura retorted dryly.

Ali considered that. "Given this group, yes, they're different. But Jake's not like them. Trust me."

Someone in the next room was calling Ali's name, and she backed to the door. "Do it now," she said before she disappeared.

Laura sighed and moved away from the wall. Ali had neglected to tell her which of the men here was Jake McClennon. She would find the house restorer at some point, but not right now. Right now she didn't think she could manage to paste a smile on her face for any man, not even the one who could restore her neglected Victorian home.

Maybe she'd made a mistake coming back, she thought wearily. This was harder than she'd expected. And the last thing she wanted was to make her daughter Molly unhappy.

But so far she was doing just that. Seven years old, Molly was uprooted from her old school and friends—and her grandmother. But if she hadn't moved here with Molly she was afraid that both she and her daughter would have succumbed to Trina Halstead's suffocating presence. Of course eighty miles wasn't a big distance, and Trina seemed to navigate it quite easily. The woman had come to see Molly several times. Laura didn't object to that. What she did object to was Trina's veiled threats and disapproval of Laura as a parent.

She broke off her thoughts as she realized she was standing in the doorway and two people were approaching her from different sides of the room. One of them was a tall man dressed in jeans. She didn't have time to dwell on the put-upon expression on the man's face because the second person reached her first, Mrs. Constance Fife Beachem, the hostess of the gala.

"Miss Halstead," the woman said, holding out a stiff hand.

"*Mrs.* Halstead," Laura responded firmly but politely, knowing that the mistake was deliberate. She shook the woman's hand and met her eyes.

Mrs. Fife Beachem insisted that her friends call her Corky, but there had been no such invitation issued to Laura.

"Well, dear, I'm glad you could come."

"You have a lovely home," Laura said, wondering what Corky was waiting to say. Bad news was lurking in her eyes and the tightness around her mouth.

"Thank you, Laura. Tippy and I just put so much effort into it, but it's well worth the money we spent." Tippy, short for Tipton, was Mr. Fife Beachem, according to Ali. Tippy and Corky. The first image that came to mind was of two poodles.

"We are about ready to serve dinner," Corky said, beginning to look somewhat discomfited. "And I thought that...well, that is, that you might be a bit uncomfortable with the others." Corky cleared her throat and glanced back over her shoulder. Following her gaze, Laura saw the precipitator of all this discomfort. Trina Halstead, Laura's mother-in-law, stood in the middle of the room, her glare fixed on Laura.

"I see," Laura said quietly.

"Trina Halstead has made a lovely contribution to our restoration efforts, and she'll be seated at the main table for dinner. I'm sure you understand why you can't stay. It's just that..."

Corky's voice trailed off, but Laura understood perfectly. The ticket for which she had paid forty dollars in advance, was no longer good. Because Trina Halstead had paid more to keep her out.

"Mrs. Halstead," a quiet voice at her elbow said, "are you ready to go? We'll miss our dinner reservations if we don't hurry."

Confused, she turned to see the put-upon man in jeans glancing at his watch. "I hate to run, Corky, but we really must. The party was up to your usual standards." The last was said in a dry tone left open to interpretation.

"But," Corky said, her startled eyes going from one of them to the other, "but, Jake, dinner's just starting."

"And I'm so sorry to miss it," the man called Jake said smoothly, lightly holding Laura's elbow with one hand. "But this lady did expect to have dinner tonight."

Corky flushed slightly as the admonishment sank in. "Well, I..." she began, then regained her composure. "I appreciate your coming."

"Good night," Jake called cheerfully, steering Laura toward the door. She just had time to plunk her glass down on a marble-topped umbrella stand in the hall before Jake pulled her toward the closet.

"What did you have on?" he asked, rummaging through the clothing hanging there.

"A navy blue knit jacket," she murmured, pointing to it.

Jake pulled it off the hanger and helped her put it on, his hands brushing her shoulders. She shivered slightly and glanced at the group of people clustered around the doorway, shuffling their feet and trying not to be too obvious about their nosiness.

"We don't want to be late, Laura," Jake said loudly, propelling her out the door. "Which car is yours?" he asked under his breath.

"The red one," she said, pointing to the used compact she'd bought three years before.

"Keys," he said, holding out his hand. She marveled that she was turning over her keys to this man she had yet to meet. All she knew was that his name was Jake, and she was going off with him without benefit of an introduction.

She had to hurry to keep up with his long stride. He didn't say anything else as he helped her into the car, then came around and got in the driver's side. They pulled into the gathering dusk, and Laura folded her arms against the chill. Early October evenings cooled quickly in the part of Illinois that perched on the Mississippi River.

Ostensibly she kept her eyes straight ahead though she was able to assess him from the corner of her vision. His hair was black, tinged with gray at the sides. She would guess that he was close to forty and that he did outside work because the hand that had cupped her elbow had been strong and calloused, and the fading tan was in sharp contrast with his white shirt. And, he was wearing jeans to a benefit dinner. The other men at the party had been paler, less muscled and certainly more expensively dressed.

Jake. Jake. The name sounded familiar. Of course! This was Jake McClennon, the man who restored houses. This was the man Ali had insisted she meet.

Well, she'd certainly met him all right. Ali couldn't fault her on that.

She turned and met a pair of frankly assessing gray eyes. Laura didn't look away, and a moment later he turned back to the road. *Nice face,* she thought. To be honest, he had nice everything. All the more reason for her to keep her distance.

"I just have one question," she said without looking at him.

"Sure."

"Where are we going?"

She could feel him weighing something in his mind, and she couldn't help herself from looking at him again. He had a strong face with a full mouth and a jaw that could only be described as chiseled. On that face she saw some of the determination that had apparently made him rescue her from the formidable Corky Beachem.

"I told Corky that we have dinner reservations, so I'm taking you to dinner."

"Are you psychic?" she asked dryly. "Or does Mrs. Beachem disinvite guests at all of her parties?"

"No, I think you're a first." He met her eyes. "Do you like hamburgers?"

"Do I like hamburgers?" she repeated. "Yes, I like hamburgers. Maybe not as much as I would have liked that forty-dollar steak dinner, but at the moment hamburgers are better than starving."

"That's the spirit," he said, sounding relieved, though she didn't know why. "I know this place where they grind their own fresh meat and then grill the burgers over a nice hot flame and smother them with catsup, onions, tomatoes and this great homemade relish." His eyes, filled with amusement, met hers again. "I know it's not steak," he said, "but you don't have to eat with Corky Beachem watching. That has to be worth something."

"Oh, that's worth a whole lot," Laura said with heartfelt relief. *And Trina Halstead wouldn't be watching, either.*

"Good. I thought that might be the case."

He must be nuts, Jake thought as he helped her from the car. He didn't even know this woman, and from what he'd overheard at the party she wasn't his type. Not that he had a type anymore.

It had been six years since his wife had died, and he'd come to the sad conclusion some time ago that there was never going to be another woman he could feel as comfortable with as he had with Beverly. He had decided that he was one of those men destined to go through the rest of his life alone, like it or not.

This Laura Halstead was an attractive woman. He liked her red hair and her soft blue eyes that had reflected such pain when Corky Beachem sent her away without the dinner she'd paid for. And she looked awfully good in the full blue skirt and high-necked polka dot blouse, the way they clung to her hips and breasts when she moved.

But he wasn't interested in pursuing her on any romantic level.

"One thing bothers me," she said, halting in the parking lot and looking up at the bright red neon sign advertising the Burger Haven. The screen door hung half off its hinges, and several letters of Burger Haven had burnt out. The cinder block construction wasn't any too inviting, either.

"What's that?" he asked, thinking that there were probably a lot of things about the Burger Haven to bother one. He found himself wondering which of the many she would choose.

"Why do you need reservations here?"

Jake found himself smiling. "Damned if I know, Mrs. Halstead. It sounded good at the time."

He took her elbow again and helped her into the dim interior. It took a moment for Laura's eyes to adjust, and then she smiled. The place was decorated, if that was the correct word for what she saw on the walls, with photographs of movie stars, past and present, some autographed and some not. Whoever owned the Burger Haven had a serious case of star struck.

She didn't have time to ask Jake because as soon as he had seated her in a red plastic-covered booth, he headed in the other direction. "I have to make a phone call," he said over his shoulder by way of apology.

"Well, of course," Laura said more to herself. Of course he'd bring her to this strange hamburger house and then make a phone call. It made as much sense as anything else had this evening.

She was looking through the menu when he came back. The restaurant was serious about hamburgers—it was the only thing on the menu. Laura realized that a slow blues song was playing on the old jukebox that sat in a dark corner like some neon-clad Buddha. It occurred to her that Jake must have put money in it when he got off the phone.

"Tell me something," she said as he sat down.

Here it comes, he thought. *She wants to know why I decided to play rescuer at the party.* And he had no answer. He supposed he just hated to see people get walked on, especially when the walker wore Corky Fife Beachem's size tens.

"Okay," he said hesitantly, forming an answer already.

"Did you and Mrs. Beachem rehearse that little scene beforehand?"

"What?" he asked, completely baffled.

"Did she arrange for you to sweep me out of there before I caused a scene upon discovering that I'd paid forty dollars for a glass of punch and a cocktail wienie?" It was a lengthy question, and she sat back in the booth, her arms crossed, her eyes on his face.

"Do you know something?" he mused. "You ask the strangest damn questions."

"I just wanted to be sure," she said, apparently satisfied after perusing his features that he was not in league with Corky.

"What were you going to do if I had planned this with Corky?" he asked, taken aback.

"Order three of the most expensive items on the menu," she said without hesitation.

Jake found himself smiling. "That still wouldn't add up to anything near your ticket price," he assured her.

"Dessert, too," she said.

"Oh, well, with dessert," he said teasingly, liking the way her eyes stayed on his face, as if she'd grown accustomed to gauging men from what she saw in their eyes.

"Hi, Jake, what'll you have tonight?" a world-weary voice asked, and Jake realized that Esther had found the time to take their order.

"May I make a suggestion?" Jake asked Laura.

"By all means," she said, shrugging. "Left to my own devices I'd probably order a hamburger."

He let that pass, though it amused him. This Laura Halstead was a confident woman, or at least skilled enough to appear confident. He couldn't imagine Beverly making that comment.

But he quickly put Beverly out of his mind.

"Esther, how's the barbecue sauce tonight?" he asked.

Esther shrugged. "Same as always. Hot. Spicy. You got sinus trouble, this'll fix it."

"No sinus trouble, but we'll take three barbecued burgers with all the trimmings." He looked at Laura for consent.

"Trimmings are fine," she agreed.

"And lattice fries," he said. "And two iced teas."

He looked at her again, and she nodded.

Apparently their order wasn't all Esther had on her mind. She had been studying Laura while Jake was talking. "I thought you were going to that fancy dinner at Madame President's house tonight," she commented.

Jake sighed. Leave it to Esther to probe what was better left alone. "I did. And now I'm here. Okay?" He was even more grouchy given the fact that he'd only now realized he'd never introduced himself to Laura. He'd just whisked her out of the house, and she'd come—willingly, which was even more of a surprise. People normally didn't allow themselves to get whisked without knowing the name of the one doing the whisking.

Esther shrugged, apparently not noticing his touchy mood. "It's okay with me. If you want a burger instead of lobster à la hoity-toity, or whatever they were eating there, that's fine with me."

"I'm glad it meets with your approval, Esther," Jake said, still annoyed.

"Probably that French cooking," Esther said to Laura. "You know, itty-bitty helpings. Jake likes enough food to cover a plate."

"Really?" Laura said. "He must eat here a lot."

"Oh, he does," Esther said, slipping her pencil behind her ear but making no attempt to leave. "Him and Billy and Frank. Sometimes I feed 'em breakfast, lunch and supper."

"Esther, do you think we could get our meal before we shrivel away to nothing here?" Jake asked impatiently.

Esther grinned. "Sure." She turned to go, then looked back, frowning. "You want a candle or something?" she asked.

"Hell, no!" Jake said, both hands coming down on the table, hard. "We want our dinner! Period!"

"Okay." Esther grinned again and left this time.

"She likes you," Laura commented, amused by his discomfort. He was looking anywhere except at her.

"People usually feed those they like."

"And she's wondering what I'm doing here with you," Laura continued, trying not to smile. It struck her that Jake was acting as if he was wondering the same thing.

"We could just tell her the truth," Laura suggested.

"Which is?"

"That I'm hiring you to restore my house, Mr. McClennon. What else?"

He was thunderstruck by two things. The first was that she actually knew who he was, when he'd been trying to figure out how to introduce the fact this late in the conversation. *Oh, by the way, my name's Jake McClennon. I may have forgotten to mention that when we made our grand exit.* And the second was that she apparently was going to ignore this whole business of Esther's curiosity about Jake being seen with a woman.

"You have a house that needs restoring?" He was beginning to think that his precipitous action at Corky's house had put him in the middle of something he didn't understand at all.

"I bought the old Connally place," she went on, unperturbed by his surprise. "To be honest, I don't have a lot of money to put into it right now, but I would like to get done whatever I can afford. Which, of course, is up to you."

Those two gossipers were right—she had to be only in her twenties, he thought, watching her. But there was a reserve about her, a way she had of masking her emotions that made her appear much older than her years—And more experienced. He was the one feeling like an awkward kid here. He hadn't handled this well at all, whatever *this* was. And he still had no idea why he'd felt he had to rescue this woman from Corky Beachem. Laura probably would have cut the woman down to size and done it deftly.

If not for the hurt he'd seen in her eyes.

"Would you like me to look at your house?" he asked.

"Yes, if that's your normal procedure. And an estimate?" She raised her hands in a vague gesture. "I don't know. I've never bought a house before, much less had any work done on one."

"There are no rules," he assured her with a smile. "I can take a look at it tomorrow morning if you'd like."

"Yes, tomorrow morning. That would be fine."

Esther set down two glasses of iced tea and then stood waiting.

"What is it?" he asked patiently.

"What should I tell Billy and Frank about this?"

"About what?" he asked testily.

"About you being here with a woman," she said in a tone that meant *What else?*

"And I'm guessing you think that's their business," Jake snapped. "Or *your* business," he added pointedly.

Esther grinned. "Men are so touchy," she volunteered to Laura. "Yes, it's my business," she said to Jake, "and it's those boys' business because we've been trying for years to get you to go out with a woman, and you always act like we're trying to match you up with some kind of... deadly insect. And we've all been worried sick about you for a long time. Now if that don't qualify us to get involved in your business, I don't know what does."

"Lord help me," Jake said. "Esther, this is not a date. Do you understand?"

"It looks like a date," she said practically.

"I don't care what it looks like. Mrs. Halstead wants me to work on her house."

So they were back to Mrs. Halstead, Laura noticed.

"Business," Esther repeated skeptically. "All right, all right. If that's what you want to call it, fine. It's just that when I been worrying over you, a thirty-nine-year-old man who acts like he's seventy-nine, for as long as I have, I think I have a right to know a little something about how things are going with you."

"Things are going fine," Jake said from between his teeth.

"You call if you need anything."

"Food, Esther, food," Jake prompted.

"Hold your horses. It's coming." She reached into her apron pocket and pulled out some kind of vine. Humming to herself, she leaned over the table and appropriated Jake's water glass. She stuck the vine in the glass and moved it to the center of the table, adjusting it until she was satisfied.

"And what's that?" Jake demanded.

"It's your centerpiece," Esther said, looking offended that he wouldn't recognize that right off the bat.

"We don't need a centerpiece," he grumbled. "And where did you get it anyway? It's not poison ivy, is it?"

"Yes you do need one if you're entertaining a lady," Esther countered. "I got it out back, and how should I know if it's poison ivy? If it is, I might just sprinkle some on your burger."

She swished away, leaving Laura trying to hide her smile from Jake, who still looked aggrieved.

"Do Frank and Billy give you as much trouble as Esther does?" she finally asked, grinning.

"They're small potatoes compared to Esther," Jake said, leaning back and briefly closing his eyes.

When he looked at Laura again she could see that he was wondering what she thought about all this. And he was worried she might put too much stock in what Esther had said about this being a date.

"Jake," she said, trying to put him at ease, "Esther seems very nice, and I'm sure that Billy and Frank are, too—whoever they are—but I'm not going to make a date out of a hamburger and a glass of poison ivy."

The instant she said it, she was almost sorry. He looked immensely relieved, and though that's what she'd intended, she felt a twinge of something akin to regret. Jake McClennon was a very nice man. And very attractive. She finally looked away from those probing gray eyes.

"Frank and Billy," he repeated, then sighed deeply and lowered his head to his hands. "There's another problem."

Laura waited, not sure how they could be more of a problem to him than Esther was.

"That was Billy I called on the phone," he said, raising his eyes. "He and Frank both work for me. Billy borrowed my pickup tonight, so I called to tell him that I didn't need him to come get me at the party." He sighed again. "What I forgot to tell him was that I needed a ride home." He folded his arms on the table and gave her a wry look. "Now I need a ride home."

"You don't do this much, do you?" Laura asked, suppressing another smile at his dismayed expression.

"Do what?"

"Rescue disinvited party goers. Tell you what," she said, pulling out her key ring and taking off a key, "why don't you take me home after we eat, then keep my car tonight. You can bring it by tomorrow morning when you come to look at the house, and we'll worry then about transportation."

He liked Laura's smile. He liked it a lot. That came as a huge surprise to him, because he hadn't liked any woman's smile in years. He liked it so much that he automatically reached out his hand for the key she held, and without so much as a token protest his fingers closed over it.

Her eyes widened involuntarily, and neither of them moved.

A second later he pulled his hand away, almost angry with himself. He hadn't meant to do that, to touch her hand a fraction longer than it took to get the key. But he had. She felt so soft and so warm that he hadn't been able to help himself. He realized suddenly that for the past five minutes he'd formed images in the back of his mind of Laura Halstead smiling at him from his bed.

The realization was so unexpected that he sat back in his seat, dumbstruck. He wasn't a prude by any means, but he had never pictured a woman in his bed upon first meeting her.

Something just happened, Laura thought. Something that made Jake look wary and guarded. She saw it clearly, but she had no explanation.

"Three barbecued burgers, heavy on the onion," Esther said with a significant look at Jake, as she set down two empty plates and a platter with three large burgers. If she was still miffed about his poison ivy comment, she didn't show it. "And fries. Enjoy."

The fries came on yet another plate, making Laura realize that this was a hamburger joint that served family style.

She and Jake ate with little conversation other than a word of praise now and then for the food.

Laura stole a glance at him, trying not to be obvious. She was still shaking inside from just the brief contact with his fingers. It annoyed her that she had so little control over her feelings, especially after her long history of learning to control them.

Mentally she catalogued what she knew so far about Jake McClennon. He was thirty-nine, he had at least one friend who was worried about his social life, and he was kind enough to lend his pickup to an employee. It wasn't a lot of information, but it was enough for her to label him a nice man. And she had no business having any interest whatsoever in a nice man. A woman with her past history brought nothing but a bad reputation to any relationship. As much as she might like to put the past behind her, people like Corky Fife Beachem and Trina Halstead would never let her.

The fact that she was having a difficult time keeping her eyes away from his compelling face and lean, muscled body only made her more determined not to let herself feel what she had when his fingers had touched hers.

"Is the hamburger too spicy?" Jake asked, making her realize that her attention had wandered far afield.

"No, it's delicious. Actually, I was just wondering about Billy and Frank." It was a lie, but not that much of one, not enough to send her to hell, as her mother had predicted often enough when she was younger.

"They're good workers even if I have to get on their cases now and then. Billy's married, Frank's divorced and they're both trying to run my social life."

"What there is of it," she suggested gently, remembering Esther's remarks.

"What there is of it," he agreed, and Laura thought he sounded sad. Had he been married? He hadn't volunteered any information.

Esther tried to talk them into a piece of pie when she brought the check. They declined, leaving Esther with the look of a woman who hadn't accomplished her mission.

The wind had picked up when they went outside, and Laura hugged her jacket to herself as she slid into the car.

Jake didn't say anything as they drove, but he looked pensive, making her wonder why the comment about his social life had saddened him. She was about to tell him where her house was, but remembered that he knew which one she had bought. They turned onto the road that followed the river, but she couldn't see the water in the dark. He turned right into her driveway and wound his way up the slight incline. Laura had forgotten to leave on any lights, and the house was barely visible under its canopy of old maples.

As Jake stopped the car, the headlights swept over another car in the driveway, and Laura's heart clenched.

She knew the car, and she knew the woman who got out.

Jake glanced quickly at Laura as he too recognized the woman. But Laura seemed oblivious to him as she got out of her car, her chin held high.

Trina Halstead's eyes swept to Jake and then back to Laura before she pointedly looked at her watch.

"I see you had a long, leisurely dinner," she observed.

"And you got to eat the dinner you paid for," Laura countered quietly, sounding much calmer than she felt.

Jake had left the car running, the headlights on, and it seemed to Laura that Trina looked even more intimidating in the artificial glare.

"I want to talk to you about Molly," Trina said, crossing her arms.

"I've told you," Laura said patiently. "You may see Molly whenever you want."

"It's not about seeing her. She belongs in a private school, not here where the teachers can barely read and write themselves."

"The school system is excellent here," Laura said, trying to maintain her composure, but feeling it slip away thread by thread.

"You're abusing that poor child by bringing her into this environment," Trina said, her voice rising. "Unlike you, I only want what's best for her."

When Laura didn't say anything, Trina turned on Jake. "I suppose this woman's tried to fool you into thinking she's some poor single parent, but she's anything but that. She tricked my son into marrying her, and she'll do the same to you."

"Trina, leave Jake out of this," Laura said, taking a step forward.

"He should know what kind of woman you are," Trina said. "He should know before it's too late, the way it is for my boy. My son's only been dead ten months," Trina said to Jake, her voice breaking. "Only ten months and now she's out with another man."

"Jake, please go now," Laura said, her voice barely audible.

He didn't think he'd heard her right. It was this other woman she should be asking to leave. "Let me take you inside," he said.

Laura shook her head vehemently. "Please, Jake. Let me handle this. Please just go."

"She keeps my only grandchild from me!" Trina Halstead was shouting at him. But Jake got in the car and began backing down the drive, feeling completely helpless.

He couldn't help Laura this time, because she wouldn't let him. And for the second time tonight he'd seen terrible pain in her eyes.

Chapter Two

Jake overslept Monday morning.

He wasn't in the habit of oversleeping, but he had tossed and turned all night. Every time he'd closed his eyes he'd seen Laura's hurt expression. It bothered him, and he was annoyed that it bothered him.

Dressing hurriedly in jeans, a chambray work shirt and sneakers, he drove as fast as he dared on the curving river road to Laura's house. He'd told her he'd be there in the morning, and morning was almost gone.

No one was around when he pulled her car up to her house. He knocked loudly, and when he got no answer he pushed open the door and walked in.

No one responded when he called Laura's name, and he looked around idly. The Connally house had been neglected for several years. The former resident, an older widow, had been either too visually impaired by age or too penurious to recognize that the house was badly in need of repairs. When she had died a year ago, after living in a nursing home for the last three years of her life, her chil-

dren had inherited the house and her apparent disregard for
its condition. It had stood empty for four years now, and it
showed.

Jake didn't like empty houses. Neglect was something he
abhorred, whether it was inflicted on a house or a person.
But he could see that Laura Halstead was not going to neglect this house.

She had already cleaned the parquet wood entryway. It
gleamed back at him, lightly reflecting the colorful quilts
piled in an open upright cabinet with doors of tin inlay, with
a punched design. An unusual piece for an entryway, he
mused, but it was warm and homey. Several brass candle-
holders were arranged on top of the cabinet, interspersed
with black-and-white photos in gilt frames. He looked at a
couple of the pictures and realized they were quite old.

Hearing nothing in the house but the ticking of a clock
somewhere in the distance, he stepped to the side into what
was once a parlor. A lot of work needed here, he noted. The
window casing was rotting, and it looked as though there
had been a serious leak above.

He went through a doorway to another room, this one
apparently for dining. Several tiles were broken on the fireplace hearth, and again there were stains in the ceiling.

Jake crossed the hallway to a small, airy room decorated
in faded and peeling flowered wallpaper. At first he thought
he'd wandered into a nursery, and he looked around uncer-
tainly.

Then he realized that it must be a sewing room. A large
wooden table in the center of the room was covered with
bolts of white fabric, some of it gauzy and some of it with
intricate eyelet patterns. Scissors, tape measures and a sewing machine far more complicated than any his mother had
ever owned, sat on a smaller table in the corner. Hesitantly
he picked up a piece of fabric lying on the table and held it
up to the light. It was a garment, he realized, but it looked
like it had been made for a very elaborate doll. Long and
flowing, it consisted of layers of frothy white lace with white
ribbon threaded through a large collar and tied in a bow.

Setting down the costume, he looked around the room. He sensed that he had found the heart of Laura Halstead, and he felt a little guilty about spying on her.

Exposed wooden rafters held hooks from which were suspended bunches of drying flowers and herbs. The window seat was piled with baskets of differing shapes and sizes and bundles of slender wood. A partially finished basket was upturned on the windowsill.

Curious, he opened the closet and found rows of shelves stacked with more lace and material. He smelled something sweet and poked around until he uncovered a small pot of rose petals.

A screen door banged, and he jerked away, hurriedly shutting the closet.

He was almost to the door when Laura came hurtling into the room, her eyes wide and startled when she nearly collided with him. Jake caught her arms to keep her from falling into him and found himself suddenly reluctant to let go, even after she straightened and blinked.

"I saw the car out front," she said huskily, her eyes still on his face. "I'm sorry I didn't hear you come in." Her voice faltered, and Jake abruptly let her go, realizing that he'd held on to her entirely too long but that he hated relinquishing the feel of her. She was soft and warm, and up close she bore the same fragrance of the rose petals in the closet. Mixed with the rose smell was a woodsy scent that came from the outdoors. She'd been working outside while he was looking over her house.

Her eyes slid away from his but not before he saw that they were troubled. He wanted to ask her about Trina Halstead, about what had happened last night when he'd in effect abandoned her, even though it was at her insistence. But the set of her mouth prohibited any questions.

"I knocked but no one answered," he said lamely. "So I snooped through your house."

She smiled briefly, though the smile looked strained. "Find anything scandalous?" she teased, her smile fading immediately when she thought of Trina's late-night visit.

Scandal was a word that seemed irrevocably linked with her name no matter how much she might wish it otherwise.

"Not unless this is something more devious than it looks," he said, holding up the lacy garment from the table and raising his brows.

"That," she said, taking the garment from him and smoothing it, "is a christening gown."

"A christening gown," he repeated, not understanding.

"For babies," she said, touching the lace. "It will become someone's family heirloom. See, look here." She held the gown forward, showing him a soft panel inset in the skirt. "This will be stitched with the baby's name and birthday, and then it will be used for that child's brothers and sisters and passed on to the next generation until all the panels are stitched."

Her eyes had grown soft as she explained it to him, and now he understood. An heirloom, she'd said.

"You make these and sell them," he said in wonder.

"Yes," she said, laughing as if she found it amusing that he hadn't known that. "I make a lot of things." She waved with her hand, vaguely indicating the window seat with its baskets and the hanging flowers. "I'm going to open a Victorian shop."

"Here? In the house?"

"Yes, of course. It's ideal."

He had never thought about someone putting a shop in one of these old homes by the river, but now he saw that it was an interesting idea. Tourists took the river road on their way to the Sandford downtown shopping district. A fancy sign out front was all she needed.

"You should do a wonderful business," he said. "These things are beautiful."

"Do you think so?" she asked, but he could see that her mind was already on something else.

"Yes, I do."

"I want to get a small shop downtown eventually," she said, "but at the moment..."

She made a small gesture with her hand and smiled, and he knew what she didn't say. At the moment she didn't have enough money for that.

The splinter in his thumb was bothering him again, and he worried his finger over it as he watched her turn to the closet to put away the christening gown. "I can do that," he said as she reached for a small step stool in the corner.

"It's no problem." She waved him away and climbed onto the stool. Jake couldn't stop his eyes from following the movement of her legs in jeans. Her fanny was pretty enticing, too, though he'd never thought of himself as the kind of man who ogled women.

This one was definitely worth ogling. She had on some kind of soft pink pullover sweater that tightened across her breasts as she reached for the top shelf, and Jake felt a corresponding tightening in his belly.

She made a soft sound, and Jake lunged forward just as she swayed and clutched the shelf. He put his hands on her waist and gently lifted her from the stool. But he didn't release her right away.

Laura stood in front of him, so close that he could see the confusion in her eyes, so close that he could smell her sweet rose scent. She looked pale and tired, and he wondered what circumstances in her life had made her that way.

Jake looked so surprised by what he'd done that Laura resisted her immediate urge to move away from him. Clearly he hadn't expected whatever was happening.

What *was* happening?

Her pulse was beating erratically, and her breathing was shallow and uneven. She hadn't felt this way—she hadn't *allowed* herself to feel this way—since before she had married Robert. Even though her own husband's ardor had cooled for her right after the honeymoon, right after some so-called friend of his had filled him in on his new wife's reputation, Laura had never let herself think about another man.

Nor had she after Robert died.

Thinking like that was unadvisable, especially with this man.

"I'm all right," she said brusquely, making herself pull away from him. Jake's hands dropped as if he'd just realized they were touching her.

"I'm sorry," he said hesitantly, his eyes clouding.

She realized that he thought he had offended her, and she tried to make amends.

"I didn't sleep much last night," she said. "I'm a little jumpy, I guess. And, come to think of it, I don't think I ate breakfast." She smiled wryly. "A woman without breakfast can be scary. Want to join me?"

His stomach was close to rumbling, and he was hungry enough to take her up on her offer despite what had just happened between them. He followed her wordlessly to the kitchen. He could bet on what had kept her from sleeping well the night before. Trina Halstead.

"I guess it's closer to lunchtime," she said, glancing at the big oak clock on the shelf over the kitchen table. "What do you say to a sandwich?"

"Only if you let me fix it," he insisted, still worried about her pallor.

She deferred to him, showing him where she kept the bread and fixings. He set to work, watching her reflection in the toaster as she sat down at the table and briefly rested her head on her hands when she thought he couldn't see. She was obviously more tired than she would admit to him.

Jake wanted to ask her what Trina Halstead had said to her last night, but he didn't want to become any more involved in this woman's life than he was already. He was supposed to be doing a cost estimate on renovations, and instead he was making lunch for the two of them. And there was the question of how he was going to get home again. He'd brought her car back, but he had no prospects for a ride. Both Billy and Frank were tied up on a job at the opposite end of town today.

He got the mustard from the refrigerator and stopped long enough to admire a quirky and colorful crayon drawing of a Halloween jack-o'-lantern. "Your child's an artist?" he asked, nodding toward the other pictures on the refrigerator, all equally cheerful.

Laura lifted her head and smiled. "She overheard Ali tell me I needed some color in my life," she explained. "Alison Newley from the party," she said to clarify, in case he didn't remember. "Molly took the comment literally, and she works very hard at providing the color. She's in second grade."

"What did Alison mean?" he asked, knowing it was nosiness on his part, but curious. How could a young woman like Laura with a big house, a child and a business need color?

"I had enough color when I was young to last me a lifetime," she said, instead of answering his question. Or maybe it was an answer, he decided.

"You're hardly old," he said, carrying two plates of sandwiches to the table.

"Twenty-seven," she said. "And I feel old. Mmm. You make a good sandwich." She took a bite, then stood and got two cans of soda from the refrigerator. "Is this okay?" she asked, setting one down by him. "Or would you rather have a beer?"

"I don't drink," he said around the bite he'd just taken.

She didn't comment but raised her brows slightly when she sat down again.

"But I don't mind if you'd like a beer instead," he said, realizing that she might be foregoing her own drink of choice because of him.

Laura shook her head. "No. Frankly I imagine I'd fall asleep if I had one now."

She didn't ask questions, he noted. She had let his comment about not drinking go by without any outward show of curiosity. He wondered if she was merely being polite or if she had been asked so many questions herself that she'd developed a strong sense of privacy. He suspected the latter.

They finished their lunch in silence, and Jake carried the plates to the sink. "I'd better start looking around if you want an estimate," he said. "Do you have something I could write on?" He smiled apologetically. "I forgot to bring my notepad."

Laura got him a pencil and some Flintstones notepaper from a kitchen drawer. "Molly's," she said, handing it to him.

She looked pensive when they left the kitchen. He followed her back to the parlor where she pointed out the wood rot and then to the entrance where she showed him some cracks in the wood parquet. He stopped to look again at the array of pictures on top of the cabinet.

"You must come from a large family," he said, surprised when she laughed.

"They're not family. At least not that I know of."

He didn't understand, and as he turned to her she took down one of the pictures. "I bought them all at antique shops here and there. I hate seeing someone's picture alone in some dusty corner of a shop. No name, no date. Just left there as if their family got tired of them. It's turned into quite a collection." She smiled wistfully and shrugged her shoulders. "In her droll moments Ali calls them my bas—well, never mind what Ali calls them. In her kinder moments she calls them my grafted family tree. Molly gives them all names. This one," she said, putting the picture back, "is Great-Aunt Ethel. Don't ask me why."

"Great-Aunt Ethel," Jake said, smiling. He was already forming a mental image of this Molly of the colorful pictures and transplanted family tree.

"This is Uncle Edward," Laura went on, moving around the cabinet and naming each picture. She concluded with a heavyset man in a topcoat. "Cousin Barney," she said. "We think he stole horses."

"And how do you figure that?" Jake asked.

"Either his collar's too tight or he has rope burns around his neck," Laura informed him.

Jake looked more closely and then laughed. The man did indeed look like he'd had a close encounter with something tight around his neck.

"No pictures of your parents?" he ventured.

Laura shook her head. "They died a few years ago. Heart disease and cancer. If you ask in town they'll tell you it was disappointment that killed them."

That remote, bleak look was in her eyes again, making Jake wonder what her childhood had been like for her to invent a whole new family for herself.

Laura took him from room to room, upstairs where there was more water damage and several fireplaces in need of work and then back downstairs where they ended up in her workroom.

"I'd really like to expand this room and turn it into a sun porch," she said. "Can that be done?"

Jake looked around. The large bay window already jutted well out of the house. It would take a little more expansion, but a lot more glass—and money. "It can be done," he said.

Laura heard stipulations in his voice, but he didn't expand on them.

She and Jake were alike in some elemental way. She could sense it. Neither was given to idle chitchat or prone to reveal much of their own volition. When talking about Molly and about her rogue's gallery of photographs she'd told him more about herself than she'd told anyone else, other than Ali. He was easy to talk to.

He harbored a deep sadness. She could feel it shadowing him like the cool vapor after a storm. Not that he was listless or unresponsive, just . . . sad.

And to her great amazement, she couldn't stop thinking about his hands. They were large, well-formed hands, clean but hardened from work. The knuckle on the index finger of his left hand was slightly larger than the others and misshapen, as if it had been broken at one time.

Laura had never thought about any man's hands before. Certainly not Robert's. Robert's hands had always been silky smooth and soft. He had carefully explained to her that he was smart, that he could make a good living sitting at a desk. He didn't have to get his hands dirty. But she saw little of that "good living." Lack of money was the main reason they had moved in with his mother, despite the fact that Laura's mail-order sewing business was already bringing in a small but decent living.

"I'd like to look around some more, if you don't mind, and make more notes. I can have an estimate ready by to-morrow."

She nodded. "Fine. Take all the time you want. I'll be working in here."

He watched as she moved to the sewing machine before he headed back to the hall and the stairs. He glanced at his watch and realized in surprise that he'd already been here almost two hours. He was essentially free today, so the time was no problem. But it had never passed so quickly before.

Jake made some notes on the stairs. A piece of the ban-ister was missing, but he was pretty sure he could match the mahogany. The main concern he had was the ceiling over the parlor. The water leakage could have weakened it consid-erably. He nosed around the kitchen until he found a broom in a small closet near the back door, then took it back to the parlor and gingerly prodded the ceiling. There was a good deal of give, making him worry. As he recalled, Molly's room was directly above.

He made notes on other things on his way back upstairs and stopped at the doorway of what must be Laura's bed-room. She hadn't indicated she'd wanted anything done there; she hadn't even shown him the room. He supposed it was idle remodeler's curiosity about a house, coupled with a man's curiosity about a woman, that made him step in-side.

Not that he was ready to do anything other than check out the room to satisfy his curiosity. He had no romantic inter-est in Laura. He had no physical interest, either, unless he counted that jolt of awareness that had swamped him when he'd lifted her from the step stool. He knew enough about hormones to understand that.

His wife had been dead for six years. He hadn't been very sexually active since then, not counting Andrea. But then, he'd been so drunk the whole time he was with Andrea that it was hard to remember how often they'd gone to bed to-gether. Now it was only natural that he would think of a woman occasionally. But that was far different from acting on impulses.

He saw more of Molly's colorful pictures in Laura's bedroom, along with some colorful rugs that looked handmade. Other than those touches, the room was sterile. There were no pots of makeup on the dresser, no bottles of fragrance, no magazines devoted to hairstyles or clothes.

His curiosity far from satisfied, he slipped farther into the room and looked around, telling himself he needed to check the floor. The floor here was fine, but still he lingered. Her closet door was open, and he gave in to the urge to take one quick look. Demure would describe her wardrobe, he thought, as he scanned the clothes hanging there. Lace, but none of it revealing, decorated several blouses. High collars, long sleeves, full skirts. Sensible shoes.

What kind of woman denied herself makeup and perfume? The same kind of woman who collected a family from antique stores. Laura's reputation was apparently painful enough for her to invent a different life for herself.

He moved on to Molly's room, carefully checking the floor. It creaked alarmingly and dipped in the middle. Not a good sign. He would have to speak to Laura about temporarily moving Molly to another room.

He did the same inspection in Molly's room he'd done in Laura's. But here he found bright nail polish designed for a young girl to play grown-up, a wild collection of beads of every shape and color, and whimsical jumpers covered with cartoon characters.

He couldn't help thinking that if he had had a child, she might have lived in a room like this.

He found a photograph beside the bed, half-hidden behind a huge children's book. A thin, serious man was holding a little girl with a headful of wavy red hair and laughing dark eyes.

"That's Molly and her father," Laura said from behind him, and he turned quickly, feeling guilty at having been caught snooping.

"She's very pretty." He set the picture down, and Laura moved closer, reaching out and picking it up again.

"She was three here. I never thought a child could be so happy."

She was smiling, but he heard what she didn't say. She hadn't believed it was possible, because she had never known that happiness herself.

"Is that her father?"

"Yes. Robert." She set the picture down again as if it had suddenly grown hot in her hand.

"He's dead?"

"Yes." She slowly met his eyes, her own troubled.

"So is my wife." She started to turn away, and before he could think twice Jake's fingers curled around her arm, stopping her. "Trina Halstead is his mother?"

Laura was quiet so long that he thought she wasn't going to answer. "Yes," she said finally with such a sad note of resignation in her voice that it made him want to take her in his arms and cradle her. "She's Robert's mother—and Molly's grandmother."

He was acutely aware of the softness of her skin beneath his fingers and the accompanying tension. But he didn't let go. He sensed that if he did she wouldn't answer his questions.

"And she's causing you trouble," Jake said.

"Yes, she's causing me trouble," Laura repeated. "Did you ever want something so badly that you didn't stop to think about what you were doing to anybody else?" she asked suddenly, her eyes meeting his.

He had to think. No, he couldn't remember wanting something that badly, unless it was for his wife not to be dead. But that kind of want was so filled with futility that it left one drained of emotion.

"I don't think so," he said softly.

"Well, Trina has that kind of want," Laura said.

"What is it she's after?" Jake asked, not understanding.

"She can't have her son anymore, so she wants my daughter."

He still didn't understand, but he apparently wasn't going to get a chance to find out more. Laura was turning toward the doorway.

"Someone's at the door," she said, pulling out of his grasp and heading for the stairs.

Her heart was pounding against her ribs in violent reaction to his touch. She would never have told a man she'd met only the day before anything about her daughter or the child's father, but with Jake's fingers feeding her pulse like some kind of drug, she couldn't seem to do anything but speak the truth.

If she was alone with this man any longer, she was liable to start imagining things that could never be. Already she was overly fond of the feel of his hands. And she caught herself thinking about the sadness in his gray eyes.

She stopped at the bottom of the stairs and took a deep breath.

So preoccupied with her troubles that he hadn't heard the persistent knocking, Jake watched Laura a moment, before following. He marveled at the fact that he was more curious about this woman than he'd been about anything in a long time. He also realized that he was being naive to suppose that his interest, if interest it was, in Laura Halstead was not going to be noticed in this town.

This latest insight of his was borne out when Laura opened the door to Billy Bartow, all smiles and curious looks as he peered over her shoulder at Jake.

Jake heaved an inward sigh and quickly made introductions, pulling Billy inside when he would have stood in the open doorway letting the cold air in. Billy couldn't seem to stop looking at Laura, and he fiddled nonstop with the red bandana he perpetually kept tied around his forehead.

"How did you find me?" Jake demanded, sounding more irritated than he'd intended.

"I called Mrs. Beachem to find out who gave you a ride home, and then when you weren't at your place I figured I'd try here."

Billy looked proud of himself, but Jake groaned out loud. Corky Fife Beachem. Word would be all over town.

"Why didn't you just put my picture on a milk carton?" he demanded in annoyance.

Billy's grin broadened. "I did better than that, boss. I asked Carl in the sheriff's office to keep an eye out for you. And I told Esther at the restaurant."

"You're a walking, talking all-points bulletin, Billy," Jake said dryly. Carl *and* Esther. A deputy and a waitress, both of whom worried too much about him. "Sometimes I think that bandana's too tight. What was so important that you had to find me this minute?"

"We've been hired," Billy said. "Big-time."

"What are you talking about?" Jake demanded. No one had phoned the business number about a job, at least not as of the time he left his home.

"Trust me, Jake. We can't afford to turn this one down. It's a simple patio and deck and garage and it pays *big.*" Billy raised his brows meaningfully.

Jake frowned. "What do you mean it pays big? I haven't done any estimates on a patio and deck for anybody."

"Apparently the lady in question didn't need an estimate. She already had a figure in mind. She says she intends to keep us working on her house for a long time to come."

"I don't have any idea what you're talking about," Jake said, his voice rising as his patience fled. "*Who* wants us to work on her house?"

"Mrs. Halstead," Billy said as if announcing the winner of a televised beauty pageant.

Jake's eyes flew to Laura as she paled noticeably.

"Trina Halstead," Billy qualified, and Jake stared at Laura. He knew at once what Trina Halstead was doing, and he wished he could have found out without Laura having to know.

She was backing away from them, her spine stiff, and at that moment Jake could have cheerfully throttled Billy. The old pain was back in Laura's eyes, the same pain he'd seen last night at Corky Fife Beachem's party.

And he didn't think he could do anything about it this time, either.

"Laura, wait!" he called as she headed for the sewing room. He caught up to her in the hall, stopping her with a hand on her arm.

When she turned to him he could see tears in her eyes.

"She has more money," Laura said stiffly, "but she's not going to win, Jake. I promise you that."

"I know," he said gently. "I know." He didn't know what else he could do for her, but he felt a strong compulsion to comfort her. He released her arm and slowly raised his hand to touch her cheek.

Laura didn't move, but her breathing quickened.

"She won't win," he said, echoing her words, wishing he could do something else for Laura. "She can't buy everything. We'll do your work, not hers."

She nodded shortly and turned on her heel, heading down the hall and closing the sewing room door behind her.

Chapter Three

No doubt Laura wanted to be alone before her tears spilled over. Not that he blamed her. It must look to her as if Trina Halstead could buy everything in Laura's life. Possibly even her child. What Trina was doing was unprincipled and callous. Jake couldn't think otherwise, not when he knew what it was like to lose a child. Carl had come to his door after the car accident, his face as ashen as his uniform.

"I'm sorry," Carl had said, and Jake had heard a life's dream disappear in those words. He'd wanted his child so much; he'd had such plans.

But he didn't have time to dwell on his own problems now.

Billy had come up behind him and now stood hesitantly, shifting his weight from one foot to the other. It was obvious that he had no idea what was going on, and he was a hairbreadth away from asking questions.

"Jake—"

"Forget it, Billy." Jake started to walk in the direction Laura had gone.

"But, Jake, what's going on? How come I mention a new job, and everybody goes off half-cocked?"

Billy was persistent if not discreet. He wanted to know, and Jake would have to answer. Jake stopped and took a deep breath. "We aren't going to bother Mrs. Halstead about this, okay?"

"Which Mrs. Halstead?" Billy promptly wanted to know. Jake had to admit that it was a legitimate question.

"*This* Mrs. Halstead," he said, nodding toward the closed door to the workroom.

"All right," Billy said agreeably. "So what do I tell the other Mrs. Halstead about her job?"

"I'll deal with that later. Right now I need you to help me move a bed."

"Why?"

Jake knew that he should have grown accustomed to Billy's questions after ten years of working together. But he still felt as if he were tutoring a five-year-old in the ways of the world.

"Because it's standing on a shaky floor that might give way. Anything else?" he asked, waiting to see what other point of interest would catch Billy's fancy.

"Big bed?" Billy asked, scratching his forehead above the bandana.

Jake gave a wry smile. "Child's bed. Come on."

"Laura," he said, leaning toward the closed door. "I need to talk to you."

There was no answer, and out of politeness he waited another half minute before trying again. "Billy and I are going to move Molly's bed. The floor underneath it isn't stable."

He thought he heard the workroom door open, when he and Billy reached the top of the stairs, but he didn't pause or look back. He had already resolved that he wasn't going to press her on anything—the work on her house, her trouble with Trina or any of the myriad other excuses he could find to talk to her about. He was simply going to let her be.

Jake decided to move the bed to the room across the hall. It was obviously used only for storage, and there were no curtains at the windows, but he was confident that the floor was good. He set Billy to work moving the packing boxes to one side, deflecting his next question before he asked it. "I don't know what's in them," Jake said. "Just be careful and don't break anything."

Jake bent to help, but he found himself listening for Laura's footsteps on the stairs. Unfortunately, he wasn't going to hear them, even if she came upstairs, because Billy had launched into one of his usual monologues. Jake had learned to listen with half his attention, because Billy enjoyed hearing himself talk. And usually Jake didn't mind. But he was still listening for footsteps today, and he didn't have a chance of hearing them over Billy.

"—and there she was with tears in her eyes kissing that stupid troll doll of hers and putting it by St. Jude," Billy was saying.

"What?" Jake asked, straightening. He hadn't thought he'd missed much of Billy's conversation, but apparently there were some points that needed more than a little clarification. Troll dolls and St. Jude for one. He couldn't imagine any kind of connection between the two.

"Esther," Billy explained patiently. "You know how much she loves those troll dolls of hers."

"Yeah," Jake said irritably, because he still didn't see any kind of connection, even one involving Esther. "They're her Bingo good luck charms."

"Right!" Billy grinned. "And you know that statue she has out back of the restaurant?"

"That statue is St. Jude?" Jake asked. "I thought it was one of the seven dwarfs."

"Yeah, well, I think it really is, Grumpy or Dopey or something. But you know Esther. She needed a statue of St. Jude, and there wasn't one anywhere around, so she decided to rechristen the dwarf."

"St. Jude," Jake repeated skeptically. He knew that Esther was a little unorthodox in her beliefs, but he had no idea that she'd turned one of the seven dwarfs into an icon. "So what was it she wanted from St. Jude?" Jake ventured.

Billy grinned. "Something for you."

"Me?" Now Jake was truly incredulous. "What could she possibly want for me?"

Billy cleared his throat and toed the floor. "Aw, you know, Jake. She's such a mother hen—"

"A very twisted mother hen," Jake added.

"It's just that she was worried about you for so long, and I guess she was feeling kind of desperate..."

"I'd certainly call a St. Jude-dwarf statue desperate," Jake agreed. "What does her church have to say about it?"

"Oh, they know she means no disrespect, and Esther gives hours of her time to the indigent family program."

"So what did all this have to do with me?" Jake asked after a reasonable length of time during which Billy volunteered nothing. "Isn't St. Jude the patron saint of lost causes?" he asked, frowning.

"Yeah." Billy grinned again. "She didn't want you to be alone like you were after... well, you know."

"After the accident. Yeah, I know." Jake bent down and slid another box across the floor. Not that he really understood yet. It was impossible to be all that alone when one had friends like Billy and Esther with her garden statues.

Billy fell silent, and Jake finally looked up. "Well?"

"Well what?"

"So how has St. Jude answered her prayers?"

"Laura," Billy said in a loud whisper, as if Jake were the most dense man he'd met.

"I took Laura to dinner, and Esther thinks that's a sign from St. Jude?" Jake asked.

"Yeah, that's about it. We were all worried, but it looks like St. Jude came through."

Jake sighed heavily. He was going to have to have a word or two with Esther's garden statue himself. About meddling friends.

"Look, Billy," Jake began, but he abruptly stopped as he spotted Laura in the doorway. All thoughts of Esther and St. Jude left his mind. He wanted to smile, but she looked far too worried.

"What should I do about Molly's bedroom?" she asked anxiously. She was talking to Billy. Her eyes refused to meet Jake's. "All of her clothes are in there."

"We'll move them," Jake said immediately. "Both dressers and everything in the closet. The floor will be fine for a while as long as there's no extra weight on it." She nodded and turned to go.

"Laura," Jake said, hurrying to catch up with her. She stopped at the head of the stairs, standing with her hands behind her back as if afraid he might try to touch her.

"I want you to understand about the other job," he began.

"Oh, but I *do* understand," she said quietly. "Better than you think. I've always understood Trina."

Jake shook his head. "She's not going to preempt your work here. I'll see to it."

"You don't know Trina," Laura told him. "Believe me, she'll keep you rolling in hammers and nails for the rest of your life. As long as you're not working here you'll never want for business. And she'll pay handsomely for what she wants."

"I told you I won't accept her job," he said simply.

"You'd be crazy not to," she told him. "It's money you can count on. Here...." She gestured briefly, then shrugged. "You aren't the patron saint of foolish prospects, are you?"

"No," he said, letting himself smile despite everything, "but I know the guy who is."

Jake and Billy were moving the last piece of Molly's furniture, an obviously old and warped oak chest, when a door slammed downstairs. Jake could hear a hurried conversation, then footsteps on the stairs. From somewhere below Laura called, "You do your homework and leave the men alone!"

Jake smiled, remembering his own mother's admonitions when he and John would arrive home and race for the fields. If it was the middle of planting or harvest they would be especially anxious to watch the tractor or the combine and maybe beg a ride.

"Are you the men?" a voice asked from the doorway. Jake turned from his position in front of the chest and wiped his hands on his knees.

The little girl twirling her red hair around one finger assessed him with large, brown eyes.

"I think so," he said gravely. "I'm Jake and this is Billy. You must be Molly."

"There's a Billy in my class," Molly said. "He throws up a lot. Do you throw up?" she asked Billy.

"On occasion," Jake disclosed. "Usually after he's had too much...pie."

"Do you like pie?" Molly asked. She seemed to be looking from one to the other, so Jake assumed it was a group question.

"I do," Billy confirmed. "I like apple pie best, then cherry. With ice cream on top," he amended.

"Blackberry is my favorite," Jake said. "But you can't find blackberries all the time."

Molly nodded in sympathy. "I like shoo-fly pie. You know, the sticky one that's got molasses," she said, in case they didn't know that particular pie. "But I don't get it every day. I guess Mama can't find shoo-flies all the time."

"Probably not," Jake agreed. "I bet they're seasonal."

"What's that?" Molly asked.

"It means something that you can only get at a certain time of the year, like fresh cherries in the summer or pumpkins in the fall."

"Oh, I like pumpkin pie too!" Molly announced, her eyes lighting up. "We're doing Around-the-World in school now."

"How are you doing that?" Billy asked.

"We're practicing being people from other countries," she told him, coming into the room and sitting on her oak chest facing them. "*I'm* a Mexican girl. I get to wear a hat and bring tortillas. Then we all eat together. We aren't using real food yet. Mrs. Foster won't let us have real food. Billy's mom is our home room mother." Molly leaned forward conspiratorially. "I heard Mrs. Foster tell Mama that Billy's mom can't cook worth beans. I sure hope we aren't going to eat beans for Around-the-World day. Do you like beans?''

The latter was directed to Jake, but it was Billy who answered. "Personally, I like beans," he said. "Baked mostly. But bean soup is okay. With lots of ham."

Molly listened politely to Billy's legume preferences, then scooted off the trunk. "This is how we sit around the table for Around-the-World day." She sat cross-legged on the floor. "I'm Maria Perez." She said it with the confidence of someone who had rehearsed the name long and hard. "And I have really long black hair. Mama's going to make me a wig out of yarn." She grinned at them, and Jake saw that one front tooth was missing. "Mama and me had to fill out these questions on a piece of paper to start school," she informed them. "Do you have to fill out questions?"

"Lots of times," Jake told her. "When you grow up they make you answer questions all the time."

"Wow," Molly said, looking suitably impressed. "How old are you?"

Jake looked to the usually loquacious Billy for help, but Billy had taken a sudden interest in the carpeting.

"Thirty-nine," Jake said. Molly looked even more impressed.

"How much do you weigh?"

"About two hundred pounds, I guess," Jake said.

"I bet that's as much as an elephant," Molly suggested.

"A baby elephant maybe," Jake allowed. He wondered if Molly intended to go through the entire list of questions for starting school, and he tried to remember if his shots were current. But apparently, age and weight were the extent of her interest.

"Want to be Around-the-World people?" she asked.

Jake and Billy should have been long gone, Laura thought as she glanced at her watch. The sounds of furniture moving had ended half an hour earlier, leaving only silence and Laura's speculation.

She knew her gregarious daughter well enough to suspect that Molly would pester the two men. But she didn't expect these two particular men to put up with it. Billy looked as if he could barely handle life's mundane aspects, much less a talkative seven-year-old.

And Jake . . . Well, Jake had no experience with kids; she was sure of that. And she was well enough acquainted with men of his age—and younger—to know that when you sprang a child on them they tended to panic.

Not that she had much account to deal with men of any age. Between Trina's harangues and her own misery with Robert, she had developed a healthy aversion to the male of the species. She would have liked to have met a good man— shoot, she would almost settle for knowing that there was actually one out there somewhere. But, to bring him home and let him into her life? No, thank you very much.

She could hear quiet voices coming from the room where she had seen them moving Molly's furniture, and she poked her head through the door. What she saw gave her considerable pause. The oak chest sat in the middle of the room and Molly, Billy and Jake sat cross-legged on the floor around it. Jake's back was to the door, and he was passing a toy teapot to Billy while he balanced a matching cup on his knee.

Molly looked up at the door and immediately said, "Uh-oh."

"Molly Ann," Laura said in a firm voice, "I believe I told you not to bother the men."

"I wasn't really bothering them, because they were here in my room," Molly reasoned. "See? This is my new room."

"Nice try," Laura told her. "Now go downstairs and do your homework. I left some cookies and an apple on the table for you."

Molly scrambled to her feet and danced past Laura, hugging her leg on the way out. Laura smiled and ruffled her hair.

Jake was having far more trouble getting to his feet.

"How long have you been sitting like that?" Laura asked anxiously as he finally made it, groaning. "You should have sent her back downstairs."

"Couldn't," Jake said, stretching painfully. "I was Niles from England. I couldn't call off teatime. Molly baked pretend crumpets." He thumped Billy on the shoulder.

"Yeah," Billy said, rotating his shoulders and arching his back. "We oughta have them crumpets more often."

He turned toward the window with a hopeful expression. "Hear that?" he asked Jake. "Sounds like Myra."

All Laura could hear was a rumbling truck engine that seemed to be drawing closer. She walked past the men and looked out. "If Myra's an old blue truck, then she's here," she informed Billy.

He grinned. "That's Myra, but she's the driver, not the truck. Hey," he said to Jake, "you got your own truck now. I'll see you later." Touching his fingers to his bandana in a sort of salute, he bounded toward the stairs. A moment later Laura heard the front door slam.

"So, does everybody around here wear tracking devices?" she asked Jake.

"Wear what?" he asked, baffled and still stretching.

It took some doing for Laura not to stare as he reached down to massage his knees. Despite his stiffness from his teatime experience, Jake was in good shape. And it showed despite the old jeans and wrinkled shirt.

"Tracking devices," she repeated, forcing herself to focus on the rug. "Billy was looking for you, and now Myra comes looking for Billy. Is this like some big game of tag?"

Jake smiled. "Not really. It's more an exercise in nosiness. You can't be up to much in this town without someone finding out about it."

But he supposed that she already knew that. She'd had enough experience with it in the past.

He took a step closer to her as he stretched again, and Laura backed away reflexively. "I need to...do some planting," she said, not sounding entirely convincing. "Please excuse me. If you're serious about taking this job, you have the run of the house." Her eyes met his and held for a long moment.

He watched her go, torn between wanting to follow and knowing he should go home. In the end, following won out. It wasn't that he had to be near the woman, he told himself. It was just that she was so damn vulnerable, and he didn't like the thought of Trina Halstead and Corky Fife Beachem chewing up a sweet morsel like Laura Halstead, then spitting her back out.

Jake passed Molly at the kitchen table, her head bent over her homework. "Mama's outside," she informed him before she went back to slowly writing the alphabet in big script.

He should just leave, he told himself again. He had a ride home, and his notes were completed, so he had no good reason to stay. No reason except the woman outside and the hurt look he hated seeing in her eyes.

"So what are you planting?" he asked, when he found her kneeling at the edge of the yard where a stand of trees began. The wind was chilly, and he shoved his hands into his pockets.

"Crocus and anemone bulbs," she told him without looking up.

"Looks like a ton of them," he said, kneeling beside her and picking up the trowel. The splinter in his thumb was still bothering him, and he absently rubbed it against his lip. He noticed that the wind whipped her red hair around her face, giving her a wild but exuberant look.

Laura nodded toward the trowel. "My tool of choice when Molly's helping. She loves the bulb planter. Says it's like cutting out cookies."

"She's a nice kid," Jake said, going to work with the trowel. The ground was still a little wet from recent rains, and he had to work to get the grass out. He thought of his own home and the unkempt yard. He should be there, raking leaves and trimming the grass, but he never got around to it. Appearances had lost all of their urgency for him. He'd discovered that it really didn't matter if the grass was cut or the groceries put away or the sheets folded. Those things couldn't change the fundamental facts of life.

Maybe they could, a voice nagged him. Maybe if he'd been driving his wife to her parents' house that night instead of sitting at home with a cold beer, the accident might not have happened. He might have been able to avoid the drunk driver. Beverly had asked him to go, but he'd declined. *I'm too tired,* he'd said. *I spent all day on my knees fitting together a hardwood floor.* And he'd felt a spurt of irritation with his wife that she'd asked again, a bit more testily. No, he didn't want to go. No, he was too tired.

He'd never had the patience he should have had. Not for marriage, at any rate.

As he turned back to the crocus bulbs, it struck him why he was so disinclined to leave Laura Halstead. It was guilt, his old friend, the reason he had once been best friends with the beer bottles of the world. He didn't want to see her hurt, but he was powerless to prevent it. So here he was, acting as if he really could do something to remove the shadows from Laura's eyes. Acting as if anything he might do could make a difference.

He should go home where he belonged.

Jake set down the trowel and sighed heavily. Laura was working a few feet away, her back to him. He dropped the trowel beside her, and she turned around, looking up at him quizzically.

"I have to go," he said. "You should go inside. It's going to be dark soon."

He had meant to turn and leave, but her hair was still whipping around, and her eyes looked wide and luminous as they watched him. He reached out a long finger to brush back the hair that threatened to cover her eyes, and she jerked away. They both stayed awkwardly motionless like a ridiculous tableau, Laura leaning away from him and Jake frozen in a half-bent position, his hand out.

Laura swallowed. "It's not you," she assured him, trying to regain her composure. "It's just that I—that Trina has made it impossible for me to let anyone into my life."

Jake straightened and fished in his pocket for his truck keys. "That's a load of bull, Mrs. Halstead," he said dryly, knowing that despite all his mental protests he was going to get involved with this woman. "I speak from experience. It's *you* who's making it impossible."

He walked off into the growing dusk, leaving Laura on her knees in the dirt, her heart pounding in her chest.

Chapter Four

"Well, well, well. What's this?" Esther demanded as she pulled her pencil from behind her ear and flipped to a new check in her pad. "Boys' night to raise a ruckus?"

Jake gave her a dry look. "I think we're a little old to qualify as boys—or to raise a ruckus," he said.

Esther grinned. "I don't know about that," she said. "Billy here looks pretty frisky yet. Though I got to admit that you and Frank are starting to show your age."

"Hey!" Frank protested. "I resent that. I am *not* old."

"Didn't say you were," Esther countered blandly. "Just said you're starting to show your age."

"Sounds like it means *old* to me," Frank retorted. "And I'll have you know, woman, that we spent the whole day doing drywall. And that's about as much ruckus as I care to raise for a week." He looked pointedly at his dusty jeans and shirt.

"Just hurry up and tell me what you want to order," Esther said. "I got Bingo in an hour."

"What do you hear from your son?" Jake asked instead, knowing that the topic would placate Esther. Jake had helped Ronnie get a job with his brother Jordan's electronics company in St. Louis.

"My son the genius," she sighed. "He throws around all those fancy electronics words like IC chips and resistors. Phones and letters he don't know. I don't hear anything unless I call."

Jake sympathized, then ordered two hamburgers with everything. He sat back and massaged his neck as Frank continued to grouse half-heartedly about the poor service before ordering the taco burgers. Billy, who looked about to fall asleep, roused himself long enough to order two plain hamburgers and fries.

"So how's Laura Halstead?" Esther asked before sticking the pencil back behind her ear.

"I thought you were in a hurry," Jake reminded her.

"I am, so make your report short. You seeing her?"

Actually, Jake had found her occupying his thoughts ever since he'd left her among her flower bulbs the evening before, but he wasn't about to admit that to Esther.

"I'll give her an estimate on her work," he said testily, "and if she hires me I'll be 'seeing' her, I guess."

"That's not what I meant," Esther said.

"I know what you meant, and it's none of your business," Jake told her. "Look, we're hungry here. How about some food?"

"I'll get you your food," Esther assured him. "I just want to know how things are going with you and your lady friend."

"There's nothing to know," Jake said. "Satisfied?"

"Hell, she's not going to quit prying till you tell her the two of you are engaged," Frank assured him. "So tell her that and we can eat."

"*Prying?*" Esther repeated, wounded. "I ask you, do I pry?" Getting nothing but raised brows from Jake's table, she turned to the only other customers, three farmers dawdling over coffee. "Do I pry?" she demanded of them.

They shuffled their feet and studied their coffee cups and cleared their throats.

"Yes, you pry!" the balding cook called from the grill behind the counter. "Now tell me what the guys want so I can cook it!"

Esther sighed and walked away. She threw one last parting shot over her shoulder at Jake. "*You're* not getting onions on your hamburger. When a man has a lady friend, he shouldn't eat onions."

"God help me," Jake murmured, lowering his head to his arms. But he was too tired to be overly irritated with Esther tonight.

"You finish the estimate for the Halstead woman yet?" Frank asked, leaning back in the booth and taking a long swallow of coffee. Frank was in his early sixties, and he swore to Jake that since he couldn't sleep anyway, at his age he might as well enjoy his coffee.

"Which Halstead woman?" Jake asked testily.

Frank shrugged. "I'm easy to please. Either one."

"I worked up an estimate for Laura Halstead," he said shortly. "We're not considering the Trina Halstead job."

"What?" Billy demanded. "Do you know how much money that woman is willing to pay us, Jake? And she said she'd put us up in the best motel there."

"Yes, I know and, believe me, dealing with her is not worth the money."

"Dealing with the other one isn't worth the money, either," Billy shot back.

"And what the hell does that mean?" Jake asked, his brows drawing together.

Billy shrugged in the face of Jake's temper. "It means she don't have any money, Jake. How's she going to pay us?"

"Maybe Jake's worked out something," Frank said, grinning.

"That's it!" Jake said, slamming his hand down on the table. "I've had enough of this." He slid from the booth and strode toward the back door, jamming his hands into his pockets.

"What's the matter with him?" Billy asked, taken aback. "He never used to get like that when we razzed him about some woman he'd met."

"Don't know," Frank said. "But he's sure been testy."

"Something to do with that Laura Halstead," Billy said. "I'll bet on it."

"Any other psychic predictions?" Frank said dryly.

"Yeah," Billy shot back. "The hamburgers are burning."

It looked like someone would have to summon the fire department in about half a minute, Jake thought as he watched the black smoke curl out through the vent in the back of the building. He shouldn't have lost his temper with Billy and Frank. He wasn't even sure now just why he'd let them rile him. They'd always had plenty to say before about any woman who hired him, but he had let it get to him tonight.

The fire was apparently out, he decided as the black smoke trickled down to nothing. He'd bet anything it was his dinner, now scorched, that had precipitated the smoke. Massaging his sore knees, he leaned back against the brick wall of the restaurant. He'd played football in college, and his knees still ached whenever he stayed in one position too long. The wind picked up, and he watched a dried leaf skitter across the parking lot to the end of the building. It came to rest against Esther's garden gnome, making Jake almost smile.

Poor Esther. Her two goals in life were to win big at Bingo and to find a mate for every single man in the county. Actually, she'd pared down the list of eligible males in need of her help to just two—Frank and him. "Just so much one woman can do," she'd explained. "Given what I got to work with."

Jake's empty stomach growled, and he pushed away from the wall. The less he worried about Esther or Billy or Frank—or Laura Halstead—the better for him.

"Look at this," Billy was whining, when Jake sat down in the booth. "Like a charcoal sandwich. I can't eat this."

"So why aren't you eating with Myra tonight?" Jake asked, biting into the extremely well-done burger, so well-done that it crunched. True to her word, Esther had made sure he had no onions. Jake opened the bun and poured on more catsup.

"She and her mother are in some homemakers club or something," Billy said. "They're at a meeting tonight. Jake, you really shouldn't eat all that junk. It's full of bad stuff."

"I quit smoking," Jake told him patiently. "I don't drink anymore. And I don't carouse with women. Eating burnt red meat with lots of junk on it is the only pleasure left in my life."

"We'll see about that," Esther called to him on her way out the door.

"I'm an old man, Esther, remember?" he teased her. She snorted before the door slammed behind her.

Jake felt like an old man later that night as he lay staring at the ceiling, the estimate for Laura Halstead on the wooden crate beside the bed. He wasn't even forty yet, and here he was with stiff knees, a burning stomach and an inability to sleep. He had to take better care of himself. This living alone did nothing for a man's health. Burnt red meat and too much coffee were half his problem. The other half had more to do with his having forgotten how to live. He went through the motions all right, but that was the extent of it. At night he watched TV or worked on his business records, something he'd sadly neglected lately with all the work he'd been hired to do.

Tonight the red meat had been pretty unsatisfactory, and the TV even less so. He needed a change.

Jake got up and turned on the light in the bathroom, scrutinizing himself in the mirror. He didn't look so old, not if you got past the dark stubble on his chin and the too-long hair. Grungy maybe, but not old.

On impulse, he got the phone book from the kitchen and looked up a number. At least he wasn't like Frank yet, he assured himself. He could still read a phone book without glasses.

A sleepy voice answered, and Jake got to the point. "I need a haircut."

After a brief verbal assessment of what he thought of late-night phone calls, the barber agreed to open the shop early in the morning.

"Now, go to bed, for God's sake!" he snapped. "Unless you can think of something else you need at midnight."

A new shirt would have been nice, but Jake knew that the barber couldn't do anything about that. Besides, the man had already slammed down the phone.

He looked different, Laura thought, when she opened the door the next morning. It was Jake and yet it was a different Jake. She let him inside, trying not to stare.

His jeans were obviously freshly washed, and the black pullover sweater looked new, but that didn't account for the change. He followed her into the dining room and sat at the mahogany table with his sheaf of papers, solemn and businesslike.

It was the hair, she decided, when he sorted through the papers long enough for her to get a good look. Yes, he'd gotten a haircut. And recently. She could tell by the small dark hairs clinging to his neck.

He looked nice, and he smelled nice, too. But he was apparently irritable this morning if his frown was any indication.

After the angry way they'd parted two nights ago she was surprised he was here at all.

Laura quickly glanced at his papers when he raised his eyes. "So," she said, taking a deep breath, "what do you think?"

Jake pushed the papers across the table. "I think we can do the work in stages. I've broken it down into each job with a separate estimate. We can tackle one thing at a time, and you can pay for it as we go." He hesitated. "Normally I require a deposit of one-third of the cost of each job before I start it."

She watched his face for a long moment, and he held her gaze. He suspected that she wondered if he was handing her some potentially expensive sham, if he would find hidden costs and more-extensive-than-I-thought damage once he started the job. As it was, the estimates were more than reasonable. He had cut them to the bone.

"The figures include everything," he said now. He knew he sounded defensive but couldn't help it.

"Impressive," she agreed, scanning the bottom line. "Are you sure you'll make any profit on this?"

"Not much," he told her honestly. "But I've always liked this house. I don't want to see it neglected."

She didn't look as if she quite believed him, but she said nothing. Sitting back in her chair, she began to read each piece of paper slowly and carefully. Glancing up once, she motioned him toward the kitchen. "Coffee's on, and there are some muffins on the counter."

He got the coffee and stood in the doorway watching her. She was frowning over the papers, chewing on her lip. She took a pencil and made some notations in the margins. Putting down the pencil she sighed.

"I think I can afford it," she said, looking up at him. "I have a lot of mail orders already for Christmas, and I should make more sales locally when we get closer to the holidays." She smiled at him, and for the first time he realized just how dazzling she could be.

"So I guess we have a deal," she said, standing and offering her hand.

Jake hastily put down the coffee cup and shook her hand. It felt small and fragile in his, and from this close he could smell the scent of soap on her skin. An ache tightened his groin, but he carefully ignored any physical symptoms Laura's closeness might cause him.

"I can start now if you want," he said, more gruffly than he'd intended. "I've got tools in the truck. I thought I'd work on the stairs first and then the parquet. That way you'll have an attractive entrance for your customers."

Laura smiled. "Yes. Thank you. That would be the place to start."

"The next thing will be to find the leakage point for the window. I think that may be what caused the floor problem in Molly's bedroom."

He was about to explain the procedure for that when someone knocked on the door, and Laura left to answer it. She came back into the room with a thin Amish girl dressed in a traditional dark blue skirt and blouse with white apron and white prayer cap. The girl stood silently observing Jake, one heavy black shoe lightly toeing the carpet.

"This is Emma Eicher," Laura said. "She's my sewing assistant, and a mighty fine one at that. Her neighbor drives her here to work."

Emma smiled under the warm praise, and Jake realized that she must be about fifteen. "Nice to meet you, Emma," Jake said. "I'm Jake McClennon."

"I know," Emma said shyly. "You buy woodwork from my brother and father."

"Ah, so you're one of Eli Eicher's children. Your family does fine woodworking."

The Amish community in that part of Illinois was relatively new, and Jake had started to have some of the woodworkers among them build custom moldings and banisters. They had also started a thriving cabinet business.

"We'll get to work, then, and leave you to the hall," Laura said, smiling as she led Emma to the sewing room.

Jake gathered his tools and went to work, soon immersing himself so thoroughly in what he was doing that he wasn't thinking about Laura. Occasionally he heard snippets of laughter and what sounded like a German song from the back room.

Some time later he was surprised when he looked up to see Laura watching him. "It's lunchtime," she said. "Would you like to eat in the kitchen with us?"

He was about to refuse, but then he thought. What harm could it do? They wouldn't be alone.

Laura felt him watching her as he followed her to the kitchen, and she couldn't help wondering again what had made him so distant today. His parting words the last time they were together? The estimate? Surely he wouldn't offer her a price that would cause him this much irritation. The reason must be the way she had avoided his touch the last time they were together. His angry words came back to her. *It's you who's making it impossible.*

Whatever his reasoning, he was giving her a wide berth now.

She offered milk or soda, and Jake chose a cold can of cola. He was opening his brown paper bag lunch when Laura nudged him with her elbow. He immediately stopped and waited while Emma prayed silently over her lunch.

Laura watched him from the corner of her eye. He had stripped off the black sweater sometime during the morning, leaving a red short-sleeved T-shirt underneath. She found the shirt more than a little unsettling, given the way it clung to his muscular arms and chest. She also had come to the realization that he wasn't going to look at her if he thought she might catch him at it. The tension between them made her sandwich stick in her throat, and she had to wash down each bite.

Emma brought out two bags of chocolate candies after they'd finished eating and pushed them toward Laura.

"Chocolate-covered raisins?" Laura asked, holding up one bag.

When Emma nodded, Laura said, "Fine. I'll buy this one, and you tell your mother to make me two more the next time you come."

Emma smiled. "Here," she said, pushing the other bag toward Jake. "You try these. They're good. Full of good stuff."

Jake knew that the Amish women often sold baked goods to earn extra money. He opened the plastic bag and popped one of the chocolates into his mouth. "*Very* good," he told her.

Emma grinned. "It's got those cereals in there. You know, the ones that look like circles."

Jake thanked her and assured her that the candy was delicious and started to rise. "Take more," Emma insisted. "That won't get you far."

He took two more and went back to work, unable to stop himself from listening as Emma and Laura cleaned up in the kitchen, then returned to the workroom, Emma chattering amiably.

Jake didn't realize how late it was until the car returned for Emma. "You'll buy a bag of those chocolates next time?" Emma asked him, grinning as she headed out the door.

"Definitely," he assured her.

Glancing at his watch, he realized that it was almost five. He was kneeling, gathering up his tools, when he heard a board squeak.

He looked over his shoulder to see Laura standing in the hall just a few feet away.

"Your check," she said, holding it out. "I made it out for one-third the estimate for the stairs and parquet work."

He didn't move to take the check right away, and Laura worked to keep her hand steady. She still couldn't understand his coolness, and it was frustrating her.

"Did Molly come home?" he asked, standing slowly.

Laura shook her head. "She's at Ali's house. I'm going to pick her up tonight."

He nodded and finally took the check from her. He didn't even glance at the amount before folding it and stuffing it into his T-shirt pocket. Laura felt herself growing even more impatient with him. She had no idea why he was treating her so impersonally, unless he had heard some new tidbit concerning her flaming reputation. She wouldn't put it past Trina.

Jake wasn't looking at her as he continued to gather his things. His back was to her. She waited, but he said nothing else. She should just let him go home and forget about his attitude. In fact, that was just what she'd do.

But she had taken only a couple of steps before she stopped and sighed. "I was planning on heating up some soup," she said. "Do you want to stay for dinner?"

"Let's go out to eat instead," he said, and when she turned around she found him watching her face. She stared open-mouthed.

"*Let's,* as in let us?" she asked, sure she hadn't heard him right at all.

"Yeah, is that okay?"

"It's fine, but—" She was at a loss.

"But what?"

"But I don't know what's going on with you," she said, deciding to be honest. "I could have sworn all day that you didn't even want me in the same room with you. Now we're going to sit at a table together and have a civil conversation?" She frowned.

"I'm sorry I wasn't the best company today," he said. "I had some things on my mind." It wasn't precisely true, but he couldn't very well tell Laura that he had been silent and withdrawn by design and that he had had no intention of asking her out to dinner until the words came out his mouth.

Laura sighed and massaged her temple.

She looked like a woman caught in a situation she didn't understand and didn't particularly want to deal with, Jake thought. And he was the one making her look that way.

"I'll go change," she said, starting up the stairs past him. "You wouldn't care to give me any clues about what to wear?" she suggested.

He almost smiled as he shook his head. He didn't know what to tell her, because he had no idea himself where they were going. He purposely wouldn't let himself look at her as she climbed the stairs. Every time he looked at her, he found himself saying things he hadn't intended to say.

She called Ali to tell her she would be with Jake before they left the house. "Do we have a destination yet?" she asked him, holding the phone in the air so he would know the information was for Ali.

"Tell her Renaldo's on the highway," he said. It was the first place that had come to mind.

She relayed the information, then glanced down at her black linen slacks and green silk blouse. "Will this get me thrown out of Renaldo's?"

Jake tried not to smile. "The way you look will get you the best service of your life and an army of admirers," he assured her. He couldn't seem to remain detached around

her, though he had tried his best. It had been the same with
Andrea Miller, he reminded himself. The difference was that
he had been far more vulnerable when she'd come into his
life. It had been a painful lesson, but he was more wary now,
far less likely to allow a woman to use him the way Andrea
had.

So why was he letting himself become involved now? he
asked himself.

"You *do* like neon to be an integral part of your dining
experience, don't you?" she asked when he pulled the truck
into the parking lot.

He had to admit that she was right. Renaldo's was nothing if not visually loud. The name in bright red, an assurance that this place served *Fine Food* in blue and various
beer logos in every hue imaginable festooned the small concrete building.

Inside it was a different story. Low lighting, tables
crowded close together and covered with red-checkered
cloths, and a polished wooden bar with brass rail gave the
place a moody, intimate atmosphere. Laura wasn't sure that
was what she needed tonight, especially with Jake, but she
figured it was either this or hamburgers again.

"It's been a while since I was here last," Jake said as he
guided her to a corner table. She could detect some other
meaning behind his words, but she didn't understand it.

As her eyes adjusted to the dark, she scanned the room
and realized they practically had the whole place to themselves. Only two other tables were occupied: one by two men
who looked as if they'd come straight from some job that
involved the outdoors and hard labor; and a back booth
where a beer drinker was about to nod off.

She looked at Jake and raised her brows.

"The place fills up later," he said. "It's early yet."

A beefy man with a faded apron emerged from behind the
bar and handed them each a stained one-page menu. Laura
noted that it was filled almost exclusively with spaghetti and
other pasta dishes.

"Something to drink?" he asked flatly.

"Coffee with cream, please," Laura said.

"Black coffee," Jake said.

The man stared at him a moment. "You planning on trashing the place again?" he demanded.

Jake shook his head. "Once was enough," he said dryly.

"Yeah, I guess."

Laura watched Jake while the man got their coffee, but he didn't meet her gaze.

The coffee was set before them, and they gave their orders. Again Laura waited for Jake to say something, and finally he did.

"The spaghetti's good here."

"The spaghetti's good here?" she repeated in disbelief. "Is that all you're going to say?"

Jake didn't pretend not to understand. Sighing, he ran a hand through his hair. "It was a long time ago."

"Apparently not long enough for that guy to forget about it."

"Three years," he told her. "I paid for all the damages, but I guess I'm still on his sh—his unfriendly list," Jake amended.

"What happened?" she prompted when he didn't continue. "Did you get a bad batch of linguine?"

That almost coaxed a smile from him.

"Let's just say that the beer flowed freely that night," he said. "And things weren't going my way. It was a bad combination."

She was intrigued, wondering what there was in his past that had been bad enough to make him tear up a bar and restaurant.

Laura fiddled with her coffee cup, but he didn't elaborate. "You said you don't drink," she ventured. "Is that the reason?"

"A big part of it. After my wife died I started drinking too much. Though at the time, there didn't seem to be any such thing as too much to drink."

Laura could certainly understand that. In a way, her teenage years had been akin to one long drinking bout. But instead of liquor she'd partaken of rebellion. In a big way.

"So, you continued drinking for three years until you tore up this place?" she prompted him.

"There was an incident or two along the way. I met another woman. I guess I thought that she was a way out of the bottle. It turned out that she was just another path back in."

"I'm sorry."

"So was I. I've hurt some very nice people along the way to sobriety."

"I'm sure they understood, given the circumstances," she suggested. She couldn't imagine this man hurting anyone, even with his sometimes studied indifference.

"That's not enough," he said immediately.

"Part of the alcoholic's responsibility to make amends?" she guessed.

"I suppose so. Though I know I had the need to make amends way before I acknowledged that I was an alcoholic. It wasn't something I reasoned out. It was just sort of there—*here,*" he said, touching his chest. "I didn't realize how badly I needed redemption until someone I respected told me flat-out what a bastard I'd become."

Laura smiled. "I'm amazed you listened."

"Oh, I didn't," he assured her. "Not at first. But he kept after me until I finally got the point. A night in jail can be a powerful argument."

"It depends on who's doing the arguing," she said mildly, and that drew him up short.

He'd forgotten about her jail time. Apparently hers had been more punitive than rehabilitative.

"I take it your jail experience was...different than mine."

She didn't know how he knew about it, but she assumed it was from the many gossips who liked to keep her past alive. Surely someone had tried to warn him about associating with the woman with a scarlet history.

"It was hell," she said without malice. "I sought out a group of girls known for their ability to cause trouble. I think in the end I was even too much of a social outcast for them. We shoplifted a lot. Makeup mostly and perfume."

Jake remembered her bedroom and the conspicuous absence of makeup and perfume. He wondered if the shame of what she'd done as a young girl still cast such a long shadow on her.

"The other girls slept around. I didn't. Not from any moral compunction, but because I wouldn't let anyone get that close to me." She was telling him this matter-of-factly, but Jake could see the effort in her eyes. "There was a tough crowd of boys from another town downriver who used to occasionally cruise our area after school. Some of the girls in my group were friendly with them. We'd all stay out late at night together, and the boys would supply beer. They got their money from small burglaries. You know, breaking into cars to steal radios and anything else they could find. A couple of them began to do houses. The girls would hear when someone was going away with their parents for the weekend, and the boys would break into the house."

"You were sent to jail for telling boys when people wouldn't be home?" he asked incredulously.

"No," she said, shaking her head. "I went to jail for shoplifting. I spent two nights there because my father wouldn't bail me out. I was sent to the juvenile home because of the burglaries. I wouldn't sleep with the boys, and one of them decided I must think I was too good for him. So when he was caught with stolen goods, he told the police I was involved in the burglaries. One of his friends backed up his story. And of course word spread around town that I slept with everyone."

"Nice guy," Jake said dryly.

"I wasn't very nice, either," Laura said quietly. "I put a lot of people through hell."

And in return she got a lot of hell she didn't deserve, Jake thought. They'd swapped sin for sin, and he felt a companionable ease talking with her. It felt good to talk freely and not worry about what the other person would think. Not quite freely, he reminded himself. He hadn't elaborated on the woman who came into his life after his wife's death. But he felt no need to discuss Andrea.

On the other hand, he was curious about Laura's dead husband. What kind of man married a woman with a supposedly bad reputation, then left her to the mercy of his mother, living in the same house?

"Laura—" he began, intending to ask the question, but the waiter-bartender appeared with their food.

The man left again, but the moment had passed when he could have asked what he wanted to know. He was left to draw his own conclusions, and they weren't pretty. It surprised him that it was important that he understand Laura and what had happened to her. That kind of curiosity was unusual for him.

They ate quietly, both concentrating on their food and their private thoughts. Finally Jake stabbed his spaghetti with a fork and decided to go ahead and ask what he wanted to know. But when he lifted his eyes to Laura, he saw that she was staring at the door, her face pale. Jake quickly turned in his seat.

Framed in the doorway like a specter, her arms akimbo, her eyes fixed on them, was Trina Halstead.

Chapter Five

Jake felt an immediate spurt of anger at Trina when he saw the now-familiar hurt in Laura's eyes.

"*There* you are!" Trina said, marching to the table and glaring at Laura. "What do you think you're doing?"

"Eating dinner," Jake responded quietly. "And what do you think you're doing?"

"Mr. McClennon," Trina said, quickly turning her voice to sugar and smiling at him. "I simply want to talk to you about those improvements to my home and give you a word of caution about this woman."

"I don't think I'm in need of guidance when it comes to my social life," Jake said, his own smile completely devoid of humor...or politeness. "I'm a big boy now."

"Yes, well, if you knew the facts about this woman," Trina began, then apparently decided to try another tact. "But let's not discuss someone so unpleasant. I was wondering when you could start on my home. The sooner the better."

"I'm sure," Jake said. "But I think you've misunderstood. I'm booked up at the moment."

Trina stared at him. "But I'm offering you a lot of money. Surely that greasy kid who works for you told you—"

"The greasy kid's name is Billy," Jake told her, enjoying her sudden discomfort.

"Well, he didn't seem too bright, but he must have told you how much money I'm offering."

"Oh, he told me all right. He was bright enough to get the figure right," Jake said dryly, but the sarcasm was lost on Trina Halstead.

"So when are you going to start?" she asked impatiently.

Not "When can you start?" Jake thought irritably. The woman apparently thought everything was negotiable if cash was involved.

"I already told you. I'm booked up."

"Surely you're not doing work for *her?*" she asked, jabbing a finger in Laura's direction.

"My work schedule is a private matter," Jake said mildly. "And so are my finances. Now, if you wouldn't mind letting the lady and me get back to dinner."

Trina laughed. "Oh, that's no lady," she said. "And don't fool yourself about finances. That's the only reason she's attaching herself to you. As for you," she went on, turning to Laura, "we're going to have that talk about Molly one way or the other."

Jake didn't care for the nasty smile on Trina's face. As she turned to go, the woman reached out one manicured hand and deliberately knocked over Laura's waterglass, making her leap back to keep it from splashing onto her clothes.

"Hey, hey, hey!" the bartender called, hustling from behind the bar. "What's going on here?"

"Just a little accident," Trina said airily. "I'll be seeing both of you later."

She sauntered out the door as the bartender and Jake rushed to mop up the water. Laura stood with her napkin balled in her fist, her jaw clenched as she watched Trina leave.

"Are you all right?" Jake asked her, the anger in his voice a residue left over for Trina.

"Fine," she said shortly, tossing the napkin on the table. "I'd just like to leave now, please."

The bartender glared at them both as Jake paid the bill. From the corner of his eye Jake could see Laura heading for the door, and he tried to hurry.

But the bartender had some parting advice for him. "I don't want to see none of you in here again," he told Jake loudly. "Not you or that woman—" he pointed at the closing door "—or the other loud broad. Understand?"

"Yeah," Jake said, glancing at the drunk now sleeping it off in the corner booth. "I can see we'd be bad for business."

Jake didn't see Laura at first as he approached the truck, and he worried that she had gone somewhere alone. But when he opened the door he found her leaning back against the seat, her eyes closed.

"You're not all right," he told her, waiting for her to tell him something, anything, about what she was feeling.

Laura sighed heavily. "For one thing, now *I'm* on that guy's list, right up there next to your name."

"That guy?" Jake repeated, then smiled as he realized that she meant the bartender who had been so relieved to see them leave. She was right, he decided. They were both definitely on the list of undesirables.

"So what did he tell you when you paid the bill?" she asked when he didn't elaborate. She had known the man would say something. He looked like the type who couldn't *not* say anything after someone deliberately dumped a glass of water in his place.

"We've both been invited to never eat there again," Jake told her.

She smiled, but not very much.

"Story of my life, McClennon," she told him. Abruptly she sat up. "One other thing."

"Yeah, what's that?"

Laura fixed him with a steady gaze. "Don't fight my battles for me. I can deal with Trina by myself."

"Right," he said mildly before turning away to start the engine. "With a little luck, she'll pour a cup of hot coffee on you next time."

"You don't understand," she persisted. "You can't come to my defense. This is a small town. You don't want to be known as the man who ruined his reputation by falling in with Laura Halstead."

"Let me tell you something," he said, turning to face her, placing one arm in a deceptively casual position on the back of the seat. "You already know what I did to my own reputation all by myself. I was tossed out of this place long before you came around. I think I can handle any fallout where you're concerned. And if I can't—you'll be the first to know." He faced forward again and pulled the truck from the parking lot.

But Laura wasn't convinced. He didn't know how persistent and mean Trina could be. He didn't know how far she would go to disrupt someone's life if that someone displeased her. No one but Ali had stuck by Laura when it came to Trina, and Laura had little hope that this man would now.

"Where are we going?" she asked, as she suddenly realized they weren't headed back to her house.

"I want to show you some molding we could use above your door. It won't take long."

Laura assumed that the trailer where Jake had stopped was his office. The yard was overgrown, and the wooden steps leading up to the door were precariously loose.

"Careful," he warned her. He took her hand to help her up after he opened the door.

When Jake flipped the switch inside the door an overhead light with one dim bulb came on. It gave little illumination. Jake was still holding her hand, but Laura decided against abruptly pulling away. She didn't want to provoke him into a fight. He was irritated enough by their encounter with Trina.

He turned to her and studied her face in the dim light. Laura could feel her heartbeat in her throat. She suddenly wanted him to touch her. Wanted him so badly. But it was the kind of wanting that she had refused herself before tonight, that she would refuse herself again.

Slowly Jake released her hand, and she let it fall to her side, still letting him look into her face. She hoped that her expression was confident and neutral enough, that her want didn't show.

"The molding's over here," he said, his voice slightly husky. He led her to a counter by the window, turning on another light as he went. While he sorted through the pieces of wood stacked there amid various tools and pieces of paper, she glanced around the trailer. It was pretty dark, but it dawned on her as she took in the sinkful of dishes and the dirty shirts thrown over a chair that he probably lived here. She could see an open door at the end of the trailer, most likely a bedroom.

"It's quite a mess, isn't it?" he said, and she glanced back at him, feeling guilty at being caught looking around. "It's been a long time since I cared about anything like this, at least enough to do something about it."

The dishes in the sink, the clothes. She began to wonder if he was saying he had made a token effort to pick up. And if so, why? Surely not for her. Even if he had planned on bringing her here to show her the molding, he had done nothing to prepare her for anything beyond that, unless she could call his holding on to her hand something.

Trying to figure him out was giving her the beginning of a headache.

"This is it," he said, handing her a piece of wood. He put his hand on her shoulder and moved her gently until she was under one of the lights. She looked at the wood in her hands, but it was a few moments before she actually focused her eyes on it.

"It's mahogany," he said, reaching over to run his finger along it. "I salvaged it from an old house that was torn down. It's the right age and style for your door frame. What do you think?"

Laura didn't know what to think. She couldn't concentrate with him standing so close. "It's beautiful wood," she said, glancing up and meeting his eyes. Hastily she handed the piece back to him.

He stood watching her, and her eyes dropped to his hands. He was worrying his thumb again, rubbing it absently.

"Did you cut yourself?" she asked, to fill the silence between them.

Jake glanced down at his hand, then shook his head. "It's just a splinter. It'll work itself out eventually."

She half smiled. "Eventually could be a while. Why don't I take a look at it?"

He hesitated, and Laura cocked her head to one side. "Regardless of what you think, I *have* done this before. Looked at splinters," she said to qualify, because her mind kept moving to things other than splinters, like the way the dim light accented the planes of his face. "Molly can't resist seesaws. I'm always digging splinters out of her legs." She was prattling, but she couldn't seem to stop. Seeing the look on his face, she added, "Maybe *dig* was a poor choice of words."

"What do you need?" he asked.

What did she need? Only to have him touch her again. But she realized that the question was in relation to the splinter.

"Some tweezers and alcohol for starters. I won't need a scalpel unless I run into trouble." At least that made him smile, and she relaxed a little. She didn't think she would be able to touch his hand if the tension remained at such a high pitch. As it was, she was avoiding his eyes because she didn't want him to read her expression.

"This way," he said, and she followed him down the hall to the darkened room she'd surmised was a bedroom. She was right, she saw, when he turned on the light. He went into the bathroom off to the side, but she hung back, surreptitiously looking around. The bed was unmade, not surprising, given the condition of the rest of the trailer. There was no nightstand, only a large cardboard box turned upside down, a flashlight resting precariously on the top. And beside that a photograph.

Seeing that he was preoccupied with rummaging through a bathroom drawer, she edged closer to the picture. This room, like all the others, was dark, but she could see enough to tell that the photograph was of a woman. A young, smiling woman standing in front of a flower garden, a tool of some kind in her hand, maybe a trowel.

"Found it," Jake said from the bathroom, and Laura jumped guiltily. He glanced over his shoulder at her and turned, looking at the place she was facing.

"My wife," he said quietly and carefully.

"She's . . . she was very attractive," Laura said, coming toward the bathroom.

"She liked flowers. Like you." He was looking at his hand and not at her as he said it. If she could read anything from his lack of inflection and the composure in his face it was that she and his wife had only that in common. Unless Laura was reading her own feelings of inadequacy into his words. She still didn't understand him, and her inability to do so left her disquieted.

He abruptly held out his hand to her, and she took it in hers, turning it to the light to inspect the splinter. It was lodged deeply in his palm at the base of his thumb, and she wasn't sure that tweezers alone would do the job. It was also red and obviously sore.

She briefly let go of his hand to pour some alcohol over the tweezers, then looked at his thumb again. Gently she tried to grasp an end of the splinter with the tweezers. His hands were rough and callused, but she felt her mouth go dry at the strength there. She found his hands incredibly beautiful. She was sure that they mirrored the man himself.

"We'd been married four years," he said, looking off into the other room. "We'd decided it was time to start a family."

She probed more deeply with the tweezers, biting her lip when he winced. But she wasn't sure if he was more hurt by her ministrations or his memories.

"We thought we were incredibly lucky," he went on, "because she got pregnant almost immediately. The whole family was excited. The baby was due in April."

Laura caught the end of the splinter with the tweezers and began gently pulling back.

"Beverly wanted me to go to her mother's with her just before Christmas. She had some cookies to deliver for a party. I was tired. I'd been working long hours all week, and I wanted to sit home and rest. She went alone."

Laura heard the guilt in his voice, and she stopped working to look up at his eyes. They were shadowed and haunted, and her heart clenched. He still wasn't looking at her.

"It was only half an hour later, I guess, when the doorbell rang. It was Carl from the sheriff's office, his cap in his hand. 'It was a drunk driver,' he said. I don't think I'll ever forget the look on his face. Or the cookies scattered and broken on the highway," he said.

Laura gave one final pull and the splinter came out. Jake sighed deeply, but she didn't think he was even aware that the splinter was gone. She stood holding his hand, letting her thumb gently caress his rough skin. She ached with the need to have him hold her, but she only stood and watched him.

When he did look at her, he was like a man waking from a dream. His hand came up tentatively and touched her hair. Laura held her breath, her blood pounding in her throat. The same hand cupped her face, his thumb stroking her lower lip. Laura swallowed hard and let him look into her eyes. She knew that he would see her want, but she was too needy to care.

"Laura," he said softly, the smallest of smiles playing around his mouth. "Why did you let me tell you that?"

"Because you wanted to," she said honestly. *Because you needed to.*

"You shouldn't be so kind to men in their trailers, Laura Halstead," he warned her softly. "Next thing you know they'll take advantage of you." His mouth hovered close to hers, and before he finished speaking he was kissing her, his lips pressing hers as if he could find some important answer there.

Her mouth parted on a soundless sigh, and Jake explored her with his tongue as she pressed herself against him.

Her breasts were warm and soft against his chest, and he lowered one hand to let his fingers trace her roundness, edging between their bodies until he could stroke the nipple. It was already hard. Her moan was little more than a throaty whisper.

He stopped kissing her long enough to lean his forehead against hers. Her eyes were closed, her mouth still parted.

He knew that if he asked her to go to bed with him she would. He didn't know if it would be kindness on her part or if she truly wanted him, but it wouldn't be right. He had had two relationships in his life, and both times they had ended in grief.

It was better if he left Laura unsullied by his own bitterness. In the long run she would suffer less. And so would he.

She opened her eyes quizzically when he put her away from him. "We should go," he said, meeting her eyes.

Laura stared back at him. "A second ago I would have sworn we were going somewhere else." She didn't sound angry, he thought, but hurt.

"I was wrong to do that," he said. "I'm sorry."

"So am I," she said shortly as she left the bathroom to retrieve her purse. "I remember the other night you telling me that I was the one making it impossible for me to have a relationship." She looked back over her shoulder as she opened the door. "Welcome to the club."

"What almost happened here wouldn't have been a relationship," he told her as he followed. "It wouldn't have even been a good start to one."

She supposed he was right, but it was hard to be understanding when she'd been as ready as a woman could be to go to bed with a man, and then be turned down. Oh, he'd been polite and considerate, but there was no getting around the fact that it was a refusal nonetheless.

Jake slid into the truck seat next to her. He put the key in the ignition, then stopped and turned to her. "I don't know if it means anything to you," he said, "but I've never... come that close with another woman in three years."

She supposed that he was telling the truth, but it did nothing to ease the ache she felt deep inside. The first nice man she'd come close to, the first decent man she'd let herself touch, and he'd turned her down. She should have figured as much.

"It isn't what you think," he said, after the silence between them lengthened, compelled for some reason to ease her hurt.

"And what do I think?" she asked quietly. She noticed that he wasn't taking a direct route to her house, probably to give both of them time to regroup their scattered emotions.

"You think I don't want to make love to you because of what other people around here think about you. You think that maybe I'm inclined to agree with them." He waited a minute, then said, "Am I right?"

"Are you?" she asked. "Inclined to agree with them?"

"Do you suppose that a man who drank away several years of his life in a very public way is going to pass judgment on someone else?" he shot back.

"Ah, but you redeemed yourself," she said.

"Did I? I don't drink anymore, but God knows I can't promise I'll never do so again. I'd be a fool to think I'm strong enough to promise that."

"Don't you see?" she said, turning in the seat to face him impatiently. "All that doesn't matter. A man is forgiven a lot more easily than a woman is."

Jake abruptly pulled the truck in front of a gravel parking lot bordered by a metal gate and fence. "And what did you do that's so unforgivable?" he asked her as he turned off the engine. "Shoplifted? Ran with a wild crowd? Got sent to a juvenile home? That's over and done with, Laura."

"It'll never be over," she insisted.

Jake grasped her shoulder. "You don't have to pay the rest of your life."

"Yes, I do," she hissed. "I do. I broke my mother's heart."

"Why? How?" He didn't understand.

But she had pulled away from his hand and was out of the truck the next instant, walking rapidly away. Jake scrambled after her, catching her by the arm and spinning her around to face him. In the moonlight he could see the traces of tears on her face before she swiped at them with the heel of her hand.

Laura looked past him at the sign on the gate. "Oh, God," she said.

Jake looked around and realized where they were. It was the county's historic jail, dating from 1860.

"Well, we've certainly come to the right place," she said with bitter irony.

"Listen to me," Jake said, grasping both her arms and making her look at him. "You're beating yourself up over something that doesn't matter now." He remembered her saying that her parents were dead, so he supposed that to her it would always matter. He knew what it was like not to be able to make amends to someone. But she also had to understand that the past was the past.

"You have to let it go," he told her. "Laura, I'm sure your mother hated what you did to yourself, but she knew you didn't do it to hurt her."

Laura shook her head. "That's just it," she said sadly. "I *did* do it to hurt her."

He still didn't know what she was talking about, and he held her away to look into her face. The eyes that met his and then fell away were filled with misery.

"I always knew something was wrong, that for some reason I was different," she said shakily. "I could feel my mother's tension, my father's anger. I didn't know what it meant, why it was there, but I knew it existed. And I knew that it was because of me. It wasn't until I got into trouble the first time that I found out."

"Found out what?" he asked, worried about the utter hopelessness he heard in her voice.

"I was eleven and out with the other kids," she said, "and I got caught shoplifting. I'd done it on a dare, but now I was scared to death. I guess the store manager wanted to teach us all a lesson, because he called all of our parents. The other mothers came and took their kids home, but it was my father who walked into that room to get me. And he took one look at me and I could see all the disgust on his face. When we got to the car he said, 'I told your mother you'd never be any good. But thank God you're no blood of mine.'"

"What are you saying?" Jake asked, holding her steady as she swayed beneath his hands.

"I asked my mother that night, but I already knew what she was going to say. It only took a good look in the mirror or a few jokes about my red hair from well-meaning relatives who didn't know. My father wasn't my father at all. My mother was pregnant before she married him. They never had any children of their own, and I think he resented me from the day I was born. No," she said firmly. "I *know* he resented me. He made it plain. And from the day I found out why, I set about proving to him and my mother that I didn't need them, that they couldn't hurt me even if they left me to rot in jail." She pulled away from him and stared up at the moon. "Even though it was tearing up my mother trying to keep peace in the house."

Jake took a deep breath. "Your mother was the peacemaker?"

"I think she tried—at least for a while. But I was so furious that she couldn't—wouldn't—see how much my father didn't want me around the house, that I resisted all of her attempts. She ended up taking his side. And eventually, after enough scrapes with the authorities and overnights in jail, I went to the juvenile detention home." She glanced up at the small, dark, bleak jail behind them. "To this day I still feel like I'm inside those walls."

"Your mother just abandoned you to the system?" Having grown up with a strong, supportive mother, he couldn't imagine a child having to endure a mother's indifference to her pain.

"I told you—I broke her heart. All she wanted was a quiet house, a kind husband and a nice daughter. I made sure she got none of those. Her patience wasn't eternal."

"What about your real father?" he asked. "Did you ever look for him?"

"I tried. At first I questioned my mother. She told me that he lied and cheated and stole from everyone he loved, and he ended up in jail. I thought my mother was lying about him until a counselor at the home found out what she could after I pestered her long enough." Laura folded her arms and looked back at Jake. "My mother had told me the truth. I think that was when I decided I didn't want to be like him anymore."

"Did you try to reconcile with your mother?" he asked.

Laura shook her head slowly. "I was still in the home when I decided to end my private war with the world. My mother was very sick, and I hadn't seen her in a long time. I think that my father—my mother's husband—wasn't especially nice to her after I was gone from home. Somewhere deep inside I'd thought that once I was gone she could be happy, that things would be right between them, if not with me. But it didn't happen."

"Then why are you still blaming yourself?" he demanded. "Can't you see the futility of it?"

She smiled without humor. "Isn't that the point of all guilt—futility?"

He wanted to press her for more, to demand that she realize how harshly she was blaming herself for something that had nothing to do with who she was or what she'd done. But he didn't get the chance. A car slowed on the highway, and headlights swept over them.

Jake released Laura's arms and turned, shielding his eyes against the bright lights, able to make out the flashing rooftop light assembly of a law enforcement car.

"Everything okay here?" a voice called, and Jake relaxed.

"Yeah, Carl, everything's fine. We just stopped for some fresh air."

"You in need of fresh air for a reason?" Carl asked in a deceptively casual voice as he got out of the car and came toward them. Jake knew what reason Carl was wondering about. *Had Jake been drinking?*

"No particular reason," Jake said, standing straighter as Carl stopped in front of him. Even though Jake towered over the deputy, he had enormous respect for the man, and he showed it. "It was a nice night for a walk." He turned toward Laura. "Carl, this is Laura Halstead. We just had dinner. Laura, Carl Morcini is a county deputy."

Laura nodded politely to Carl but said nothing. Carl, for his part, stepped closer to her, his hands on his hips.

"You wouldn't lead this fellow astray, would you, Ms. Halstead?" he asked somberly.

Laura wasn't sure if he was serious or not.

"I don't know, officer," she said. "So far I haven't led him much of anyplace."

"Ah, well," Carl said, shrugging, "he's not an easy one to lead." He looked significantly at Jake.

"You can rest assured that I don't intend to do anything of the sort," Laura told him.

"Too bad," Carl said with a hint of a smile. He swatted the side of Jake's arm as he passed him on his way back to the car. "There's something I'd pay good money to see."

It amazed Jake that Carl could joke about Jake's or Laura's intentions, given Jake's past history with Andrea Miller. She had led Jake down some dark paths. But the more Jake thought about it the more he realized that there had been no leading then, either. He had chosen his own way, a way that led inevitably to bars and liquor. He had blamed Andrea for his behavior, but though she might have been an accelerant, he was the one who lit the fire. A fire that had nearly consumed him.

If not for Carl...

"Do you have a screening committee to interview every woman you're seen with?" Laura asked him dryly, and he turned his attention back to her as Carl's car pulled back onto the road. "I'm surprised there isn't a questionnaire for me to fill out."

"What?" Jake asked, hearing the note of resignation in her voice more than her words.

"Your friends. There are apparently a lot of people who pay close attention to the women in your life."

"Women in my life?" he repeated, feeling suddenly as if she saw him as some kind of ladies' man. His brother Jordan maybe, but not Jake McClennon. One thing he didn't have was a string of women lining up for him or even a string of phone numbers in a little black book somewhere.

"I don't have women in my life," he told her, starting back to the truck and hoping she would follow. He didn't need this discussion in the middle of the night in a public place.

He held open her door for her, glad to see that she was a few steps behind him.

"For a man who doesn't have women in his life you have a lot of interested onlookers," she said.

He grunted and decided not to answer that, well aware that she had successfully deflected the conversation from her abysmal adolescence to his nonexistent love life. And he still didn't know anything about her late husband.

Laura watched him covertly as he drove. He was obviously uncomfortable talking about his past relationships, and she couldn't help but wonder about the woman he'd mentioned in passing, the one who came along after his wife died and caused him so much grief. She didn't want to be curious about this man, and she certainly didn't want to feel any attraction to him, but she seemed to have no choice in the matter. The way other people treated a man said a lot about him, and everyone seemed to care about Jake.

She was afraid that she was beginning to care for him, too. And not just because she wanted to go to bed with him.

When they pulled up at her house, he walked her to the door and as she unlocked it she could hear the phone ringing.

"I'd better get that," she said, hurrying inside and immediately worrying about Molly. Jake stepped into the hall and closed the door, his practiced eye already envisioning how the molding would look around her door. He was vaguely aware that Laura was giving short, succinct answers to whoever had called her, but he tried not to listen.

She was obviously worried and in a hurry when she came back to the hall, fumbling with her purse and keys.

"I have to pick up Molly," she said.

"What's wrong?"

"It's Trina again. Ali said she came there to see Molly. Now Molly's upset."

"I'll drive," he said, making an immediate decision to get involved, even though she hadn't indicated she wanted help.

"You don't want to do this," she told him.

"I'll decide what I want to do. We'll take my truck." He went out the door before she could refuse his help, but he waited at the bottom of the porch steps while she locked the door.

Laura looked at him sharply when she came down the steps, and he knew that she must be wondering what his motivations were now. He supposed that she had legitimate reason to wonder, given the way he had turned her down in the trailer.

I'm not the least bit good at this, he thought, *this* being the way he dealt with women in general and Laura in particular. He was pulled in opposite directions. He wanted to help Laura, but he didn't want to become emotionally entangled. And that was becoming increasingly difficult. He wanted to touch her whenever he looked at her, just the way he had always wanted to touch Andrea. But Andrea had used his need to touch her for her own ends, while Laura didn't.

Ali's house was two miles north on the highway, and the porch lights were on when they pulled into the drive. Laura got out and immediately hurried to the door. Jake followed but at a distance. He needed to let Laura set the tone with her daughter.

Ali opened the door and hugged Laura briefly before she had a chance to ring the bell. She gave Jake a strained smile.

"She's in the kitchen having some cocoa," she told Laura in a low voice. "She's frightened."

"What happened?" Laura asked.

"Trina rang the bell, and when I answered she stood on the porch loudly announcing that you are a terrible mother and Molly needs someone who cares about her. Molly heard her voice and came running. I don't know how she knew that Molly was here."

Laura's shoulders sagged. "She found us at the restaurant. I think she knows Jake's truck."

Ali nodded. As Laura started for the kitchen, Ali put one hand on her arm. "Laura, she said some awful things about you."

"Doesn't she always?" Laura said in a brittle voice. But she forced aside her bitterness in order to deal with Molly.

"What's this?" Laura asked brightly when she entered the kitchen. "Are you having a nightcap, Molly?"

Laura took care to keep the worry from her voice and face, but it broke her heart to see Molly look at her with such solemn, frightened eyes. As she knelt down beside Molly's chair and ran her hand soothingly over the child's hair she noted that her cup of cocoa was untouched.

Ali went to her own daughter and touched her on the shoulder. "Come on, Beth," she said quietly. "Molly's mom needs to talk to her."

Laura knew that Jake was nearby, but he wasn't hovering. He had discreetly positioned himself on the other side of the kitchen doorway, and she could hear Ali talking to him in a low tone.

"Come here," Laura said gently, and Molly immediately threw her arms around her mother's neck. "What is it, sweetie?" Laura whispered. "What did Grandma say that frightened you?"

Molly hugged her for another long moment, on the brink of tears and gulping hard to hold them back. "She said you're a bad person," Molly whimpered. "She said you're going to go to jail."

"No, no, of course not," Laura said, stroking her daughter's back. "I'm not going to jail, honey."

"But she said you were in jail before, and they were gonna take you back." She was hiccuping now with the effort of holding in her tears.

Laura sighed heavily. Trina had never told Molly that before, and Laura supposed that it was her trump card where her granddaughter was concerned. Laura took a deep breath and held her daughter slightly away so she could see her face.

"I was in jail once, Molly," she said, and she felt a searing pain as her daughter's eyes widened. "It was a long time ago, and I was a teenager. Older than you but still young. I stole some things and that was wrong. But that's over now, honey. I'm not going to jail again. Do you understand?"

Molly nodded slowly, her face still apprehensive. "Can Grandma make you go to jail?" she asked timidly.

"No, honey, she can't." Laura smiled and brushed back Molly's hair. That was one thing to be thankful for. "Do you want to go home now?"

Molly nodded, and Laura became aware that Jake had moved into the room behind her. His smile was strained, but he stooped and picked up Molly.

"Come on, sunshine," he said, ruffling Molly's hair. "Let's take you and your mom home."

Laura was quiet on the short trip, but Molly, apparently over her recent trauma, chattered on about the toys she'd played with at Ali's. There were several things Jake would have liked to tell Laura, but nothing he could say in front of Molly. His distaste for Trina Halstead had increased tenfold in the aftermath of her underhanded attack. She and Andrea would have made a good pair, he thought darkly.

At her door, Laura thanked him, but she made no move to invite him inside. "I don't know if I can go anywhere with you again, McClennon," she said, attempting a smile. "We keep getting thrown out of places."

"Don't," he said, because he saw through her attempt to cover her pain. "Tell me what I can do."

Laura shook her head. "You've done enough already. Thank you." She dredged up another shaky smile. "Good night, Jake."

He stood on the porch for a few moments, listening to the dry leaves rustling in the wind. He strained to hear any conversation from inside the house, but it was futile. He didn't know how she would get through tonight, having had to tell her daughter that she had been in jail.

And Trina would revel in it.

Jake strode down the steps and got in his truck. He couldn't just walk away and leave her to deal with this.

Back at the trailer he sat at the table and pushed around piles of papers, thinking. Then he made a phone call.

Chapter Six

"This is against my better judgment, you know," Rowen Pruitt warned Jake, taking another long gulp of coffee.

"I'm asking you as my friend, not my lawyer," Jake told him, trying not to show his impatience. He'd called Rowen the night before last, the night Trina had showed up at Ali's house, and asked for a favor.

Jake had badly wanted to see Laura the next day, but Frank ran into problems with the drywall where he and Billy were working. The wall was bowed, and Jake had spent the entire day helping them work around the problem.

He planned to go back to Laura's house today, but first he wanted to know what Rowen had found out.

"More coffee?" Esther asked, appearing at their table with the pot in hand.

"Yeah, and some skim milk to put in it," Rowen told her, and Esther sniffed.

"If you want those *fancy* coffee things, you got to go to that new shop on the highway with the boy waitresses in monkey suits and a menu that needs subtitles."

"They're called waiters," Rowen told her, leaning back in his chair and grinning. "And I want skim milk because my cholesterol is too high. I'm fifty-two years old, and all my numbers are going up—my weight, my cholesterol, my blood pressure and my eyeglass prescription. Everything except my damn hourly rate," he added wryly, looking pointedly at Jake. "Half my work is for free."

"Couldn't guess it by the price of your clothes," Esther told him as she eyed his three-piece suit, but she headed back toward the counter, presumably to get skim milk.

"I'll write you a check if that's what you want," Jake said, still waiting for the information.

"No, no, I won't take money from you," Rowen said, leaning forward to rest his elbows on the table. "Lord knows you did enough work on my house without charge. I owe you a few free hours at the least."

Jake waited, knowing that Rowen would get around to the point sooner or later. He did, after Esther brought him a small pitcher filled with milk.

"I want to ask you something," Rowen said, pouring the milk.

"What's that?"

He set the pitcher down and met Jake's eyes. "Do you want this information for business reasons—or is it personal?"

Jake gave a heavy sigh. He supposed he had to tell Rowen, especially in light of the fact that Jake was the one asking for a favor.

"It's personal."

"Are you interested in this woman?" Rowen asked, his brow furrowing.

Jake chose his words carefully. "I'm interested in her welfare, Rowen. Some people around here are giving her a hard time about things that happened a long time ago."

Rowen grinned again. "People like Corky Beachem?"

"Among others."

"Man, I wish I hadn't missed that party," Rowen said. "Now there's something I'd pay to see, Corky Beachem with her mouth hanging open while you escort her leper-at-the-wedding guest out for dinner.''

"I take it there's been some talk about the party?'' Jake asked warily. Just what both he and Laura needed, he thought. The recovering alcoholic and the jailbird keeping company. Now, there was a juicy topic of conversation for Corky and her friends.

"Talk!'' Rowen hooted. "My friend, if we had a local tabloid you would be front page news. I heard it from my stylist, and then my secretary was all abuzz at lunch the other day, after she heard it from a friend.''

"You go to a stylist?'' Jake asked, raising his brows.

"Don't change the subject,'' Rowen said, pointing his spoon at him. "I must say, I've enjoyed hearing the accounts of your little rescue at Corky's party. You've gone chivalrous on me, Jake.''

Jake sighed in resignation. He'd known that Rowen would want the details of his relationship with Laura. But he'd hoped he could sidestep most of the questions. Apparently not. The same thing that made Rowen a good attorney, a microscopic attention to detail, also made him a difficult friend at times.

"I didn't like what Corky was doing to her,'' Jake said. "And I don't like what her mother-in-law is doing, either.''

"Ah, the mother-in-law,'' Rowen said, shaking his head. "Worse by far than Corky Beachem, I'm afraid. She's the kind who gives barracudas a bad name. From what I gather, she wants that granddaughter badly.''

"What kind of chance does she have of getting her?'' Jake asked.

"I haven't checked into that fully yet,'' Rowen said.

"And what *have* you checked into?''

"What you asked,'' Rowen said, offended. "Laura Halstead's financial position. And,'' he added, putting on his reading glasses and looking at Jake over the rim, "her position is precarious, I'd say.''

"How so? Wasn't she her husband's beneficiary for his life insurance?''

"Well, yes," Rowen said, pulling a piece of paper from his breast pocket and perusing it, "but apparently he didn't carry a whole lot of coverage to take care of a young widow and a child. Looks like her benefit was forty thousand dollars."

"Forty thousand?" Jake repeated in disbelief. "I thought his family had money. At least Trina made it sound that way when she tried to hire me."

"Yes," Rowen said dryly. "I heard about that, too." He consulted the paper again. "From what my sources tell me, and I don't want this repeated because my source told me this in confidence," he said, leaning forward to give Jake a significant look over his glasses, "the husband's mother, Trina, controls the purse strings for the whole family. If sonny behaved she supplemented his salary. She was the one who took out the life insurance policy and paid the premiums."

Jake stared incredulously. "So she made sure her daughter-in-law and granddaughter would get some money in the event of the son's death but not enough to give them any freedom."

"You got it," Rowen said succinctly. "She wanted them right where she could control them. Fortunately for your lady, she makes a modest living with her business. She's not dependent on her mother-in-law."

"Which is giving her mother-in-law fits," Jake said. Another thought occurred to him. "But why would Laura come back here and buy a house that obviously strains her budget?"

Rowen smiled. "I know the answer to that, too. Apparently the owners of the Connally house were distant cousins of Laura's. The old lady's will stipulated that the house be offered to a relative before going on the open market. None of the other relatives wanted the place, so they contacted Laura and she was interested. I'm sure she would have preferred not to come back to her hometown, given past circumstances, but all in all she got a good deal on the house."

"That's about the only thing she's gotten a good deal on," Jake said dryly.

"You sure you want to get involved in this?" Rowen asked. "I mean, it wasn't that long ago that you had to deal with... well, you know."

"Yeah," Jake said. "I know. Andrea." At first, he had thought Andrea needed his help. Alone, with no family and a small income, he'd felt sorry for her. And Andrea had played him for a sucker. She'd gotten everything she could from him financially and emotionally before she'd moved on to look for greener pastures.

"*I* don't think there's any comparison between the two," Rowen said carefully, "but I'm not sure if you do or not."

"If she were anything like Andrea I'd have left her in Corky Beachem's hands," Jake said.

Rowen studied him a long moment, then looked down at his coffee. "Things didn't go well with Andrea. I wouldn't want to see that happen again."

"What you're trying not to say in so many words is that I was an uncontrollable drunk. You know I can't promise that it'll never happen again, Rowen."

Rowen shook his head. "Not you, Jake. You're too hard on yourself. The guilt alone will keep you away from liquor. What I mean is the aftermath of a woman who leaves you high and dry." He paused and raised his brows. "Maybe dry is the wrong choice of words. You lost your wife, Jake, and then you got involved with a woman who only saw you as a means to her monetary goals. As it was, you got away with losing only a car and a big chunk of dough."

Jake gave a grunt of dissent, and Rowen held up his hand. "And your self-respect. Don't forget that. She laid you pretty low, son, and there was no one around to pick up the pieces. Do you want to risk going through that again?"

Rowen had a valid argument, and the same thought had occurred to Jake. It was why he had worked so hard to keep Laura at arm's length. All to no avail. Getting involved again was like wading into a tangle of undergrowth. It would be just as difficult to turn around and go back as to go on. And perhaps equally painful.

"You haven't answered me," Rowen said. "What if this turns out badly, Jake? What happens then?"

"I don't know," Jake said honestly. "All I know is that Laura needs help, and I think I can give her that."

"At what price?"

"If you mean financial, I don't think that will be a problem," Jake said. "As for personal, time will tell."

Rowen shook his head. "I think you're about to do something foolish," he said. "And hell, I don't even know what it is you're planning."

"I don't know, either," Jake admitted. "I just know that I'm going to do something."

"So," Esther said, reappearing with the coffeepot, "you two gonna jabber some more or do you want breakfast?"

Rowen winked at Jake. "Jabbering seems safer around here. But I guess I'll have two eggs over easy and a strip of bacon."

"A man who drinks skim milk in his coffee has no business eating bacon and eggs," Esther informed him. She pulled her pencil from behind her ear and read aloud as she wrote. "Scrambled egg substitute and two pieces of unbuttered toast." She held up her pencil as Jake was about to order and said, "And pancakes for you, right?"

"Of course," Jake agreed, smiling.

"You're so predictable, Jake McClennon," Esther said with self-satisfaction before she walked away.

His predictability might just be about to change, Jake thought. And Esther wouldn't be the only person surprised. Even he wasn't sure what he was going to do.

"My prediction," Rowen said when Esther had left, "is that you're going to get very involved with this, like it or not. And I'm not sure I like it."

"Laura has this idea that she can't get involved with anyone because of her history," Jake said.

Rowen paused before answering. "I can understand that, given the gossip I've heard."

"Half of it's not true," Jake said. "And the rest is probably exaggerated."

* * *

Jake ate lunch with Laura and Emma again. He wanted to say something to Laura about the night at his trailer, but with Emma there it was impossible. He knew that things between him and Laura were muddled at best. He wanted her to understand that he hadn't meant to hurt her.

He was aware of Emma watching him through the silent meal. She found him in the hall after she'd helped Laura clean up the kitchen.

"Your stomach is hurting you?" Emma asked directly, her hands on her hips.

"No," he told her, smiling down from the ladder. "My stomach is fine."

"Your throat then?"

"My stomach, my throat, everything's fine," he said.

"Then I don't understand your face."

"What?"

"Your face says that something hurts. I'm good at fixing what hurts."

Jake climbed down from the ladder and sat on a lower rung, facing the girl. "I don't hurt here," he said, touching his throat, "but here—from something I've done." He put his fingers over his heart.

"Ah," Emma said. "That's different. Then it's words that hurt you. They're caught inside you, and they need to get out. I know how that is."

"Do you?" He was amused but didn't want to smile and hurt her feelings.

"Yes. I have two older brothers and two younger sisters. I'm right in the middle, so a lot of times I'm a bother to my brothers. And sometimes my sisters bother me, and I'm mean to them even when I try not to be. It isn't easy," she concluded with a shake of her head.

"No, it isn't," he agreed.

"But it stops hurting there when you say soft words," she advised him.

"Thank you, Emma," he said gravely. "I'll take your advice."

She went back to the workroom and soon he heard her singing a German song. He couldn't help smiling as he climbed back up the ladder.

Emma was right, he thought. He needed to say soft words to Laura to make both of them feel better.

Emma gave him a significant look as she left that afternoon, but Jake's smile faded as he closed the door after her. He stood in the hall a moment, then turned resolutely toward the workroom. Molly would be home from school anytime now. Laura wouldn't be alone much longer.

Jake stopped inside the doorway, struck by the sight of Laura bent over the work table, patiently sewing one of the christening gowns. The sun was low, and the light bathed her hair, turning it to fiery copper. Her lips were pursed in concentration, her slender fingers gracefully cradling the fabric. She was humming softly, the same German song he'd heard Emma singing. Jake just stood, listening and watching in fascination.

It struck him that when he looked at Laura he didn't think of either Beverly or Andrea. *Laura.*

She glanced up and jumped, startled to find him standing there. In her distraction she poked her finger with the needle and cried out, hastily removing her hand before it bled and stained the gown.

"Here," he said, quickly moving to her. "Let me see."

Laura clutched her hand to her chest protectively, then, blinking slowly, she held it out to him. Jake took out a clean handkerchief and pressed it to her finger, then held it firmly in place. He looked down at the gown.

"It's beautiful work," he said.

"This one was ordered by a woman in Michigan," Laura said, trying to fill the uncomfortable silence and take her mind off the fact that he was still holding her hand. "Her first grandchild's about to be born, and this will be her gift."

She abruptly pulled her finger away and unwrapped the handkerchief to check it. "I started making these after Molly was born," she said, staring down at her hand. "Before that my mail-order business consisted mostly of lace collars and blouses. Now I do mostly christening gowns. Emma does the majority of my blouse and collar orders.''

The mention of Emma reminded him why he had come in here, but he was still curious about Laura's work. "Does Molly's christening gown have a place for her name like this one?" he asked.

She didn't answer right away. "Several of them," she said finally. "I guess I thought I would have other children and then Molly's children would inherit the gown."

Other children. He hadn't thought much about it until now, but he had always hoped he would have lots of children. When his wife and unborn child died, the dream seemed to have died with them. Andrea had certainly shown no maternal inclinations. And since then there had been no one in his life.

Laura checked her finger and carefully folded the handkerchief. "Sometimes things don't work out the way we'd planned. I'll wash this for you."

"No need," he said, but she was already heading for the laundry room off the kitchen.

Laura dropped the handkerchief into the overflowing laundry basket of dirty clothes and turned to find Jake right behind her. *What?* she wondered. He seemed to need to say something, but he wasn't getting to the point at all.

"I was wondering," he said. Abruptly he looked around the laundry room. "You know, I could build some shelves in here, and you could use it as a pantry as well as a laundry room."

"I think it was probably a pantry in the first place," she said, watching him with her arms folded and speculating on what he had been wondering.

"It's big to have been a pantry originally, but maybe someone knocked out a wall along the way to enlarge it."

"Jake," she said, and he stopped surveying the room to look at her. "What is it? Is there a problem with the work here?"

No, he thought. Not with the work. With us. With me.

"I wondered if you liked to ride a bicycle?" he asked, noting her incredulous look. Obviously it was the last thing she'd expected him to say. "I saw two of them in the garage when I drove up today."

All right, she thought. We'll talk about bicycles.

"Molly and I used to ride a little. She loved it, but Trina...didn't want us doing anything in which she couldn't participate as well." Laura ran a hand through her hair. "I'm sorry. That was petty."

Jake wanted to touch her, to let her know that she had every right to be angry with Trina. But he didn't. The memory of her in his trailer was still so fresh. If he touched her he might not be able to stop what he had halted that night.

"I thought maybe we could all go for a ride. You, Molly and me," he qualified as though she might think he meant the whole town.

"Yes. Okay." She was totally baffled by his strange invitation, if that's what it was.

"Is the day after tomorrow all right?" he asked. "It's Sunday, so Molly won't be in school."

So it was an invitation after all. "That sounds fine."

"I have to help Frank and Billy tomorrow, so I won't be here." He stopped, thinking that he sounded like a man making excuses. Which he probably was. He had never felt so insecure about asking a woman to go on an outing. He couldn't make himself even think the word *date*.

The front door slammed. "Hey, where are you guys?" Molly called anxiously, the wood floor creaking under her sneakered feet.

"In here," Laura called back, her eyes still on Jake. "And wipe your feet."

The creaking temporarily stopped. "We had cupcakes today, and I had to give them to everybody, and the only one left for me was squished, and Jessica was laughing," Molly poured out, burying her head against Laura's hip.

"Poor starving baby," Laura crooned, kneeling down and pulling Molly against her in a big hug. She held her away and smiled. "Do you think it might make you feel better if we had hamburgers tonight and watched a movie?"

"A cartoon movie?" Molly asked hopefully.

"I think that could be arranged."

"And another cupcake?" Molly was smiling now herself.

"How about a cookie and an apple instead?"

"Okay!" That business settled, Molly bounced up on her toes and grinned at Jake. "Hi, Mr. McClennon! Look at the book I made in school today."

Jake knelt beside Laura and oohed and aahed over the picture book Molly had colored. On each page she'd laboriously printed a simple sentence telling what she did that day. "My mom and me go shop," read one page.

Unaccountably, Jake felt his throat constrict. He remembered lying in bed at night before the accident thinking about his unborn child and what they would do together. *As if we had all the time in the world to get to know each other.*

He knew that he and Laura had one thing in common at least—neither of them took anything or anyone for granted anymore. They'd both learned what thieves time and circumstances could be.

"And can we go get some leaves for school?" Molly was asking her mother as Jake tore his attention away from things he couldn't change now. "I got to have them for Monday."

Laura's eyes met Jake's over Molly's head. "Mr. McClennon is going to go bike riding with us Sunday. I imagine we can collect all kinds of leaves then."

"Do you know trees?" Molly asked Jake, obviously worried that he would take her to a place devoid of flora.

"Yes," Jake said, smiling at her. "Yes, I know all kinds of trees. We'll find a whole bunch for you."

"All right," Molly said, reassured. "I guess you know where some good trees are. Can we go get a hamburger now?" she asked her mother.

"It's too early, Mollster," Laura said, making Molly giggle. "Go get an apple."

Molly dashed around the corner to the kitchen, and Jake could hear her scraping a chair at the table.

"I should go," Jake said as he stood. "I have some bookkeeping to catch up on." He was hoping for an invitation to dinner, but apparently none would be forthcoming, judging from Laura's staid expression. He took responsibility for this breach between them, but he couldn't think of a way to end it and still keep their relationship on a level with no intimacy. The bike ride was a start, though.

"We'll see you Sunday then," Laura said, standing and holding Molly's book against her chest. "What time should we be ready?"

"Ten okay?"

"Fine." She nodded and followed him to the front door.

When he had gone she continued to stare at the closed door. Jake McClennon wasn't like any other man she'd known. If not for his rejection of her, they would have made love the other night, and yet now he was asking her to go bicycle riding with him. Men usually conducted that scenario in reverse order. First the man tried to get the woman to sleep with him, then the man stopped asking the woman out.

Not that she had firsthand experience. She hadn't gone to bed with any man other than her husband. But she knew the routine from the countless stories she'd overheard in grocery stores, from acquaintances and, yes, on talk shows. *Why don't women know better?* she often wondered. It happens over and over, but we don't learn. She had long ago come to the uncomfortable conclusion that her husband, Robert, would have left her, had she not become pregnant.

But Jake didn't fit the bed-them-as-fast-as-possible-then-leave-them stereotype. He seemed in no hurry to do anything with her, other than work on her house.

Molly called from the kitchen, and Laura sighed. Maybe she'd never understood what men wanted.

Laura didn't feel assertive enough to jostle with teenagers at the closest fast-food chain, so she drove Molly to the Burger Haven where Jake had first taken her.

"Look at that!" Molly cried as they pulled into the parking lot, fascinated by the giant neon hamburger on the roof.

"Spiffy, huh?" Laura said, smiling. "Your mom knows how to dine out, kiddo."

Laura covertly checked the parking lot, relieved not to see Jake's truck. She didn't feel up to second-guessing his motives again tonight.

Esther grinned at them from behind the counter, making Laura hope fervently that she hadn't walked into an inquisition.

"By yourselves?" Esther asked, making an obvious display of peering behind Laura.

"Ladies night out," Laura explained. "We wanted to get a couple of hamburgers to go."

"And who's this?" Esther asked, smiling toward Molly as she pulled her pencil from above her ear.

"My daughter, Molly. And she *really* likes hamburgers."

"Yeah," Molly agreed, grinning. *"Really."*

"You've come to the right place," Esther said. "How about two with the works? And two orders of fries."

"Sounds good," Laura said.

Esther scribbled their order, then fastened it on a carousel above the grill. "Special customers," she told the cook who grunted in response.

Looking around, Laura noticed that most of the booths were filled, generally with men in their twenties and thirties, all wearing work clothes. Not a suit to be seen. Somehow that didn't surprise her. And she kind of liked it.

"So," Esther said, leaning over the counter to speak to Molly. "What are you going to wear trick-or-treating this year?"

"I want to be a spider," Molly told her, "but I don't think my mom has time to make me a costume."

"Emma and I have to finish those christening gowns," Laura told her, wishing she could just give in to her guilt and promise to make the costume. But she had to put their income first. She probably should have turned down Jake's invitation to go bike riding so she could sew instead, but she couldn't let autumn slip away without getting herself and Molly outside for a time.

"It's what you call," Molly began, stopping to search for the right word, "it's...hopeless."

"I have just the remedy for hopeless causes," Esther told her, winking. "You come with me."

Not sure where they were headed, Laura put her hand on Molly's shoulder and followed Esther around the counter and out a side door. She adjusted Molly's sweater as the wind hit them in the face when they rounded the building to the back. All she could see was a Dumpster and a weedy plot of grass with a concrete statue in the middle. Laura decided that the back of the Burger Haven certainly qualified as a hopeless cause in its own right.

"This," Esther said proudly, stopping in front of the statue, "is St. Jude, patron saint of hopeless causes."

"He looks like—" Laura began and then bit off her comment. Esther no doubt would not appreciate having her saint called a dwarf. He even sported what might have once been a pointed hat but now was broken and chipped to the point of looking like a beret. "Like a very kind saint," she amended.

Esther beamed. "I've always considered him my own personal patron," she said fondly.

"I didn't know saints were so short," Molly observed.

"Big things come in little packages," Esther quoted. "And I'm going to share him with you, Miss Molly. Feel free to ask St. Jude for what you want. I have, many times. And I'm here to tell you that if it weren't for him, why that Jake McClennon would still be on the path to ruin."

Now there was an interesting topic, Laura thought.

"He seems very stable now," she observed.

Esther snorted. "Too stable, if you ask me. That man might as well check into a retirement home for all the enjoyment he was getting out of life before you came along."

"Me?" Laura said, startled.

"After that Andrea woman got her hooks into him I thought he'd end up in jail or dead for sure," Esther went on, unperturbed at Laura's obvious shock. "She had everyone thinking she was so sweet and innocent when all the time—" Esther snorted again. "Well, don't let it be said that Esther Wardlow doesn't know a rotten floozy when she sees one. I told everyone as much. It took some doing on St. Jude's part to get Jake back on the right track. And then the man turned into a stick-in-the-mud." Esther sighed. "Well, no matter. Things will be fine. Now, Molly, you go ahead and have a chat with St. Jude if you want." Esther winked at Laura and put a beefy hand on her shoulder, turning both of them back in the direction they'd come. "Those hamburgers ought to be about ready."

Laura glanced over her shoulder and saw that Molly was apparently taking Esther at her word as she stood gravely studying the statue. They had almost reached the side door when Molly caught up to them.

"Now," Esther said in her booming voice, "who wants hot sauce on their burger?"

They were on their way back home, the bag of hamburgers and fries filling the car with their aroma, before Molly broached the subject of the statue again.

"Do you think St. Jude listens to little kids?" she asked.

Laura tried to think of a satisfactory answer. "I think that anyone that short and chunky would probably listen to everyone," she said at last, smiling at Molly.

Molly grinned back. "That's what I thought."

She didn't say anything else about St. Jude, and Laura found herself going back over what Esther had said about the woman who had nearly ruined Jake. *The rotten floozy.* Esther's description was certainly colorful, but Laura suspected that half the town would describe Laura in the same terms.

Maybe she ought to start talking to St. Jude herself.

Chapter Seven

Laura couldn't decide what to wear, and it annoyed her that it mattered. She couldn't seem to overcome her sartorial insecurities when it came to Jake.

She finally decided on jeans and a long-sleeved green blouse, topped with a black pullover sweater. She pulled her hair back and secured it with a small cloth band. She looked too plain, she thought critically as she surveyed her reflection in the mirror.

On the spur of the moment she rummaged through her drawers and came up with a plastic tube of mascara she hadn't used in at least a year. It was dry, but not too dry to use. Quickly she brushed the mascara over her lashes before she could stop to worry about whether or not she would get an infection from old mascara. Then she reached up and pulled a few tendrils of hair loose and let them fall softly around her face.

The woman looking back at her from the mirror was almost a stranger. She looked younger, more vital, alive. She looked like a woman who was looking forward to seeing a man. She looked like a happy woman.

Don't get too used to happiness, she told herself. *Because it doesn't last.*

She didn't have time to worry any longer about her state of mind because Molly called from downstairs.

"Mom! He's here!"

Laura looked great, Jake thought as Molly opened the door for him. He could see her coming down the stairs, and if Molly hadn't tugged him by the hand toward the sewing room he would have stood and stared.

"What's this?" he asked, nodding toward the pile of black cloth on the work table.

"My spider costume!" Molly cried, dancing up and down in her excitement. "Mom and Emma are doing it for me! Isn't it great? I'm going to be *so* scary."

"Yes, you are," Jake agreed, smiling at Molly's enthusiasm.

"She wanted it so much," Laura said from the doorway. "And Emma and I decided we could make it and still finish the christening gowns on time."

She noticed that he was looking at her when he turned, really looking. And he seemed to like what he was seeing. Unaccountably, she could feel herself blushing.

"It's a nice day for a bicycle ride," she said, grabbing on to any topic to cover her discomfort.

"Yes, nice," he agreed, but he was still looking at her, and the comment took on an added meaning.

"Well, I guess we're ready to go," he said after another long moment of silence.

"I made some sandwiches," she offered, "unless you had something else in mind."

"There's an ice cream stand near the river, but all they have is overcooked hot dogs and slushy ice milk. Sandwiches sound much better."

"And brownies," Molly advised him. "I helped."

"Then I bet they're extraordinary," Jake said, making Molly laugh again.

Jake followed them to the garage and checked Molly's bike, filling the tires with air and tightening the seat.

"I haven't ridden for years," Laura said by way of apologizing for the condition of her own bike.

"It doesn't matter," Jake said, turning toward his truck. "We're not taking your bike."

"We're not—" Laura began, confused. She stopped short when she saw the tandem bike in the back of his truck. "You're not getting me on that thing, McClennon," she told him ominously.

"*Somebody's* got to get on it with me," he said, grinning, "or I can't go. And Molly's legs are too short. Yours are just the right length."

"Yeah," she said dryly. "They reach the ground when I stand up. And my hands are just the right size to fit around your neck. I'm *not* riding that thing, Jake."

Her protest seemed to amuse him more than anything. At length she gave up and decided he would just have to see for himself that this wouldn't work.

The problem was that it did work—after a fashion. Laughing, Jake had insisted that Laura sit on the back seat while he held the front handlebars, then pushed the bike to get it started. When the bike was moving, Jake hopped on, and he and Laura went wobbling down the drive. Molly trailed behind, laughing so hard that she nearly fell off her own bike.

Laura couldn't help but smile. She had never heard her daughter laugh so hard, and she was treated to Jake's rare laughter as well. The whole thing seemed to do them all a world of good. Maybe it wasn't such a bad idea after all.

"See?" Jake called over his shoulder. "No problem."

"Watch where you're going!" she shrieked as the bike wobbled back and forth, and Jake laughed again, a sound she was learning to like a lot.

"Yes, ma'am," he said with mock contrition, teasing her as he deliberately swerved the bike again, earning himself a thump on his back. He really enjoyed teasing this woman, he admitted to himself, something he couldn't have imagined a few weeks ago. He also couldn't have imagined enjoying this kind of outing. But he was—immensely.

Laura soon fell into a rhythm of pedaling and tried to concentrate on the scenery. But every time she looked ahead she saw Jake's firmly muscled back and shoulders. His arms were sinewy and hard from physical labor, as were his thighs. *His thighs.* She had to stop looking down. His sculpted backside moved on the seat as he pedaled, and from there it was an easy glance to his thighs. Laura nearly groaned. She had never been prone to particularly erotic thoughts before, but they were running rampant now.

This wasn't fair, she thought. For so long she had considered herself almost sexless, and now the man who inspired heights of libidinous fancy was the same man who had turned gallant on her. She was going to have to think of something else.

They followed a bike path that paralleled the Mississippi River, and Laura forced herself to watch the sparkling water and the glorious parade of trees in full autumn regalia.

"Look, Molly!" Jake called out. "Mallards!" He pointed to the river, and Molly squealed in delight.

Although Jake was doing the lion's share of the pedaling, Laura was beginning to tire from the pace he was setting. As if he read her mind, Jake said over his shoulder, "Do you think Molly's getting tired?"

Excitement was still propelling her daughter, but Laura decided they could all use a rest. "She's probably ready for a break."

They settled the bikes against a tree between the path and the river and sat down on the grass to savor the day.

Jake lay back and stared up at the clouds. Molly flopped back beside him, imitating the way he bent his arm beneath his head. Jake sighed, and Molly did the same. Laura smiled.

"Mr. McClennon?" Molly ventured. "Will the river freeze like the ponds do?"

"If the winter's cold enough it'll freeze partway," Jake said. "But it's deep, moving water, Molly. It won't freeze completely. And you can call me Jake."

"Okay," Molly said agreeably. "What's that tree?" she asked, pointing to a spiny tree with a crooked trunk and yellow leaves.

"That's an Osage orange," Jake said, sitting up to look. "Native Americans used the wood for their bows and the settlers got a yellow dye from the roots. Let's go see if there's any of the fruit on the ground."

Molly jumped up and hurried after him eagerly, leaving her mother to look after them wistfully.

Robert had never spent more than half an hour at a time with his daughter, and that grudgingly. Laura often wondered how Molly had escaped with no feelings of abandonment. But Trina had doted on her only grandchild, maybe too much. She had made excuses for Robert and her own husband who also had had little use for children. And she had taken every opportunity to remind Laura that Robert would not have married her had she not gotten pregnant. Laura had miscarried soon after her marriage, another source of blame from Trina. Robert had been indifferent.

She thought of Jake losing his unborn child in the accident and remembered her own bereavement. Loss came in different ways, but it still left pain in its wake. She could clearly see Jake in his grief, turning to drink. She had done her own howling against the fates in an effort to block the pain. In the end, one had to go on. And that's what they'd both done, despite Jake's brief history with the woman he was so reluctant to discuss.

When Molly was born Laura saw her as an unexpected gift from life, a gift that made up for all the things that had come before. For the first time in her life she understood unconditional love. It was Molly who gave Laura the strength to leave Trina's house after Robert died and to withstand Trina's vigorous efforts to reclaim her granddaughter.

"Mom! Look!" A breathless Molly fell to her knees beside her mother, holding out her cupped hands. They were filled with leaves, a few nuts and a large, greenish orange ball. "This is that Osage orange," Molly explained, rolling the bumpy ball onto the ground. "There's little nuts inside. Isn't it cool?"

"Yes, it's cool," Laura said, smiling as Molly painstakingly told her the name of the tree that had shed each leaf, sometimes with a little prompting from Jake.

Laura glanced up at Jake, who was standing beside them, and flushed when she saw that he was watching her.

"What?" she asked, when she realized that Molly was saying something else.

"I said that Jake's going to take me trick-or-treating, Mom. We've already got it planned."

"I don't think you should ask Jake to do that," Laura said. "It's almost two weeks away, and he may have other plans."

"No, I'd enjoy it," Jake said, and Laura looked at him again. He seemed to mean it. But she didn't understand why he said he wanted to do it. This wasn't the kind of activity single men liked. Was he trying to impress her?

If that was his reason she was even more baffled. He had no reason to impress her. He knew that she would have slept with him. What more could he want?

"Mom? Please?" Molly danced on her toes.

"If Jake's sure it isn't an imposition," she said, giving him a hard look. Jake met her eyes and smiled. "Are you going to split your candy with him?" she teased Molly.

It was obvious from Molly's expression that that particular contingency hadn't occurred to her. "You don't eat much candy, do you, Jake?" she asked.

Jake pretended to consider. "Only licorice," he said.

Molly beamed. "I *hate* licorice! You can have all of mine! Wow, this is going to be great!"

"She's not usually this enthusiastic about everything," Laura said when Molly danced off to pick up some more of the Osage oranges. She realized that what she'd just said implied that she didn't offer her daughter many opportunities to be enthusiastic. She started to amend her statement, but Jake interrupted her.

"She's thrilled with the costume you're making for her," he said. "I think Molly's one of those lucky kids who finds pleasure in all kinds of things the rest of us take for granted.''

Yes, he was right, and she was surprised that he'd seen that in Molly. She wondered briefly how such an astute man had come to be involved with that woman who had nearly made a shambles of his life. Grief, maybe, she thought. Or anger at the loss he'd suffered. It was anger that had made her so rebellious that she'd nearly ruined her own life.

She realized suddenly that she hadn't felt that anger in a long time now. She no longer hated the father who had rejected her. In fact, all she felt was a dull melancholy that she hadn't reconciled with her parents before they died.

"What are you thinking about?" Jake asked, startling her away from her reverie.

"That it's time for lunch," she said, summoning up a smile and standing. No matter what her regrets, she wasn't ready to share them with Jake McClennon.

They were all tired by the time they got back to Laura's house. Jake had ridden the last three miles with Molly on the back of the tandem bike. "I'm bushed," Molly had said, and Jake had smiled at that particular expression, one he had heard often from his mother.

Jake saw the new car when they turned into the drive, and for a moment he worried that Trina was back. Then he recognized Rowen's late-model, low-slung sports coupe. "A friend of mine," he called over his shoulder to Laura who was behind him on Molly's bike.

Jake briefly made introductions when Rowen walked around the corner of the house in his three-piece suit, leaving out the pertinent fact that Rowen was a lawyer.

Laura waited, but neither man said anything about what this was all about. "Would you like something to drink?" Laura asked when what she really meant was "What's going on here?" Jake thanked her and said no for both of them, so there was nothing for Laura to do but excuse herself and take Molly inside.

Jake watched them go. He thought about how much he'd enjoyed just being with Laura and Molly, and he wondered if what Rowen had to tell him would change that.

Laura stopped to take one assessing glance at him over her shoulder before she went inside.

"I felt like a Sunday drive, so I thought I'd come find you. Esther said you might be here," Rowen said as he dusted off the porch step, then sat down. "This is a nice house. It needs a lot of work, but I imagine she realizes that. I don't guess she would have hired you otherwise. She seems like the type who likes to keep things in good order."

When Jake didn't say anything, Rowen went on. "It seems she tried to be as independent as she could during her marriage, given the circumstances."

"Well?" Jake prodded him impatiently when Rowen didn't say any more. At the moment he wasn't inclined to put up with Rowen's habit of leading up to a subject by the most casual path possible.

Rowen raised his brows but didn't comment on Jake's hurry.

"Well," he said, "Laura Halstead started her needlework business over her mother-in-law's objections. She targeted her market through magazines that cater to antique aficionados and the like. And the mother-in-law was quite an impediment."

"Speak English, Rowen," Jake said testily.

Rowen gave an exaggerated sigh. "Laura Halstead had to take out a bank loan to start her business. And do you know what she put up for collateral?"

"No, and I hope you plan on telling me sometime soon."

Rowen gave him an arch look and went on. "Her husband had a small piece of property left to him by his grandmother. He cosigned the loan with her. Apparently this so infuriated his mommy that she took back the Porsche she'd given him for his birthday." Rowen lifted his gaze to his own car. "A shame. I do so hate to see a sports car gathering dust in a garage."

"A real shame," Jake said dryly. Given his own modest upbringing, he couldn't imagine the kind of wealth that provided a sports car along with the birthday cake.

"Anyway, it was apparently the last time the boy stood up for his wife. He caved in when his mother insisted she had heart trouble and needed her child at home. Laura and her husband moved in with his parents after Trina stopped supplementing their rent on a fancy apartment."

"What did Trina's husband think of all this?" Jake asked.

"He doesn't seem any more effective at curbing her behavior than the son was. All the money is on Trina's side of the family, so all the weapons are apparently in her arsenal."

"What kind of man was Trina's son?"

"I'm a lawyer, not a psychiatrist," Rowen said dryly. "But from everything I hear he was molded at any early age by his mother, and the boy never quite escaped that."

"Meaning he let her control him," Jake said with distaste.

"Some unfortunate souls haven't got the strong will you have," Rowen told him. "Or her," he added, jerking his head toward the house. "She was determined to get out of Trina's financial clutches after her husband died. The older Mrs. Halstead offered the younger one mucho bucks to continue living in the house with her, but Laura opted out."

"And that's why Trina's after Molly?" Jake ventured.

Rowen shrugged. "I think she truly believes that Laura isn't a good mother for her only grandchild."

"What kind of a case does she have?" Jake said, deciding to cut to the chase.

Rowen made an elaborate display of pulling his reading glasses from his pocket, putting them on, then consulting a small notebook he fished out of his jacket pocket.

"Your friend's been arrested." He peered at Jake over his glasses. "Did she tell you that?" When Jake nodded, Rowen looked at the notebook again. "And she was in the juvenile home for a long stay after she assaulted her father with a knife. Mixed up with some kind of gang thing, too, though they didn't think of them as gangs so much back then. Crowd of tough kids into burglaries."

But Jake didn't hear any more of what Rowen said beyond the words "after she assaulted her father with a knife." Laura hadn't said anything about that to him. She hadn't even glossed over it. She just plain left it out.

Had he misjudged her so badly?

"There are some points against Laura if this comes down to a custody battle, but so far as I know Trina hasn't consulted an attorney yet," Rowen said, his voice winding down in the sudden realization that Jake wasn't listening. "Is there a problem with this?" he asked, folding his glasses and putting them away.

"I don't know," Jake said honestly.

"Then you'd better get yourself clear on that point before you do anything else," Rowen advised him.

Jake nodded. "Thanks, Rowen," he said, shaking his hand. "I appreciate the help. Send me a bill."

"Bills are for clients, not friends," Rowen said, standing and stretching. "Besides, I may need a hot tub installed in the future."

Jake rolled his eyes. "The Rowen Pruitt mansion grows ever more splendid." He sighed. "Take care."

"I will," Rowen said, eyeing Jake and clearly not entirely satisfied with what he saw. "And might I suggest that you do the same?" He looked at the bicycles parked in the yard and then back to Jake. "And that's completely free advice."

Jake sat on the step for a long time after Rowen left, going over what he'd been told. But no matter how many times he did, he couldn't reconcile the woman who had sat behind him on the bicycle with the girl who had assaulted her father with a knife.

Laura tried not to speculate about what was going on at the top of her porch. But she found herself straying close to the window on one pretext or another.

She grew increasingly irritated that they were using *her* porch to discuss something from which she was excluded.

And she strongly suspected that she was the topic of conversation. She didn't deserve Jake's suspicions, and it was time he damn well understood that.

The man in the suit left, but Jake still sat there, alone.

When he finally stood, she hurried back to the kitchen and pretended to be busy putting away the dishes that were in the drainer, determined not to discuss this until she was over her anger.

"Where's Molly?" he asked from the doorway.

"Upstairs," she said, pausing and looking around at him. He looked unsettled, the same way she imagined she looked to him.

"I think we need to talk," he said, pulling out a chair. Then he took another look at her face, and his own closed. "No, not now," he said, shoving the chair back in. "Maybe when I'm feeling different about this."

That was too much for her, and Laura crossed to him and jerked the chair away from his hands.

"*Don't* put me off like a child," she said furiously, despite her resolve not to talk to him while she was still angry. "I have a right to know what you were talking about on my porch."

"Yes, you do," he said, facing her across the chair. "It was about you."

Laura let go of the chair and crossed her arms, waiting.

"Sit down," Jake said.

"I prefer to stand," she told him, and Jake shrugged. "Suit yourself."

They didn't sound anything like the two people who had shared a day of bike riding with Molly, Laura thought in distraction. Somehow, something had gone wrong.

Jake paced the length of the kitchen and stopped at the window. When he faced her she couldn't really read his expression because of the bright light behind him. "Rowen is my lawyer," he said.

She raised her brows, but she wasn't really surprised. "And?"

"I asked him to check into some things for me," Jake said. "Things like your financial status when you were married and after. Why Trina is so concerned about Molly."

"Rowen dresses well," she said sarcastically. "He must charge a fortune."

"He's my friend, as well."

"It must be nice to have a lawyer for a friend," she said, the sarcasm still in place. "A little free work. And a deputy for a friend as well. The right side of the law is a fine place to be."

"I was always straight with them," he said, looking into her eyes. "Except when I was drinking."

There was a message in there for her. She could feel it in his gaze. But she didn't understand.

"So what did you find out about me?" she asked coolly. At the moment she didn't know if she was more angry with him for discussing her with someone else or the fact that he'd done it here on her porch.

"I think I found out more about your husband and his mother," he said, still holding her gaze. "He wouldn't—or couldn't—stand up to his mother, so she controlled his life in every way. Then she tried to bind you with her purse strings to keep you and Molly there after he died. And you infuriated her by leaving, anyway."

Laura could still hear the carefully controlled anger beneath his words, but she didn't understand why it was there. Her marriage was far less scandalous than her history before her marriage. He already knew the worst about her.

"The one time Trina couldn't control Robert was when he wanted to marry me," she said with quiet reserve. "I think it was his defiance then that made her dislike me so. Is there anything else you'd like to know about Robert?" she asked brusquely. "Or do you prefer to get your information secondhand?"

"I prefer to get it from a reliable and thorough source," he said, and she drew in her breath quickly. Anger mounted to the surface again.

Laura gripped the back of the chair. "I would have told you anything you wanted to know," she said through clenched teeth. "All you had to do was ask. *Me*," she added pointedly.

"And what would you have told me about assaulting your father with a knife?" he demanded quietly.

He noted with satisfaction that the color drained from her face. "He told you that?" she asked. "The lawyer?"

"Right out there on your porch," he said, pushing himself away from the window and approaching her. "When did you plan to mention that little incident to me?"

"Never," she said, closing her eyes.

"You must have really hated him," Jake said bitterly.

To his surprise Laura gave a short, mirthless laugh. "I did after that night."

"Why didn't you tell me?" he demanded. "It was a very important detail you left out."

"I didn't want to ever think about that again," she said angrily, gripping the chair so tightly that her knuckles turned white. "But to this day I can remember every detail. I was fifteen, and he brought me home from one of my many scrapes with the police. We were in the kitchen alone. Mom had run upstairs crying, and he told me to look what I'd done. Then he reached out and pulled up my blouse and started to fondle me." Laura wasn't looking at Jake now. Her eyes were focused past him. "I kept backing up," she said, "but I couldn't get away from him. And when I was pressed up against the counter I reached back, and my hand closed on a knife." She shuddered. "I just swung it, like it was a bat. And I cut his arm. He was so furious he called the police. It was on my record when I was sent to the juvenile home. But at least he would never touch me after that."

Jake's stomach turned in revulsion, not at Laura but at what had happened to her.

"Oh, God," he groaned. "I'm sorry." He reached for her, but she wouldn't let him touch her. Jerking away, she hugged her arms to herself. "Go home," she said in a flat voice. "You don't belong here."

"Laura," he said softly.

"Just get out, Jake." She sounded tired and defeated and vulnerable, but he knew that he could do nothing to help her now. He'd already messed things up enough.

She was right. He didn't belong there.

Chapter Eight

When Jake went back to Laura's house to work two days later, on Tuesday, it was Emma who answered the door. He didn't think he was imagining the reproach in her eyes, but Emma said nothing.

Jake worked alone in the foyer, and if Laura ever left the sewing room she didn't come anywhere near him. At lunchtime he sat on the step and ate his sandwich alone.

He had never felt more shunned in his life.

When Emma stepped past him to leave that afternoon, she stopped and looked back over her shoulder. Jake knew what she was going to say.

"I don't think soft words will do it this time," he told her gently.

"Then soft deeds," she said. "You study on it."

Molly came home from school, stopped long enough to fill him in on her day, then ran to find her mother. Jake resolutely gathered up his tools and went out the door, trying not to think about where Laura was in the house or what she might be wearing or how she would smile as she listened to her daughter.

Things weren't any better when he got home. The trailer felt unnaturally empty, and even the television couldn't fill the silence. Jake paced, he poured himself a glass of milk and then let it sit as he riffled through the newspapers piled haphazardly on the couch. Nothing settled him down.

Laura was right to be angry with him. He hadn't considered her feelings when he'd asked Rowen for information. And he'd further hurt her by letting Rowen tell him what he wanted to know while he was at Laura's house. He would have been equally furious if he'd been in her position.

There wasn't much he could do to make it up to her, he realized. The damage was already done. But, still, he wasn't willing to let it go. "Soft deeds," Emma had said.

The knocking on her door sounded awkward, as if someone was having a great deal of difficulty with the task. Kids, Laura thought. Probably out selling something for a school project.

But it was Jake she saw when she opened the door. Jake, balancing a large flat box that smelled like pizza, a couple of videotapes, a six-pack of soda and a bakery box. No wonder the knocking had been strained.

"Don't shut the door," he said quickly before she had time to even think of it. "I need to talk to you."

"You need a lot of props to talk," she noted wryly, nodding toward the pile in his arms.

"I didn't know what to bring to show you how sorry I am, so I brought—"

"Everything," she finished for him.

She still hadn't smiled, and Jake thought that she probably hadn't softened toward him at all. He had a sudden fear that she might never want to see him again.

He briefly wondered why he was doing this and why he feared not seeing her again. He had certainly made it plain to her that he didn't want any intimate involvement. Yet here he was, acting like a desperate man.

He couldn't stand seeing her hurt, he told himself. That was what drove him back to her door.

"The pizza has everything on it," he said hopefully. "And the videos are for kids—*Snow White* and something with three dogs and a cat. Cupcakes for Halloween," he added, trying to hold up the bakery box.

"It's not Halloween yet," she told him, but he thought he detected a softening in her voice.

"I always liked to get an early start on things."

"I shouldn't do this," she said, shaking her head. "All right. Come on in."

It was the novelty of it, she told herself. She had never had a thirty-nine-year-old man bring her such ordinary gifts and make them seem extraordinary. She had never known a man who could apologize in such an original way.

She led the way to the kitchen, eliciting a "Wow" from Molly who was sitting at the table working on her homework.

Jake deposited his offering and stood back. Laura tried not to stare at him. He had changed into clean jeans and a crisp white shirt topped with a red sweater. His dark hair was mussed, his eyes still worried and his jaw shadowed with a day's growth of beard. He looked incredibly good to her.

"Am I forgiven?" he asked.

"Are the cupcakes chocolate?" she asked in return, trying not to smile.

Jake nodded.

Laura sighed. "All right. Let's eat pizza." She met his eyes before turning to the stove, and Jake saw that though she might have forgiven him, she was still holding a part of herself away from him. He couldn't blame her.

"I was cooking vegetable soup," she said. "Do you want some with the pizza?"

"Sure," he agreed, hunting for plates in the cabinet. "The more vegetables the better, right, Molly?" he said, lightly thumping her head with one hand as he walked past.

"Right," she said, giggling. "As long as they're not Brussels sprouts."

Jake feigned disappointment. "Oh, no. And I ordered extra Brussels sprouts on the pizza."

He kept the mood lighthearted through dinner, teasing Molly and avoiding any further mention of what had happened on Sunday. After they ate he insisted on washing the dishes while Laura checked Molly's homework. Then Laura made a big bowl of popcorn, and they adjourned to the parlor to watch *Snow White and the Seven Dwarfs*. After Laura assured him that she'd had all the fireplaces checked out, Jake brought in some logs from the pile behind the house and built a fire.

"I've never had this much fun on a school night before," Molly said happily. "Pizza, cupcakes, popcorn and a video. Yum!" She grinned and kicked her feet enthusiastically. Smiling, Laura looped her arm around Molly's shoulders, her fingers just barely grazing Jake's arm. He felt himself respond to her immediately, but he deliberately held himself still.

It had been so many years since he'd seen *Snow White* that the movie was almost new to him. Molly's eyes widened when the dwarfs appeared, and she leaned forward excitedly. "Look, Mom!" she cried. "A bunch of St. Judes, except they got big caps on!"

Jake met Laura's eyes over Molly's head. "St. Jude?" he asked, painfully aware that he was already pretty sure where Molly had gotten that idea.

"We ran into Esther in the restaurant," Laura said, shrugging uncomfortably. She didn't want Jake to think that she'd been looking for him in his usual haunts.

Jake nodded slowly. "And you saw St. Jude?"

Molly interrupted. "I asked him to let me be a spider for Halloween—and now I am."

"Ah, St. Jude came through," Jake said. "Esther will be thrilled."

"You didn't ask him for anything else, did you?" Laura asked Molly.

"Well, no. Nothing right away, anyway."

Molly sat back, apparently quite satisfied with St. Jude's accomplishments. But Laura couldn't help worrying about whatever else it was Molly wanted St. Jude to do for her.

Molly made few protests at bedtime. She practically danced up the steps, first planting a kiss on Jake's cheek. He was taken aback but hugged her and smiled. He was helping Laura clean up the parlor when Molly sang down the steps that she was ready for bed.

Laura went up to tell her good-night, leaving Jake standing alone in front of the fire.

Tonight had been food for his soul, the kind of peace he hadn't experienced in a long time. He wasn't looking forward to going home to the empty trailer with its messy but sterile atmosphere. He'd almost forgotten what a real home felt like. His mother, during one of her visits prompted by worry about him, had called the trailer a boar's nest. Yes, he thought, that was an apt description.

"Do you want some coffee?" Laura asked from the foot of the steps, and he turned to look at her.

She was wearing jeans, a white blouse and blue sweater. And she looked absolutely beautiful to him. *Stop it,* he told himself.

"I'll help." He followed her to the kitchen, and they went about the task silently. Jake got down the mugs while Laura put decaffeinated coffee into the automatic drip machine.

They settled back in the parlor, together on the couch, but with a definite physical distance between them.

An old movie was on TV now, the sound muted, and neither of them seemed to care. Laura glanced at Jake now and then as she sipped her coffee. She didn't know what to make of this evening, Jake's sudden gift-bearing appearance and the resultant entertainment.

"Esther loves this movie," he said suddenly, and her eyes shifted to the screen. She recognized Spencer Tracy and realized the movie was *Captains Courageous.* "Deep down she truly believes that things always turn out right in the end, even in real life," Jake said, smiling.

"That must be why she's apparently decided that I'm all right despite my reputation," Laura said, sounding more bitter than she'd intended.

"No," Jake said, leaning over to touch her jaw and turn her to face him. "Esther's an astute judge of character. She knows exactly what kind of person you are."

"Does she?" Laura asked over the sudden rush of heat to her face.

"And so do I. Though I've done a bang-up job of convincing you otherwise."

"Don't, Jake," she said, but he pressed one finger to her lips to silence her. She should pull away, she told herself. She didn't think she was strong enough to go through another of Jake's rejections tonight.

She was right, he told himself. He shouldn't be doing this. He didn't have the right to touch her, not after he'd hurt her so badly. But the selfish side of him wanted it.

Jake slid closer to her as his fingers drew her face toward him. Her face, scrubbed clean of makeup and showing her soft freckles, looked like a child's beneath the cascade of red hair. But her luminous eyes were all woman. And they were filled with worry.

He started to tell her once again that he was sorry, but her lips parted slightly and her eyes widened, and he was lost. His mouth brushed hers, and he nearly groaned out loud. She tasted so clean and sweet. He could feel an urgency filling his loins.

For a moment she stayed quiescent beneath his tentative kisses, then with a soft sound she caught his sweater with her hands. Jake pressed his mouth against hers, wanting more. His hand tangled in her hair, caressing. His tongue entered her mouth, seeking.

And through all this she kissed him back with reckless abandon. Some detached part of him could only marvel that she was so generous in her giving after what he'd done.

He could feel heat everywhere, from the point where their thighs touched to the place where their mouths joined. Glorious heat. It made him want so much more.

One hand slid down to cup her breast, and Laura arched sharply against his touch, moaning softly when his thumb stroked her to hardness there.

Her breath came in short, sharp exhalations against his mouth, and when he drew back fractionally to look into her eyes, he saw a dazed need.

"What do you want from me?" she whispered hoarsely, and he realized how completely he had confused her. He could barely think straight himself, but the one thing he knew was that he didn't want to hurt her any more than he already had.

"I don't know, Laura," he murmured hoarsely. "God help me, I don't know." He levered away from her while he was still capable of such an act, and stood. Looking down at her, he knew that she would go to bed with him if he asked.

But he couldn't ask her. He wouldn't take Laura into his bed when he couldn't give her any kind of commitment in return. For a brief moment he wished he were one of those men who viewed sex as casually as food. The next bed, the next meal they were all the same.

But Jake couldn't do that. He'd had a marriage based on respect, but he knew how easily a person could devalue a bed partner. He couldn't act as though lovemaking mattered no more than a change of clothes.

"I seem to have a habit of backing out on you," he said with a wry half smile. "Would you forgive me one more time?"

Laura heard what he didn't say. How much he didn't want to leave just now. Then why was he?

"This is the last time," she told him solemnly, her mouth looking soft and swollen from his kisses. "And I really mean it, McClennon."

He smiled and nodded, even though he was sure that at the moment she really did mean it. "I know," he said softly. "I know." He reached to push back a tendril of her hair, then thought better of it and backed away. "I'll see you later."

Laura didn't move even after she heard the door close behind him. She tried to get her thoughts in order, but after what she'd felt as Jake McClennon had kissed her, it was nearly impossible. And that was precisely why she wasn't going to let him do that to her again. No, he wasn't going to leave her breathless and aching and with all of her resolve scattered to the far corners of the globe. "I'll see you later." What the hell kind of good-night was that for a man who'd just kissed her like that? Why did he think he could...?

But she didn't even complete that question. Another, more pressing question had taken priority. When would she see him again?

"This is crazy," she muttered, dropping her head into her hands and sighing. She, Laura Halstead, despite all the bitter experience of her past, despite a concrete resolve that had carried her through the past ten years, was falling for Jake McClennon. And falling hard.

Laura sat on the couch, her knees drawn up like a frightened child. She hadn't felt this vulnerable in so many years. The feeling was nearly overwhelming.

Jake hadn't arrived by the time Emma and Laura set to work the next morning. After sticking herself twice with the sewing needle while she was paying more attention to traffic sounds on the road than to the fabric in her lap, Laura gave up.

"I need to pick up some things in town," she told Emma. "Do you want to come?"

Emma was always game for a trip to town, especially when she could ride in a car. They shopped at the grocery store, the fabric store and then had a cup of coffee and a doughnut before starting home again. Laura was finally relaxed, until she saw the note on her door.

Jake had been there and gone again. She nearly swore until she remembered Emma standing beside her, her solemn face studying Laura's expression.

"Things have not gone well today," Laura noted, shaking her head.

Things grew worse that night. It had been a dry summer and fall after the flood of the previous year, but now the rains came. In torrents. And driving the downpour was a wind that screamed like a banshee, swirling around the house and alternately sucking and blasting at the windows.

After Molly got ready for bed, Laura let her curl up on the couch under a blanket, and together they listened to the storm raging outside. The lights flickered, then went out, and Laura reached for the flashlight she'd laid by the couch.

A few minutes later a loud banging and screeching shot them both to an upright position.

Reassuring Molly that everything would be all right, a sentiment she decidedly did not feel, Laura climbed to the top of the stairs to locate the source of the noise. She shone the flashlight around, seeing nothing at first. Then she heard a steady dripping sound.

Moving into the doorway of Molly's old bedroom, she aimed the light at the noise. Her heart nearly stopped. Water was dripping in a steady stream from the ceiling and pooling on the already rotten floor. Beneath the window another insidious stain grew.

Over the racket created by the howling wind, she heard a pounding at the front door and she groaned. "I don't think I can stand it if another thing goes wrong tonight," she warned no one in particular.

"Mom, someone's at the door!" Molly called, sounding scared.

"It's all right, honey," Laura said with more assurance than she felt as she hurried down the stairs. She tried to peer through the window at the side of the door to see who was knocking so forcefully, but the rain reached even there, under the porch, turning the glass to a lake surface. But over the howl of the wind she could recognize Jake's voice calling her name. She jerked the door open.

"A section of your roof's gone," he said as he slipped inside, dripping water onto the small rug. Seemingly without thought, he reached out to touch her shoulders while he looked into her eyes. Despite all her worry, she wanted to ask him how he was. "I thought I'd better get over here when I saw how bad the storm was," he went on. "When I pulled into the drive I could see shingles in the yard. I couldn't tell for sure, but it looks like they came from the peak over Molly's bedroom."

Laura told him what she'd seen upstairs, and Jake ran up to take a look for himself. He was back down a few seconds later, his eyes obviously worried though his face betrayed nothing. Molly had come to stand beside Laura at the foot of the stairs, the blanket wrapped around her, her eyes wide with anxiety.

Jake knelt and smiled at her and gave her a few words of encouragement. When he stood, his face was grave. "You really shouldn't stay here tonight. I'm going to call Billy and Frank to get over here and help me get everything secured down," he said, then pulled his key chain from his pocket and took off one key. He grabbed Laura's palm and dropped the key there. "But I want you to take Molly and go to my place. Okay?"

Laura nodded, then looked at the parlor. "Shouldn't I move things?" she asked. "What if they're under a leak?"

"Don't worry," he assured her. "I'll take care of everything. You two go on. You can put Molly to sleep in my bed." Catching her eye, he smiled and said, "I changed the sheets today."

About to tell him that she wasn't going to quibble over housecleaning, she realized that this was no time to engage him in chitchat. Jake had already headed for the phone in the kitchen. Laura put on a coat and helped Molly into her raincoat and boots. With one last, worried glance toward the kitchen she opened the door on a blast of wind and sprinted for the car with Molly.

Laura jumped up from the couch when she heard a truck rumbling up the drive. She must have fallen asleep. Pushing her hair away from her face, she leaned forward to see the dial on the alarm clock that sat on a box next to the couch—1:00 a.m.

Laura opened the door just as Jake reached for the handle. He looked drenched and cold and exhausted, but the first thing he did was look into her eyes and smile. "Is Molly asleep?" he whispered.

"Yes, but don't worry. She's out like a light. She exhausted herself with worry about all her things at home." Laura hesitated. "I told her everything would be fine."

Jake knew she was afraid she'd lied to her daughter. He took off his coat and dropped it on the mat in front of the door.

"It *will* be all right eventually," he told her. "But not right now, I'm afraid." He ran a hand through his wet hair and headed for the small kitchen, Laura following.

"I found some soup in the cupboard," she said, flipping on the light over the stove. "Want a bowl?"

Jake nodded and sat down heavily on one of the folding chairs set up at the card table jammed against the wall. He propped his elbows on the table and stifled a tired groan as he rested his forehead in his hands.

He waited while she opened the soup and heated it on the stove. When she put the bowl in front of him and sat down opposite he raised his head. He wanted to see her face while he talked to her.

"There's been some bad leakage, Laura. We got the hole covered with tarps and stopped most of it. But before we were done, part of the floor in Molly's old room collapsed."

Laura paled, thinking about Molly in that room just a week before.

"Is it . . . repairable?" she asked, her voice weak.

Jake nodded. "Yes, honey, but it's a major job." He looked at her, assessing her state of mind.

Laura held her breath. Though she was hovering on a state of emotional shock, she clung to the sound of Jake calling her "honey." "What else?" she asked quietly.

"Trina called after you'd gone. We were working inside by then, and I answered. I thought it might be you," he added apologetically.

"It's all right. What did she want?"

Jake took a long breath. "The usual." His eyes caught hers and held. "She wanted to know where you were and who was with Molly. I told her part of the truth. I said you were staying at a friend's house, and Molly was with you. Laura," he said, reaching over to touch her hand on the table, "this time she said she has a lawyer. It sounded like more than an idle threat." He hesitated. "I could ask Rowen what he knows—if you want."

Laura looked away briefly, giving herself time to think about what he'd said. It was too much to assimilate at once. Her house was now in need of even more repairs, and her mother-in-law was threatening legal action to get her daughter. Had she escaped Trina's house only to have everything fall apart around her?

It wasn't fair, but Laura had never been one to waste tears where they did no good. She would just have to meet this latest crisis head-on.

She turned back to Jake, started to speak and then momentarily forgot what she intended to say when she looked into his face. His gray eyes were dark with weariness and concern—concern for her, she realized. She wondered how a man who had never shared any physical intimacy with her could worry this much about what happened to her. She hadn't known anyone like him.

The only word that came to mind was *old-fashioned,* a word she had once scoffed at. But applied to Jake it was a graceful, gentle word that connoted only good things.

"I think we both need to get some rest right now," she said, trying to smile. "We can worry about everything tomorrow."

"It *is* tomorrow," he reminded her, smiling himself.

"I don't know how to thank you for coming to my rescue tonight," she said. "I'm afraid it's getting to be a habit, my leaning on you for things. I shouldn't."

Jake shook his head quickly. "It was time to dust off my white horse." He traced her hand gently with his finger and she turned her palm up, closing her fingers over his. "Go get some sleep, Laura. I'll take the couch, and you can share the bed with Molly."

Laura rose, slipping her fingers from his, and murmured her thanks again before heading down the short hallway to bed.

Jake leaned back and flipped off the wall switch, throwing the room into darkness. He sat there for a long time, thinking about the idea that had come to him while he was in the middle of the emergency work on her roof. Over the rain and the wind and the cold it had come to him like a bolt of lightning. He knew what he should do.

But how Laura would see it was another question entirely.

Laura dreamed about phones ringing and alarm clocks buzzing, but when she woke it was to find Jake sitting on the edge of the bed, smiling at her.

"You look lousy," she muttered as she took in his unshaven face, weary eyes and tousled hair. He had apparently slept in his clothes, as she had, and they were wrinkled and disheveled.

"Hey," he said, laughing softly. "That remark could seriously compromise your chances of getting a fresh cup of coffee around here."

"Lousy but wonderful," she amended, smiling too. "What time is it?"

"Seven. I wasn't sure what time Molly had to be at school."

"Oh, Lord," Laura groaned. "In an hour."

"I grabbed some of her things last night and left them in the truck. I didn't know what she needed, so I just emptied a couple of drawers."

"There you are on that white horse again," she said gratefully, sitting up and pushing the hair from her eyes. "Just let me splash some water on my face, and then I'll wake her up."

Despite the change of scene and the lack of sleep, Laura managed to get Molly ready for school and reassure her that the house would be all right. Molly ate cereal while Laura drank her coffee, and for the first time since she'd stepped inside last night, Laura looked around the trailer. It looked different, and she couldn't quite put her finger on it.

Cleaner. That was it. Jake had picked up all of the flotsam that had lain over chairs and the floor the first time she was here. It looked as though he'd swept the floor and dusted as well. And a full box of cereal along with the cans of soup she'd found the night before attested to the fact that he'd also gone to the grocery store.

Jake insisted that Laura eat some breakfast while he drove Molly to school, and, still half-asleep, she agreed.

She could see that something was on his mind, but she knew that he would tell her when he was ready.

He didn't meet her eyes when he came back, and she waited while he walked around inside the trailer, picking up things and then setting them down again. It was his preamble, and she realized that she'd learned somehow to read some of his moods. This one was apprehension. But it was mixed with something she couldn't identify.

Jake finally came to rest on the same chair at the card table, and Laura settled across from him again, her coffee cup between her hands.

"I talked to Rowen early this morning," Jake said, "and he called me back. I don't know how he managed to dig up information at that hour of the morning, but he did." He lifted his eyes to hers. "Trina does have a lawyer now. Someone from where she lives. No lawsuit has been filed yet. Apparently they're still in the investigating stage."

"Investigating?" she asked.

"To see if a custody suit is feasible."

"Oh." She had suspected that it might come to this point. "I've been considering my options," she said carefully. "Concerning the house and concerning Trina. And I've come to a couple of decisions." She looked out the window to avoid having to tell him while she was watching his face. "I'm going to sell the house, and I'm going to move back near Trina. Not in her house," she said quickly, holding up her hands. "But close enough that she can't complain that I've taken Molly too far away."

"Do you really think that's going to solve anything?" he asked.

"It will take off some of the pressure," she said, sounding as if she needed to convince herself as well as him. "Jake, I just can't afford to have anything more go wrong with the house right now. And if I don't fix it up I won't have a business. And as for Trina, I don't have the money to fight a lawsuit for my child. It's as simple as that."

Jake admired her for the decision she'd made. He admired her strength in facing her problems and her refusal to lie down and cry. But he had other plans.

"Listen, Laura—"

"No," she said, interrupting. "I know what you're going to say. I can't take money from you, Jake, not even if it's a loan. And I can't let you work for nothing. For heaven's sake, you're nearly doing that now. No, there's no other way."

"I know of another way."

She looked at him in exasperation. Didn't he understand that she had come to this decision by a hard, painful recognition of the truth? She was a woman with few resources, and she couldn't squander any that she had left.

"There is no other way, Jake," she said quietly.

He shifted in his chair, his eyes searching her face.

"Yes, there is. We could get married."

Chapter Nine

Laura stared at him. He was waiting for her reaction, looking far more composed than she felt at the moment.

"You can't be serious," she breathed.

"I've given it a lot of thought," he began.

Laura shook her head vehemently. "No. You couldn't have. It's impossible. I can't believe you even mean it."

"I've never been more serious about anything," he told her, and she saw that he did indeed mean it.

"Married," she repeated, shaking her head. "No, Jake, it's impossible. It just wouldn't work."

"With any two other people, maybe not," he agreed. "But, think about it, Laura. Neither of us wants the kind of marriage other people have. We both know all the things that can go wrong with a head-over-heels-in-love kind of marriage. We've both heard the bells ringing before, and we know what happens when they stop. This would give Molly two parents and go a long way toward ending Trina's harassment. I'll think of Molly as my own child, Laura. And if we live in your house I'll pay half of everything. I'd assume half ownership of the house and continue to work on it at my own expense."

"But what about you?" she demanded. "What do you get out of this?" It was a blunt choice of words, but she didn't know any other way to ask.

He searched for the right words before answering her. It was important to him that she understand. "I get a home, someone to come home to," he said. "It's not easy when you've been married, having to live single again. I don't like coming home cold and tired and opening the door on an empty trailer that has all the atmosphere of a tin can. I want to come into a warm house and know that a woman lives there, too, that there are sounds and scents there other than my own. And I want to hear a child's laughter. I didn't know how much I'd wanted that until lately."

He waited, watching her face as she tried to assimilate everything he'd said.

"You know what people think of me," she said, raising her hand to stop him when he would have protested. "Do you really want that kind of person for a wife?"

His sharp oath was to the point. "You're *not* that kind of person," he said. "And I don't care what people think. Hell, do you think they've forgotten the sight of me being dragged out of a bar by Carl, my shirt half-off and my face bloated from too much alcohol? Do you think they don't still talk once in a while about the time I was so drunk that I staggered into the convenience store on the highway and fell into a shelf of videos? Isn't that a pretty picture, Laura? Do you really want that kind of man for a husband?"

He had matched her, anguished memory for anguished memory, and all she wanted to do was reach across the table to him and ask him to hold her forever. But she couldn't take what he offered, not yet.

She realized that she was actually considering his strange marriage proposal, and her heart quickened with all the implications.

"Jake," she said tentatively, "there are other things to marriage besides a warm house." She flushed and fell silent, not knowing how to broach the subject she found so uncomfortable.

It took Jake a moment to realize what was worrying her, and then he nearly blushed himself. But he'd known that this too would have to be addressed. And he'd thought about it. Agonized about it, actually.

"The sleeping arrangements?" he guessed, and she nodded, dropping her eyes. Mentally she chided herself for acting like a silly schoolgirl instead of a woman with a colorful past.

Jake cleared his throat. "There are several bedrooms in your house," he said carefully. "If we lived there I could take a bedroom next to yours. As for sex," he continued thinking how cool and unemotional that word sounded for what he felt when he looked at Laura, "we could..." He stopped and cleared his throat again, suddenly unsure of himself. "We could begin a sexual relationship once we felt comfortable with each other."

Comfortable was not a word that described her feelings when it came to sex with Jake. Heated, hungry and electric were better words for the reaction she had whenever she looked at Jake or accidentally touched him. No, not the least bit comfortable. It made her wonder if she could live with the knowledge that *comfortable* might be all he wanted from her.

Only a few days ago, it seemed, she'd been rock solid in her determination never to let another man near her. And now she was falling head over heels for this man. This man, who might not want her the same way she wanted him. She might as well face the fact that he might never want her that way.

Laura bit back a sigh as she looked at his face. He wore the lines of experience well. His face was mature, but still rugged and handsome and gentle at the same time. His gray eyes looked as uncertain as she felt at the moment. She fought off the urge to brush back the lock of black hair that fell across his forehead. If she touched him she would be lost.

"Think about it," Jake said, breaking the silence. "I'm going to go do some work at your house. You stay here and get some more rest."

"I've slept more than you have," she protested.

"It's all right," he said, smiling as he stood. "I don't think I could sleep now, anyway. Come on over later."

She suspected that he needed some time alone now, and so did she. What he was proposing was too momentous for them not to think about it long and hard.

"Laura," he said from the door, his coat half on. "I guess you know that I can't offer you anything other than emotional and financial support. I wish I could, and I do care about you, but I don't think I can ever fall in love with anyone again." His eyes caught hers and held, as gray and unyielding as granite. "I'm sorry it has to be that way, but you should know what you're getting."

He left before she could respond, and she resisted the urge to bury her head in her hands and weep.

Jake had been honest with her, and she almost wished he hadn't.

Sleep was impossible. She lay on the bed awhile, but her mind refused to quiet itself. It assailed her with each of Jake's words in perfect clarity. He cared about her but he didn't love her, and he never would.

But he would marry her.

Was that enough?

She had asked that question of herself once before, when she had just told Robert that she was pregnant. "I don't love you," he'd said immediately, making her heart contract. But he'd liked the idea of a wife and family, because, Laura suspected now, it would give him someone to act as a buffer between him and his parents. And she'd been a buffer all right.

When she'd lost the baby, she'd felt as though she had nothing. Robert still didn't love her, at least not the way she imagined that a man should love his wife. But despite Trina's efforts to get Robert to divorce her, he had remained married to her for his own reasons. It wasn't until Molly was born that Laura finally understood what it was like to be truly loved in return.

Now she was facing the same dilemma. Was it enough to live with Jake, to occasionally share his bed, but to know that she couldn't have his heart?

She had never let herself want even that much before. She was the "bad girl" with a reputation. She couldn't have any man who was decent or good or kind. She didn't deserve a man like that. And no man like that wanted her, anyway.

Except for Jake. He was all of those things and more. And he was asking her to marry him. Her reputation didn't matter. Neither did the prospect of gossip. He understood what it was like to be the outsider, the sinner.

Laura knew she could be very happy married to a man like Jake. She would have all of the things she'd thought so far out of her reach that it was pointless to even dream of them. All of them except his love.

She knew what her decision would be.

Laura got up from the bed and went to check her reflection in the bathroom mirror. She looked tired. And when she went to him she wanted to look her best.

So she brushed her hair and splashed water on her face and made herself as presentable as she could. Then she took a deep breath and got her coat.

"You know," she said to him when she walked in her front door and found him on a ladder in the parlor, working on a large hole in the ceiling, "that wasn't precisely the marriage proposal I dreamed of from childhood." It had taken all of her control not to run screaming into the house to assess the damage, after she pulled into her drive and saw the huge tarp draped over her roof. But she was determined to confront one thing at a time.

"It wasn't very good, was it?" he said, half turning to her and almost smiling.

"No," she assured him. "But it was better than the proposal I got when I told Robert I was pregnant. Two men have asked me to marry them over the course of my life, and neither one of them seemed terribly thrilled by the whole prospect. I, on the other hand," she went on, trying not to look into his face for fear of stumbling over her words, "am a hopeless romantic. Thrill or no thrill, I accept."

"You . . . accept?" he repeated, and then he did smile.

She really liked his smile, and she vowed then and there to make sure it happened more often.

They just looked at each other for a long moment, and Laura almost expected him to climb down from the ladder and shake her hand. But the moment passed, and he shifted his weight.

"The house looks better than I expected," she lied, needing desperately to change the subject. "I guess I thought the whole roof would be caved in."

Jake shook his head. "With all the rain we had last year there was a lot of roof damage. It's a crime that the owners didn't see to the repairs."

Jake climbed down from the ladder then, wiping his hands on his jeans. His blue chambray shirt was rolled up to the elbows, and he fiddled with the sleeves, pushing them higher in his need to have something to do with his hands. He wanted so badly to reach out for Laura, to pull her against him and drown himself in her sweet scent. But she looked like she was about to bolt the room at the slightest provocation. It amazed him that she had accepted his proposal. It amazed him that he'd even made it. Mostly, it amazed him that he was feeling as giddy inside as a schoolboy, instead of a man who had been married once before and had put affairs of the heart in the past.

But this one didn't involve the heart, he reminded himself. It was an arrangement, a contract, mutually beneficial to both parties.

Laura was looking at the ceiling, but he didn't think she was really seeing it.

"Jake?" she said quietly, her hands clasped in front of her. "Is it going to be all right?"

Some instinct told him that she wasn't asking about the ceiling or her house. She was asking about the two of them, about this strange, impersonal union they were about to begin.

Jake stepped in front of her so that he blocked her vision. "Everything's going to be fine, Laura. I promise. I'll go see Rowen and have him draw up an agreement for us. Just to be sure that what you're entitled to is in writing," he quickly assured her when she paled.

"Does *everything* have to be in writing?" she asked, sounding suddenly like a young girl who was unsure of herself.

He didn't understand what she meant at first, but one look at the heat creeping up her face and he knew.

"No, no, of course not," Jake said, trying not to smile. "Some things will remain private, just between the two of us. I won't say anything to Rowen."

Laura looked relieved, relaxing her hands somewhat. "Thank you, Jake."

He couldn't help himself then. He didn't mean to do it, but it was as though he was no longer in control of his hands. They reached out and touched her shoulders, drawing her closer to him. He could feel her trembling slightly beneath his touch.

She looked so pretty and so fragile, still wearing her clothes from the night before, her hair mussed and tangled around her face. Young and uncertain.

Jake knew better, but still he pulled her yet closer until her hands came to rest on his chest, her fingers warm and soft through his shirt. Her eyes, wide and shy, were on his face.

"Laura Halstead," he said softly, "you are one pretty woman."

She actually blushed at that, and that made him hold her even tighter. This woman who thought she had such a dirty reputation that she wasn't fit for any decent man was actually blushing.

Jake tilted her chin up and let her look long and hard into his face. He wanted her to see how much he wanted her and how much she excited him. Then he slowly brought his mouth down on hers, nearly groaning out loud at the first touch of her soft, warm lips.

She kissed him back with no reservation, her mouth parting and seeking, needing him as much as he needed her.

He moved one hand to cradle her head, tangling his fingers in her red-gold hair and marveling at the feel of spun silk against his hand. His heart began to pound raggedly as her breasts pressed against his chest. He traced her spine with his other hand, cupping her bottom and drawing her against his own arousal. He could feel her breath quicken against his mouth.

Laura was still trembling when he gently pulled away from her. It took all of his control to do it, but he wasn't going to make love to her here, not when she was so tired that she nearly swayed on her feet, not when her house was about ready to fall down around her ears.

"Do you have a wedding dress?" he asked, realizing even as he said it how inane it must sound.

"A wedding dress?" she repeated as if he'd asked if she had a moon rock. Slowly she shook her head. "No, I never..."

She didn't finish the sentence, but he guessed that she had ɔeen about to say that she'd never had a wedding dress. It would have been just like Trina to deny her future daughter-in-law a real wedding.

"Then I think we should go buy you one," he said.

"Now?" She could hardly think of anything at the moment, much less a wedding dress. She was still tingling everywhere her body had touched his. Heat and hunger chased each other around her bloodstream... and *he* was talking about clothes.

Jake could think of a couple of other things he would rather do now, like make love to Laura until he was finally sated with the feel of her. But it was suddenly important to him that Laura have a real wedding.

"Do you have a minister?" he asked, that detail coming to mind.

Laura managed a smile. "Hey, I'm the person who doesn't have a dress. Where would I be hiding a minister?"

Jake smiled back. "We'll add *minister* to the list."

"The list?"

"Yeah. Minister, church, cake, all of that."

Laura's smile faltered. "Jake, you're talking about a wedding."

"I think that was the general topic," he agreed.

"No, I mean a *wedding* in a church with a lot of people." He saw that she was knitting her fingers together again, betraying her nervousness.

"If you don't want that, it's fine," Jake said gently. "We'll have whatever kind of wedding you say."

"It's not that I don't want it," she said, and he heard the wistfulness in her voice. "It's just that..."

"You don't deserve it?" Jake finished quietly for her, and Laura nodded.

"Something like that," she said. "I think people would be outraged if I had a church wedding with all the trimmings."

"Trina, yes," he agreed quickly. "But no one else, Laura. You have the right to get married the way you want."

She hesitated, thinking about her first wedding, about the judge in his chambers and how scared she felt because she'd only come before a judge before as a result of her misdeeds. She hadn't even had any flowers, and her dress had been the only good one she'd owned, worn several times before. She'd felt like she hadn't belonged. And when she had looked at Trina she'd seen the triumph in her face. Clearly, Trina had wanted Laura to feel like that.

Laura looked at Jake's face, into his patient eyes, and she knew what she wanted. With this man she wanted to do it right.

"Well," she said, taking a deep breath, "let's go get a dress and a preacher."

Jake smiled broadly, making her heart turn over. She lived for those smiles.

"And a cake," he reminded her, propelling her toward the coat closet. He wanted her to have a good day today, a day filled with things she would enjoy. He didn't want her to have a single moment to worry about her ceiling or her roof or the rest of her life.

* * *

Jake took her to the nicest dress shop in town. She'd ve-toed the tiny bridal shop, telling him that she had no desire or intention of getting married in the typical wedding gown. She knew just the kind of dress she wanted.

Laura stopped hesitantly inside the door. Peering over her shoulder, Jake saw the problem straight ahead. Corky Fife Beachem stood in front of a full-length mirror, a salesgirl at her side like a lady-in-waiting, admiring her reflection in a long, gray cashmere coat.

"Enemy aircraft at six o'clock," Jake murmured in her ear, squeezing her arm. Laura turned her head to him and smiled, realizing that no matter how good a customer Corky was she couldn't throw Laura out of the store.

Corky turned around and swished toward the rack of coats as Laura was passing, nearly colliding with Jake. Her startled eyes slid from one to the other before she pulled herself together and smiled frostily as she snatched up two more coats. Jake realized that the woman probably would never forgive him for making her look petty when she threw Laura out of her fund-raising party.

"Discount store too crowded?" Corky asked tightly.

Jake just smiled and propelled Laura toward the plump salesclerk heading their way.

"Anything in particular I can help you find?" the clerk asked amiably.

"As a matter of fact, yes," Jake said. "A wedding dress."

He smiled in satisfaction as from behind him he heard the coats hit the carpeted floor with a muffled thud. Glancing at Laura, he saw that she was trying very hard not to laugh. Her eyes met his, and she squeezed his hand.

This was how he always wanted to see her, full of happi-ness. Her blue eyes laughing.

He sat on one of the expensively upholstered chairs and waited while the clerk took Laura to the fitting room with several dresses. She came to stand in front of him with each one, seeking his opinion. He didn't have a preference until she waltzed out in the third outfit, a two-piece dress in an-tique-white silk. The dress was elegant, the top flaring at her hips and the skirt falling in soft pleats to her knees. Laura was adjusting the pleated cuffs at her wrists, and when she looked at him her eyes seemed larger and bluer than he remembered.

"That's the one," he said, not bothering to worry that he might sound pushy.

"And if I don't like it . . ." she teased him.

"Then we'll buy it, anyway, and you can wear it another time for me."

Laura laughed. "It just so happens that this is my favorite, too. Emma and I can make a little hat to go with it."

Jake didn't care whether she wore a hat or not. He just knew that she was a vision in that dress. And she was smiling. He'd buy the entire town if it would make her smile like that.

When they left the shop he pointed her in the direction of the small bakery and told her he had something else to attend to at the moment. Laura's gaze scanned the street and stopped on Rowen Pruitt's door.

"I'd like to come with you, if you don't mind," she said, suddenly serious.

"Are you sure? Not that I'm going to say anything that I don't want you to hear, but . . . I won't vouch for Rowen's comments." Just so she knew.

Laura nodded. "It's all right."

They caught Rowen on his way to an early lunch, stopping him in his two-hundred-dollar-leather shoe tracks when he heard what they wanted.

"I can always order in lunch," he said laconically, one brow raised as he led them back to his office.

"Married, you say?" he repeated, his brow permanently stuck high on his forehead as he gestured them to the plush leather chairs in front of his expansive mahogany desk.

"As in 'I do' and 'forever and ever,' et cetera, et cetera," Jake said impatiently. He hadn't expected Rowen to be this surprised.

"And you want the et cetera in a written contract," Rowen said, sitting forward in his chair and pulling a legal pad and pencil toward him.

"I want certain protections for Laura," Jake said.

"All right." Rowen sighed and ran two fingers over his glossy hair. "Let's get this party-of-the-first-part stuff down on paper."

Jake told him what he wanted: a financial agreement that would put the house in both Jake's and Laura's names but specify that Jake was responsible for its maintenance and mortgage. In addition he would assume financial responsibility for Molly.

By this time Laura was sitting bolt upright in her chair, her hands gripping the armrests.

"And in the event of a divorce?" Rowen asked, giving them both a look over the top of his glasses.

Jake named a settlement sum due Laura in the event either of them decided to end the marriage.

"No!" Laura said suddenly. "You're not going to do this, Jake. This contract is just a way for you to give me money. I don't want that."

"She has a point," Rowen said dryly.

"It's for your protection," Jake said, turning to Laura. "I don't want any circumstance to leave you without resources."

"This isn't protection," Laura said tightly, gesturing toward the pad in front of Rowen. "It's the sales receipt for a wife. And I don't want anything to do with it."

"Very nicely put, Mrs. Halstead," Rowen said, grinning. "She has a *good* point, Jake. As much as I hate to drag reality into this, if this doesn't work out you're going to be supporting a woman who is no longer your wife."

"That's fine with me," Jake said stubbornly.

"Well, it's not fine with me," Laura retorted. "I'm not signing something like this. Not with these terms."

"And what about the wedding?" Jake asked quietly.

"I'll marry you anytime you want, Jake McClennon. But I won't sign a piece of paper that puts a price tag on either one of us. I don't want to be Mrs. Party of the First Part." She looked at Rowen who was grinning openly at her.

Jake sighed heavily. After staring at the carpet a long time he raised his head to Rowen. "Draw up a contract that provides for Laura and Molly in the event of divorce." He shot Laura a searing look. "And make it something she'll sign."

"Fair enough," Rowen said, chuckling. "Oh, Lordy, I'd love to be under the dryer at the Klip 'n' Kurl when this news hits."

"You probably will be," Jake said dryly, looking pointedly at Rowen's hair.

When they were back in Jake's truck, Laura leaned back and closed her eyes. "Jake, I don't think I'm up to ordering a cake right now," she said wearily.

"Let's go back home," he agreed. He cast a sideways glance at her, his eyes worried. "There's something else we should do, and we should do it soon."

"What's that?" she asked, opening her eyes.

"Call Trina and tell her. And hope that Corky Beachem hasn't called her first."

Laura groaned. He was right. Trina should hear the announcement of the impending wedding from Laura first. "You're right," she said, sighing heavily. "Let's go get that out of the way."

The call was as bad as she'd expected. At first Trina was surprised that Laura was calling her. But when she heard the reason why, she sputtered for about thirty seconds, then lit into Laura with a lecture on her morals, her manners and her impending marriage. About the time Trina called the whole marriage idea scandalous, Laura had had enough. She quietly said goodbye and hung up the phone while Trina was in mid-harangue. She sat and stared at the phone, wondering how Trina could nurse her bitterness for so long.

"Rough?" Jake asked quietly, coming to stand behind her and massaging her shoulders.

Laura nodded. "You understand, of course," she said dryly, "that my first husband was a saint and far too good for me."

Jake laughed softly. "It's a good thing mothers aren't in charge of canonization, or we'd be overpopulated with saints." He continued to rub her shoulders in silence.

"There's someone else we need to tell quickly," he said finally.

"Molly."

"Right. Any idea how she'll take it?"

Laura considered. "She likes you a lot, Jake. And she doesn't talk about Robert much. I think he's more a shadowy memory for her than a real father. He wasn't at home very often. He took a sales job that kept him on the road."

"And how did Trina take that?"

"Not very well. But she convinced herself that it was his way of avoiding me."

"She never missed a chance to get her digs in, did she?" Jake asked.

Laura shook her head. "I think she had a right to be disappointed in the wife her son chose, but she never understood where her rights ended."

"She had no right at all to be disappointed in you," Jake said flatly. "No one does."

Laura smiled, closed her eyes and leaned her head back against his chest. This was how she always wanted to feel—safe and unjudged. With a husband who didn't hold her past over her head and who didn't care that someone else might judge him because of his wife. With a husband who loved her.

The last thought followed unbidden on the heels of the others, leaving her suddenly sad and pensive. Jake had told her that he cared for her but could never love her. And she'd settled for that. She'd lived with a lot less in the past, and at least she could call Jake hers. In name. And on a marriage license.

"Go get some sleep," he murmured. "Your bedroom's all right. No damage there. I'll try not to make too much noise. You're almost asleep on your feet."

It was true, but it was a pleasant sleepiness. For once in her life she felt cared for. She had someone to share the future with.

She was too tired to fight the feeling that washed over her. It was love, pure and simple. She would do anything for this man, and just being near him made her feel incredibly good.

Laura stood and stretched, a dreamy smile still on her face. She looked into Jake's eyes a long moment, then headed for the bedroom and some sleep.

Laura woke shortly after three, amazed at how long and how soundly she'd slept and mortified that she was still lying in bed as Molly came home from school. She could hear Molly's clear, high voice downstairs, asking Jake about the roof and ceiling. Laura couldn't hear what Jake said, but it apparently satisfied Molly, who went on to another topic.

Laura quickly sat up and pulled on her shoes, then hurried down the stairs. She drew to a halt at the bottom, smiling as she watched Molly, hands on hips, head cocked, pouring out recess woes to Jake. "And then he said, 'If you won't get your jump rope off the playground, I'm gonna kiss you.'" Molly's voice was filled with outrage. "Who does he think he is, Jake, to just kiss me?"

Laura saw Jake hastily hide a smile. "Did you kiss him back?" he asked solemnly.

Molly shook her head adamantly. "No way...! I know how boys are. Let 'em kiss you and the next thing you know they want to share your ice cream cone."

Laura coughed to stop her own laughter, and when her eyes met Jake's she saw the merriment there, too.

"Give 'em an inch and they'll take a mile," Jake agreed, holding out his hand to Laura to draw her into the room with them. She came, letting her fingers nestle in the warmth of his much larger ones, and she smiled at her daughter.

"Let's get some milk," Laura suggested. "Jake and I want to talk to you."

Jake held on to Laura's hand as they settled in the kitchen around the table, Molly diving into her milk and cookies.

"Jake and I," Laura began, but then found she wasn't sure how to continue. Jake waited, letting her find her own words. Molly, sensing the importance of whatever was to come, dipped her cookie in her glass and swished it back and forth, watching her mother.

"Jake and I care about each other very much," she said, "and we want to live together as husband and wife. The way your father and I did before he died. So we're going to get married. We'll have a wedding. Then our family will be three people instead of two."

"Are you in love, Mom?" Molly asked, wide-eyed. "Like those girls from high school on the bus, the ones who giggle and wiggle their eyes?"

"Something like that, sweetie," Laura assured her, hoping Molly wouldn't ask the same question of Jake. "But I don't do much giggling and wiggling anymore."

"Are you going to be my daddy?" Molly asked Jake.

"If you want me to be," he told her. "But you'll always have your first daddy in your memory, too."

Molly nodded. "Lots of kids got two dads. Only they see them both." She shrugged. "I'll just see one of mine."

"That's true," Jake told her.

"Can I come to the wedding?" she asked, brightening.

"Of course, honey," Laura said, reaching across the table to squeeze her daughter's hand. "In fact, you can wear a pretty dress and stand up in front with Jake and me."

"When are we getting married?" Molly asked, and Jake grinned. This was what he wanted, a family affair, a display of unity that told the world they were all in this together.

He scratched his chin. "We have to get the blood tests and the license and find a minister, but I guess . . . we could get married a week from Saturday."

"Saturday!" Molly and Laura cried in unison.

There was a moment of silence, then Laura said, "I guess there's no reason we couldn't. Do you think your family could come on such short notice?"

Jake grinned again. He knew his family, and nothing—but nothing—would keep them away from his wedding. "They'll be here," he promised her.

Laura lifted her brows. "Okay," she said softly. "The wedding's a week from Saturday."

"I've got to find my necklace!" Molly announced, pushing back her chair. "And my barrette! I've got to wear my best barrette at the wedding!" She ran for the stairs, giggling excitedly.

When Laura looked at Jake he was studying her, his gray eyes soft and reflective.

"What?" she asked.

"You're worried," he said.

It was true. Beneath all the excitement, she wasn't sure she was doing the right thing, marrying a man who would never love her.

"Don't worry," he said, covering her hand with his. "Everything's going to be all right."

But even his assurances didn't quell the little voice inside that warned her it would never be enough if he didn't love her.

Chapter Ten

Somehow they did it.

They pulled together a wedding on notice so short that the minister kindly asked them if there was some emergency, all the while looking furtively at Laura's stomach. She was tempted to laugh, tempted to call it all off, tempted to run.

Today, dressing in a small women's room down the hall from the sanctuary, she felt like a cat at a pit bull picnic. Everything made her jump, and she was sure that her panic was evident to anyone who came within ten feet of her.

She and Jake had invited only immediate family and friends. It was a hell of a way to meet her new in-laws, but they had been impossibly kind to her since their arrival that morning. Jake's mother, Elizabeth, had offered to help wherever she was needed. His younger brother, Jordan, had picked up the cake and flowers. And Rachel, married to Jake's brother John, had informed her that there was never a dull moment when a woman was married to one of the McClennon brothers.

Laura had wholeheartedly agreed.

The door opened, and Elizabeth slipped inside, smiling as she paused to look at Laura in her off-white dress. "You look beautiful," she said, closing the door and reaching up to help Laura adjust the veiled hat she and Emma had managed to produce in a day.

"I don't feel beautiful," Laura breathed. "I'm scared to death."

Elizabeth laughed. "Now you sound like Rachel. She and John went through so much, and when they finally got married she was so worried that he might change his mind."

Laura didn't want to admit that similar thoughts had crossed her mind. But she'd heard from everyone who stopped to wish her well that Jake was indeed already in the church, chafing in his suit and grumbling that the wedding was never going to start.

Jake had told her about John and Rachel and the son John hadn't known he had. Laura thought that surely she and Jake could manage to make a life together if his brother had overcome even more insurmountable obstacles. But still she worried.

"I just wanted to tell you," Elizabeth said, standing back to admire Laura again, "that I'm so glad Jake found you. He's been through so much, losing Beverly and the baby and then nearly drinking himself to death with Andrea. I know this wedding is sudden, but you two will be wonderful together."

"I hope so," Laura whispered, feeling near tears. She couldn't help wondering how she would survive if Jake changed his mind, or, worse yet, if someday he found someone else he *could* love.

The door opened again, and Elizabeth turned to frown at Jake. Laura couldn't stop staring at him. In the dark suit, a carnation at the lapel, his hair so black except for the sprinkling of gray, he looked impossibly handsome.

"You aren't supposed to see the bride before the wedding," Elizabeth scolded him.

"I have to, Mom," he said softly, his eyes riveted to Laura. "How else am I going to know if this is the one I proposed to? Besides, this is important."

Elizabeth grumbled, but with one last look at the two of them, she left, closing the door behind her.

Jake turned the lock and pulled the papers from behind his back. "Rowen just got these done," he said apologetically. "He's waiting out front, complaining to anyone who'll listen about the cleaners ruining his tux."

Laura managed a smile. "He's not actually wearing a tux, is he?"

Jake shook his head. "A five-hundred-dollar suit and a salon hairstyle. I told him he looks like a perfume commercial. If he were smaller we could put him on top of the wedding cake."

Laura smiled, but sobered quickly as she looked at the papers Jake held out. She took them hesitantly. "The financial settlement?" she asked.

"See for yourself," he told her, flipping the page.

Laura scanned the figures. In the event of a divorce, no matter which party initiated it, she would receive eight hundred dollars a month for herself for three years and another four hundred for Molly until she turned twenty-one.

"Jake, it's still too much," she protested, looking up to find him watching her with an unreadable expression.

"It's not," he assured her. "You're just used to making do. Sign it, Laura, and let's get married." His hand reached out to brush back a strand of her hair. "One part of the contract isn't on paper," he said quietly.

"What's that?" she murmured, her heart leaping to her throat.

"We both know that this isn't a love match, Laura. I don't want you to even hope that it will be. No emotional entanglements. We have honesty and friendship, but if love becomes an issue, then the marriage will be dissolved."

He had said the words in a kindly voice, but she knew that he meant them. Slowly she nodded.

Jake took a pen from his inside pocket and held it out to her. She took it, their fingers brushing, and stared into his eyes. Why was he doing this, making sure she was so well taken care of? Was it just his way of ensuring that she'd take his money? The terrible thought struck her that he might be planning to divorce her quickly after the wedding, leaving her financially better off but emotionally broken.

No, Jake wouldn't do that. She knew him well enough to know he was the kind of man who honored his obligations, no matter how painful they might be. But that was the last thing she wanted to cause him, pain.

She broke her probing gaze and put the contract on the edge of a small table, signing quickly.

"Don't we need witnesses?" she asked, handing it back to him.

"Rowen's right outside," he assured her. "I told him I wanted to do this alone." He caught her expression and smiled gently. "It's all right, Laura. Really."

She almost told him then. Almost said that she was marrying him even though she'd already broken the contract. That she was desperately in love with him. But she didn't.

"Okay," she said, attempting a smile.

Jake folded the papers. "All right, Party of the Second Part," he said, "Are you ready to marry Party of the First Part?"

This time her smile was genuine.

Laura would always remember her wedding to Jake. She would remember Molly's glowing smile as she walked down the aisle by Laura's side. And Ali's misty eyes as she walked ahead. Esther dabbing at her eyes during the ceremony and praising St. Jude afterward. Emma hugging her outside the church, and Jake's family, genuinely happy on this day.

But most of all she would remember Jake, so tall and handsome, his gray eyes like pewter as he watched her walk toward him. And then he had reached out his hand, looked into her face and smiled just for her. How she loved to see that man smile.

They had reserved a back room at a small restaurant on the river, twenty miles from the church, and now Jake and Laura, Molly, Jake's family, Ali and her daughter Beth, Rowen, Frank, Billy and his wife Myra all sat finishing their steak dinners, the laughter coming easily, now that the formality of the ceremony was over. Laura stole glances at Jake beside her, feeling suddenly shy now that they were married.

He always seemed to sense her moods, and now he reached for her hand under the table, knitting their fingers together.

John made a toast to the newly married couple, wishing them long life, much happiness and short arguments.

"I have to admit I do enjoy those arguments," he said. "We have a new one going now." He looked at his wife, Rachel, sitting beside him, and they both smiled. "We can't agree," he said, "on what to name the new baby."

Elizabeth made a small exclamation, then beamed. Everyone else applauded. In answer to the immediate question, Rachel said the baby was due in March.

"Looks like you're next in line to the altar," John told his younger brother Jordan who had arrived dateless for once.

"That's one line I'm not joining," Jordan said adamantly, but he smiled at his brothers. "You and John are the marrying kind. Not me."

"Famous last words," John laughed. "You'll end up just like Jake and me. The harder you protest the harder you'll fall."

Laura laughed with the rest of them, and she clung tighter to Jake's hand. He hadn't fallen for her, she thought in misery.

It was dusk when the party broke up. Jake's family headed south on the highway, toward home. Esther, Billy, Myra and Frank went to the Hamburger Haven for another round of coffee. Ali and her daughter went to their own home after a last hug.

Molly chattered in the car all the way to the house, going over every detail of the wedding. Laura was glad for the distraction. She felt a fresh shock each time she glanced sideways at Jake and realized yet again that they were really married, that he was her husband now.

That morning Jake had brought over some things from his trailer and left them piled in the foyer. Now Laura helped him carry them upstairs to the bedroom next to hers. Molly trailed after them, and Laura breathed a sigh of relief when her daughter said nothing about the separate bedrooms.

His room was sparse, furnished with only a twin bed that Laura had bought before her first marriage and a pull-down shade at the window. Somehow during the past week, amidst all the wedding preparations, Jake and Frank and Billy had managed to fix the roof.

Laura and Jake set the boxes on the floor and made another trip for the two suitcases. Jake set them on the bed.

Laura apologized for not having a chest of drawers in the room, but Jake waved aside her worry. "I'll bring mine over tomorrow," he said.

She hovered in the room as he opened the suitcase. Molly flitted in and out, still wound up, singing meaningless syllables to the Wedding March. Laura knew she should go, should change her dress, but she wanted to stay. She was Laura Halstead McClennon now, and she wanted to try on the feel of it like a new perfume.

Her husband. She wanted to be with her husband, even if it was just to sit on the end of the bed and watch him take underwear and shirts out of a suitcase.

Jake made a pile of his clothes on top of one of his boxes. When he got to the jeans, he started another pile on the box next to it. Molly bounced into the room, still singing, and when she bumped the box, the jeans fell on the floor. She was out of the room again before Laura could warn her to slow down.

Shaking her head, Laura knelt beside Jake to pick up the clothes. He smiled at her as Molly's voice went drifting down the stairs. Her songbird. She'd almost begun singing before she could talk.

As Laura lifted the jeans she noticed a small white jeweler's box open on the floor, and her fingers brushed a piece of metal. She turned the jeans over and saw a small heart-shaped picture frame caught in the belt loop. Carefully untangling it, she pulled it through and cradled it in her palm. There was no picture in the silver heart.

When she looked at Jake, she saw that his smile had faded. The lines at his eyes seemed deeper, and the gray eyes lost some of their luster. He carefully took the frame from her and stared at it a moment before laying it back in the jeweler's box.

"It was for the baby?" she guessed softly, trying to make herself breathe normally.

"I was going to put the baby's first picture in it," he said. "I don't know why I've kept it."

Laura knew. He'd kept it because he had loved his unborn child, and because the silver heart was like his own, solidified in his grief.

"I'm sorry," she said. "I didn't mean to make you face painful memories, especially...today."

Jake's hands reached out and clasped her shoulders. "Don't apologize, Laura. You haven't done anything wrong. You can always ask me anything you want. All right?"

She nodded, but she didn't really believe him. They were married, but they weren't husband and wife. She still didn't believe she had the right to ask anything of him, not when all she wanted was something he couldn't give.

Molly's wavering song started up the stairs again, and Jake stood, pulling her upright with him. He looked into her face and started to say something else, but Laura backed away from him. She was afraid that he might have already seen too much in her eyes.

"I'd better go change clothes," she said, hurrying for the door.

Jake started to follow her, but Molly got to her first, grabbing her mother's hand and demanding help in finding a bedtime book with a wedding in it. "Will Cinderella do?" Laura asked, following Molly, and Jake heard the anxiety that lingered in her voice.

This was harder than he'd imagined. Somehow he'd thought that the wedding would solve everything, that Laura would be safe and he would settle into a comfortable household routine.

But he wasn't at all settled. He was fighting the urge to prowl the house and the coming night like a stranger seeking something he couldn't define. He wanted to go to Laura, to take her into his arms, to feel her body yield to his on the softness of her bed, but he didn't know the right words, the right cadence of a wedding night like this. And he didn't want her to feel that she was a bride bought with a contract.

Jake knew what it was she needed to hear, but the words were impossible for him to say.

He changed into jeans and a black sweater. They had coffee in the kitchen, hot chocolate for Molly, and afterward Jake helped Laura clean up the dishes. They sat in the parlor awhile, Jake paying scant attention to the TV, Laura reading while Molly got ready for bed.

Jake kissed Molly good-night, then sat alone a long while listening to Laura moving around upstairs, getting ready for bed herself. It was early yet, but neither he nor Laura seemed to know what to do with themselves.

She reappeared downstairs, settling onto the couch, her hands fluttering over some needlework, but her attention obviously elsewhere.

Jake kept stealing covert glances at her. She was wearing a blue chenille robe, and he caught glimpses of a long silky peignoir underneath when she crossed her legs. It was white with hints of blue in the fabric.

He felt his throat constrict and heat race to his groin. But he turned his attention deliberately to the television. He was going to give Laura plenty of breathing room and time to adjust to this sudden change in both their lives.

Time crawled, but finally she stood and stretched. "I guess I'll go up to bed," she said hesitantly, her eyes everywhere but on him.

"Okay. I may stay up awhile." He stole another look at her as she headed for the stairs, and every muscle clenched. She was so soft and pretty. And probably tired, he reminded himself.

He waited another hour before climbing the stairs. Her bedroom door was closed, but there was a light underneath. Jake sighed. She probably wouldn't find it any easier to sleep tonight than he would.

He checked the hall again after he cleaned up in the small bathroom. It had no tub, just a toilet and sink, which served his purposes tonight. Her light was still on, and he tapped lightly on the door.

He thought she said something, but he couldn't be sure, and he waited another few seconds.

The door opened, and he swallowed hard, his eyes looking over her shoulder because he was afraid he'd openly stare if he looked anywhere in the vicinity of the peignoir.

His brief glance had been enough to burn her image indelibly on his mind. The peignoir was soft white and as tempting as Eve must have been to Adam. Pale blue ribbons served as straps for a fitted bodice with a lace inset that allowed glimpses of the creamy skin of her breasts. The rest of the thing rustled when she moved and hugged her hips in a way that made the heat in his groin burn hotter.

"I... brought you something," he said hesitantly, shifting his weight.

"Come in," she murmured, scanning his face as if assessing his mood. She closed the door after him and tried to smile.

Jake looked into her face and for a moment forgot why he was there. Beyond her composure he could sense uncertainty. She was waiting, he realized.

Jake reached into his shirt pocket and pulled out a small box. Opening the box Jake let the gold chain pour softly onto her palm. Laura looked up quizzically. "What is it?"

"A key," he said, liking the way she looked at him.

A soft smile flitted over her face as she held it up to the light. "A key," she repeated. "It's so delicate."

"You told me once that you felt as if you were still in jail," Jake said. "You're free, Laura. I just want you to understand that. You don't have to be afraid of anything again. This is to remind you."

She felt tears spring to her eyes, and she looked down a moment until she could control herself. "Thank you," she said hoarsely. Quickly she turned around, holding the necklace around her neck.

Jake stepped up behind her and took it from her trembling fingers. He worked at the clasp longer than necessary, because he was entranced with the delicacy of her slender neck and the sheen of the coppery hair she held up out of his way. It would be so easy to bend just slightly and kiss her nape, to test and taste the soft skin there. He forced his attention back to the necklace, closed the clasp and stepped away.

"Thank you," she whispered again as she turned around and lifted the key to look at it. The smile on her face was more reward than he deserved, he thought. It was a simple gift, but Laura looked as though he'd given her the key to a kingdom.

He knew he should leave now, but he couldn't seem to make himself turn away from her. She let the key fall back against her throat and looked at him, her eyes soft and beguiling. Impulsively she took a step toward him and quickly hugged him.

"It's beautiful, Jake," she murmured.

His arms came up automatically to wind around her back. He closed his eyes and briefly inhaled the sweet scent of her.

Laura made no move to break the embrace, and Jake found himself drinking in the feel of her soft body against his. He could feel her breasts pressed against his chest and the quickening of her breath. So soft. He wanted to hold her like this forever.

But he wouldn't. He would let her sleep tonight, and then tomorrow they would talk about this brand new marriage of theirs. Gently he disengaged his arms and held her away. "Sleep well," he said softly.

"Jake," she murmured tentatively, "you don't have to go."

But he did. He was afraid that she was offering herself out of some unwritten obligation. Almost as if Rowen had indeed included a shared bed in the contract. He didn't want a woman to give herself to him because of some perceived payoff. The way it had been with Andrea. But with her the payoff had come much later.

"No," Jake said softly. "Not tonight. I want you to have some time ... to be sure."

Laura nodded, afraid to say anything as she watched him edge toward the door. If she spoke, she might not be able to stop herself from telling him how much she wanted him in her bed tonight. And she wouldn't risk another rejection.

Jake lay stretched out in his bed, staring at the ceiling in the dark. He'd put on pajama bottoms but left his chest bare. He was still consumed with heat just from touching Laura.

It wouldn't have been the kind of wedding night Laura deserved if he had done what he'd wanted and taken her to bed. It would have been fast and furious and explosive. No gentleness or tender love words. Just a consuming hunger.

He wouldn't go to her until he could give her what she needed, a tenderness that kept her safe.

A floorboard creaked in the hall, and a minute later the door closed softly downstairs. Jake got out of bed and went to the window, lifting the shade enough to see into the backyard. He couldn't see anything for a while. Then he heard the quiet scrape of a chair on the porch.

The porch ended at the corner of the house, but by looking out at the edge of the window he just caught the corner of the railing and the Adirondack chair there. He could make out Laura's shadowy form, what looked like her coat pulled up around her shoulders and neck.

She moved her leg, and he saw a flash of white, the peignoir shifting around her knees. His eyes were adjusting to the dark, and he could make out her hand at her throat. Her fingers lifted something and stroked it delicately.

Jake rested his head against the glass. The key. She was out there alone in the dark with the necklace he'd given her.

He wanted to go to her, to reassure her again that everything was going to be all right. But he didn't know how much his reassurances were worth. He was the man, after all, who enticed her into marriage with a financial contract. He knew that the arrangement still didn't sit well with her.

Maybe it was just time they needed to get this marriage right.

With a soft oath he turned back to bed, knowing even as he did so that he wouldn't sleep.

Jake brought his chest of drawers over to the house the next morning and wrestled it upstairs to his bedroom with Laura's help. "I know you don't have much room here," she said apologetically. "If you want to put your clothes in the drawers, I'll organize the rest of your things."

"You don't have to do this," he said, wishing she were still wearing that white peignoir instead of jeans and a plain pink blouse. Still, she looked tantalizing enough that he searched for something else in the room to study.

"I know I don't have to do it," she said, hands on hips as she scanned the three boxes of his belongings. "But I think we need something to break the ice here."

She was right, and he realized it immediately. Maybe this would be better than that little chat he'd planned. It would certainly be a lot less formal. Molly was downstairs watching a video, and Jake was feeling restless and uncertain. He should have had Rowen include a list of instructions in the marriage contract, he thought wryly.

"Okay." He saw her relax before she bent to sort through the first box.

"There's a wicker shelving unit in the bathroom," she said. "I'll put your shaving things in there."

Jake watched surreptitiously as she moved back and forth between the bedroom and bathroom, finding a place for each of his belongings while he dealt with the clothes. Laura possessed an unconscious grace, both of the body and spirit. He knew she was working hard to recapture what little serenity she'd earned for herself before this marriage.

He wasn't making it any easier on her, he reminded himself.

"Come here a minute," he said, catching her hand when she swished past again. He pulled her down beside him on the floor and tried to smile.

"What's this?" she asked, intent on rummaging through the second box. "Business records?"

Jake nodded. She was avoiding this discussion.

"I'll have to work in the evenings. I'm way behind."

Laura pulled out a cardboard box filled with receipts and looked at him questioningly. "Sure looks like it. How do you plan on keeping up with your regular work, fixing up this house and doing your bookkeeping?"

Jake shrugged. "I'll manage. Laura, we need to talk about more than my schedule here."

She sighed and sat back on her folded legs. "Yes, I suppose so. We need to establish some ground rules."

"Ground rules?" he repeated.

"Isn't that what you had in mind? A few simple guidelines to make this easier? I've got a plan."

The word *guidelines* wasn't the one he'd had in mind, but he supposed it was good enough for the moment.

"I want one thing understood," she said solemnly. "I do the cooking."

Jake cocked his head. "That doesn't sound very liberated to me."

Laura smiled. "Only because I appreciate a good meal. I saw your cupboards, McClennon. You're solely responsible for keeping the canned chili manufacturers in business. And, believe me, I make a much better chili than what comes in that can."

"Oh, do you, *McClennon?*" he retorted, beginning to smile himself. He liked it when she gave him the business.

"So I do the cooking. You get to be assistant chef and chief bottle washer."

His brows went up again. "KP duty?"

"Molly helps, too," Laura told him. "I figure we can do the rest of the housework together, you know. Whoever has time does the laundry and the vacuuming. That should take care of the basic rules."

But it didn't. It didn't even begin to cover the intricacies of this relationship. This was small peanuts compared to some other issues he wanted to settle. Like the sleeping arrangements. How did he explain to her that the assistant chef was burning up inside with the need to kiss the chef's body from head to toe?

"And I can help with your bookkeeping," she added, picking up one of his account books and paging through it. "It's only fair, with all the time you're spending on the house."

"All right," he agreed, and he could see that he'd surprised her with his readiness to comply with her plan. "If you'll agree to a couple of little stipulations from me. Sort of my own rules."

Suddenly wary, Laura dropped the account book back into the box. "And what are they?" she asked.

"We eat dinner out two nights a week, one time with Molly and one time without."

Laura frowned. "I can't afford a sitter."

"I can."

"All right," she said reluctantly. "What else?"

You smile for me, he wanted to say. But he didn't. There was something else he needed to make clear—*I don't want you to sleep with me because you think it's part of the contract.* He wanted her on her own terms, no strings attached. No past, no debts. No past lovers in the bed like ghosts. He wrestled with a way to say it and found he couldn't.

"Another rule. I pay you for doing my bookwork." It wasn't even close to what he wanted to say to her.

Laura shook her head adamantly. "Absolutely no way. You're working on the house."

"Which is also my house now," he said. "If you take a salary for the bookwork it's a tax break for me."

He could see that she didn't believe him at all.

"I think you're still trying to find ways to give me money," she challenged him, her chin jutting out.

He cupped that chin in his hand and smiled. "You'll change your mind when you see my books," he assured her. "You'll want a raise in salary."

She started to protest, then somehow lost herself in his eyes. Smoky gray, they reminded her of the deep fog that often swirled in from the river on winter mornings. She had sometimes thought that she could lose herself in that fog, and now she made the analogy with his eyes. So soft and promising and unfathomable.

Laura started to say his name, but he leaned toward her, and she took a shaky breath instead. "I think you're using these rules for your own advantage," she managed to say before his mouth brushed hers.

She thought he said, "You better believe it."

The problem was there were no rules when it came to this kind of contact. His kiss deepened, and Laura tried to hold herself in check. She didn't want to throw herself at him, to succumb only to have him turn away. So she closed her eyes and willed her mind to blankness. The teasing pressure at her mouth nearly undid her, but she bit back the moan in her throat and remained rigid and unresponsive.

When Jake pulled away, his gray eyes were stormy and filled with questions. His hands tightened on her shoulders. They stared at each other, their breathing gradually slowing.

It was a long minute before Laura realized that the phone was ringing. She rose to her feet and hurried for her own bedroom, her fingers flying involuntarily to her sensitized lips.

It took her another several seconds to realize that it was Ali on the other end.

"You sound out of breath," Ali said. "Were you busy?"

Laura assured her that she wasn't, all the time trying to collect her scattered thoughts. Ali wanted to know if her daughter and Molly could go trick-or-treating together, and Laura had to summon all of her faculties just to remember when Halloween was.

"I'll let you go," Ali said, and Laura could picture her smile on the other end. "I know how it is with newlyweds on their honeymoon."

It wasn't anything like Ali imagined, Laura thought as she hung up the phone. It was an ache that wouldn't go away, that only grew each time Jake touched her. And he seemed determined not to let the touches become anything more.

She hugged her arms to herself and leaned against the wall. She didn't know how she was going to live with this ache.

Chapter Eleven

Laura's mind was elsewhere as she zipped Molly into her spider costume. Molly couldn't contain herself in her excitement, and the stiff black legs that protruded from the costume bounced as she twirled and laughed.

"Hold still," Laura said automatically as she adjusted the black cap with its red eyes, but her frown wasn't for Molly. She hadn't heard from Trina since the wedding, and it wasn't like Trina to go away quietly. Then there were the christening gowns she and Emma were working on into the evening hours. Several new orders had arrived recently, throwing them into a frenzy of sewing. Finally, there was Jake. The last two nights he hadn't come upstairs until late, well after she had gone to bed. She had lain awake until she heard his footsteps, unable to think of anything but him.

The night before, Laura had gone to bed and lain there listening to the refrigerator door open, the chair scrape back in the kitchen, the soft clink of a mug against the counter.

Now she found herself listening for the sound of his truck as surely as she listened for him to come upstairs at night.

A rumbling motor that could only be Jake's truck stopped in the driveway, and Molly squealed. "Jake's home! Let's go trick-or-treating!"

Laura applied a last smudge of rouge on Molly's lids before her daughter danced away from her.

"Jake!" she cried as soon as the front door opened. "Look at me!"

"Where's the flyswatter, Laura?" Jake called in a mock-worried voice. "There's a giant spider in here!"

Molly laughed, and Jake smiled, kneeling to inspect her costume. "Oh, it's you, Mollykins. I thought I was going to have to get a giant can of bug spray." He admired her eight legs and her bright red eyes while Molly preened in front of him.

Laura stood by the stairs, smiling indulgently. Jake had brought a new dimension into Molly's life. Molly had always been a confident child, but with Jake here she suddenly seemed glad to be a little girl.

"Let's go, Jake!" Molly called, trying to pull him to the door.

"Give me a minute first," he told her, still smiling. "I need to wash my hands." He stood and walked toward Laura. Then, as if it were the most ordinary thing in the world, he stopped and kissed her.

It was a brief kiss, the kind a tired husband gave his wife when he came in the door. But Laura savored it, precisely because of what it was.

She felt the heat climbing her neck, and when she looked at Molly, her daughter was grinning. Laura mumbled something about finding a treat bag for Molly and scurried for the kitchen.

"Don't forget to pick up Beth," Laura called from the kitchen when Jake came back downstairs. Molly and Ali's daughter had spent so much time planning this on the phone that she knew there wasn't a chance Molly would let him forget Beth. She didn't hear any answer and went back to putting away the lunch dishes.

"Why aren't you going with us?" Jake's voice asked from behind her, making her jump.

She didn't want to tell him that she was already as nervous and flustered as a schoolgirl around him. Going along would only rattle her some more.

"I need to stay here in case any trick-or-treaters come," she hedged, turning to find him far too close. She pressed her backside firmly against the sink.

Jake studied her a moment, then shook his head. "I think this is something we should all do together."

He was right, but she didn't know how much more time she could spend with him and not go out of her mind. By the time she went to bed each night she was so keyed up she couldn't sleep.

If Jake tossed and turned as much as she did, he gave no indication in the mornings.

Laura's eyes slid away. "Molly will have just as much fun with you as with the two of us."

"But I won't," he said, gently putting his hands on her shoulders and pulling her away from the sink. She thought he might kiss her again, and her pulse rocketed in anticipation. But he propelled her toward the front door, stopping long enough to pull her coat from the closet.

Laura remembered to grab the treat bag for Molly and a flashlight before Jake maneuvered the two of them into Laura's car. Beth was as excited as Molly, and Laura began to relax as the girls made enough noise for a dozen people.

By the time they got back home after touring the neighborhood and dropping Beth at her house, Molly was still wound up and pawing through her bag of candy.

"I think I got *three* candy bars at that last house," Molly chortled, plunking the bag onto the kitchen table. "You know, I oughta make a map for next year, so I know where all the good houses are."

"A future executive," Jake observed lazily, dropping onto a chair with a smile.

"Or a pirate," Laura amended with a raised brow. "Come on, Mollster. Leave the candy for after dinner."

Jake heated some soup and bread for dinner while Laura worked on one of the christening gowns. They all sat together in the parlor after dinner, Molly coloring in a book

Jake reading the newspaper and Laura working on Jake's ledgers. When Molly's bedtime came around, Jake took her upstairs and read her a story.

It was the perfect domestic scene, Laura thought as she continued to enter material bills into the book. But underneath it all it wasn't so typical. She couldn't keep her mind on her bookwork, had been having problems with concentration all evening. She couldn't seem to think of anything but Jake and how he must look stretched out on the bed next door to hers. She wondered if he slept in pajamas all the time or underwear—or nothing.

"Nothing," his voice said from the doorway, and heat suffused her face as she worried that she had given voice to her erotic speculations.

"What's wrong?" he asked, frowning as he sat down beside her on the couch.

"Nothing," she lied. "I guess I was daydreaming."

"Well, I was saying that I asked Molly what she wanted for Christmas, and she said nothing. I don't know if she really means it, or if she just wants to sound good in case Santa's listening." He grinned, and Laura tried to smile back. All she could focus on were his gray eyes and the warmth and humor there.

Jake, I need so much more from you than this.

But she didn't say it. She lowered her eyes and said something about Molly never deciding what she wanted until the last minute.

And Jake nodded and stretched out his legs, propping his head against the back of the couch. Laura had to make herself look back down at the book in her lap. He looked so lean and strong and handsome. Her husband.

Laura realized her hands were shaking.

"I think I might turn in early," she said, striving to sound casual.

She offered him a brief smile and started upstairs. She hesitated, hoping he would follow, but he stayed where he was. Suppressing a small groan, Laura set about mechanically getting ready for bed.

She was still wide awake when he came up later. She could hear him moving around the small bathroom and then the creak of the bed. She did groan softly then as she thought of him lying there in the state of undress that had stuck with her since her too vivid daydream.

Sleep was impossible. Outside her window a bare branch scratched against the side of the house as the wind picked up and whispered under the eaves.

Laura slid out of bed and pulled on a thick white terry-cloth robe. She would just sit on the porch until she calmed down, she told herself. Just until she could sleep.

The wind was cold, but the corner of the porch with the Adirondack chair was sheltered. She curled her feet under her, hugging her arms to herself.

Laura was outside on the porch again. Jake could just see the edge of her robe in the chair. He started to go back to bed and give her the solitude she apparently needed. But then he changed his mind.

He padded downstairs in his bare feet and slipped out the front door. Quietly he made his way around the corner of the porch and stopped beside her chair. The wind was blowing, and though a floorboard had creaked Laura hadn't heard him.

"You don't have to hide out here, you know," he said, and she jumped violently.

"You scared me to death," she said, clutching one hand to her lapel.

"If you want time alone, all you have to do is tell me," he said.

"You're going to freeze to death," she said, noticing that he was wearing only pajama bottoms. Actually it was hard not to notice with his bare chest only inches away from her. Laura nearly groaned. Dark springy hair matted that chest and tapered down to the flat abdomen partially visible where his pants had slipped.

He crossed his arms which only served to accent the hard muscles of his torso.

"Come inside," he said.

Laura nearly bolted from the chair. "Maybe I could use a cup of hot tea," she muttered, trying not to look at him as she brushed past.

Jake was right on her heels when she entered the kitchen and flipped on the light switch. Bad move, she thought as she realized that she could now see his chest and arms in stunning detail. His skin was darker than hers, the flat, hard nipples even darker. She could imagine her hand there, stroking over his skin and testing the hardness beneath. Just thinking about it made her fumble with the mug she had pulled from the cabinet.

"Here, let me—" he began, reaching for the mug, but Laura jerked away.

"No, I can do it," she insisted, sounding desperate even to herself. She whirled away from him a little too quickly and bumped the counter. That was all it took to dislodge the mug again, and it went thumping to the small area rug in front of the sink.

"Laura," Jake said, and she could hear a wealth of what he didn't say behind that simple word. He snagged her arm with one hand when she was about to bend for the mug. But she would not let him touch her tonight. She would break into a million pieces if he touched her and then left her alone in her bed again.

She swore angrily and pulled her arm free, hurrying for the stairs. Behind her, she could hear him swear softly in turn.

She didn't know if he followed or not. Her only goal was to reach her bedroom and shut the door, to close him out before he made her night a hell of aching need.

Laura didn't get the door closed before he jammed his arm against it. She backed up and stood stiffly, hoping to end the confrontation quickly before it got out of hand.

"I don't understand what's going on," he said sharply, coming inside and closing the door. He reached over to flip on the small light on top of the dresser. "Why are you running away from me, Laura?" He took a step toward her, his jaw tight, his gray eyes a deep pewter.

Laura backed up, then decided to stand her ground. If she didn't know this man she would have found him more than a little intimidating. But this was Jake, and Jake would never hurt her. Of that she was sure.

"Jake, please be reasonable," she said. "It's late. We should both get some sleep."

He gave his watch an impatient glance. "It's ten-thirty, Laura. It's not that late. Now what's the matter?"

She could hardly keep her eyes lifted to his face. His bare chest was so close, so tantalizing. She had to grit her teeth to keep from reaching out and touching him.

"It's . . . *this,*" she said finally.

"What?" He frowned, clearly not understanding.

"This," she said again. "You and me."

"Laura, you're not making sense," he said, reaching out and drawing her closer. "What are you talking about?"

She couldn't think with his hands on her like this, with his half-naked body so close. Her senses were swimming in the intoxicating aura surrounding him. She could feel herself drawn closer, like an iron filing to a magnet. She let one hand touch his skin, trail down his chest, the springy hair tickling her palm. She nearly groaned.

Jake's eyes darkened.

"So this is what's bothering you," he murmured softly. His arms dragged her even closer until she rested her head against his chest.

"Yes," she said, her breath catching. "Yes." It was an answer to his question, and it was an acknowledgement that she was succumbing yet again. This was what she wanted, for Jake to hold her like this and to touch her, his fingers sparking fire wherever they skimmed.

Laura turned her head and gently kissed his shoulder, eliciting a moan from Jake. That made her smile despite her tension. At least she wasn't the only one suffering from this excruciating frustration.

"What do you want?" she whispered, lifting her head to search his face in the dim glow of the light. *Tell me.*

"I want you." The words were uttered with a nearly gutteral harshness. "But I want you of your own free will. Not because of the contract."

Laura shook her head slowly. "It's not the contract, Jake. I want you because of who you are. I want you to be my husband in more than name. Make love to me tonight."

She had never been carried by a man before, and when Jake lifted her and carried her swiftly to her bed she clung to him, her heart racing. This was what she had craved every night since their marriage, her husband claiming her as she claimed him.

Jake set her on her feet and ran his hands caressingly over her shoulders and down her arms, making her shiver in anticipation. Her eyes locked with his, and she felt herself drowning in a stormy pewter sea.

Smiling slightly, he untied her robe and pulled it from her, tossing it over a chair. His hands reached again for her, then stopped as he saw what she was wearing. His gift to her, the gold chain with the small key, hung around her neck. Jake touched it experimentally, and Laura shivered as his fingers traced the key and then her collarbones.

"That nightgown," he said in a husky voice, "has been driving me crazy from the moment I saw it." He hooked a finger under each strap and lifted, sliding them down her arms. Moving closer, he tasted her lips slowly, his tongue rimming the inside of one and then the other. Laura shifted restlessly against him, whimpering softly with the need for more.

As the pressure of his mouth increased, Jake cupped her breasts and stroked the nipples with his thumbs.

By instinct alone Laura thrust her pelvis against his, finding him as ready for joining as she was. But Jake was in no hurry tonight. He was driving her into a mindless state of only sensation with the ministrations of his mouth and hands. Her knees trembled as his fingers moved to her sides and began sliding the nightgown lower.

A moment later she stood in the darkened room with the gown at her waist, Jake gently tracing patterns on her naked breasts.

Her breasts were beautiful, he thought in wonder. They were creamy and smooth with small, round nipples almost the color of the key at her throat. His thumbs strummed those nipples to pebbly hardness. He loved the way she trembled as he touched her.

He loved everything about her, he thought in distraction. The way the shadows captured the hollows beneath her cheekbones and between her breasts. The way her skin turned pearly where light skimmed it. The way she responded to his touch.

One quick tug, and her nightgown fell to the floor. Her hands caressed his chest, then drew lower until one hand slid beneath the waist of his pajama bottoms. Jake groaned and repressed the urge to take her right then and there. He had waited this long he was determined to make this last for both of them.

Laura brought her mouth to his chest, her tongue flicking at one flat brown nipple until he groaned again and clutched her more tightly against him. She could feel his muscles clench beneath her mouth and hands, and she reveled in her sense of power.

Jake couldn't stand any more. He scooped her up and laid her on her bed. The patchwork quilt was already pulled back, and he stood beside the bed, pausing to drink in the sight of her ivory skin against the dark green sheets. Her hair spread out around her face like a cloud of flame, beckoning him to the fire.

"You," he said softly, punctuating his words with short, sweet kisses to her mouth, "are the most beautiful sight I think I've ever seen."

Laura twisted in her need to pull him closer to her. "I don't feel very beautiful," she said, trying to smile. "My hus— No one ever told me that before."

"Then he was blind," he said quietly. "You're very beautiful."

She did smile then, opening her arms to him.

Jake slid off his pajama pants and lay down beside her, noticing with some pleasure that Laura was overtly studying him. His pleasure was short-lived as he realized that she might not necessarily like what she saw.

"Laura," he said hesitantly, "my hands and my body aren't so pretty. I do hard work, and unfortunately it shows." He knew that it showed in his callused hands, in his myriad bruises and small scars and on his skin, still darkened from outside work.

Laura found his body breathtaking. For the first time in her life, she was realizing what lust felt like.

"It's not unfortunate, Jake," she said, smiling as she stretched a hand down the length of him, making his muscles clench. "I can't imagine any other man I'd want in my bed more than you."

The uncertainty began to ease from his eyes. One last worry needed to be settled out loud. "You're sure you're not doing this because of the marriage contract?"

Laura's smile widened and she shook her head. "Party of the First Part," she said, teasing him, "are you going to make love to me or not?"

"Party of the Second Part," he said, leaning over her to begin a sizzling exploration of her body with his mouth and hands, "I am."

Laura quickly found herself overtaken by a passion she had never known before. It both startled and bemused her. Sensing her uncertainty, Jake forced himself to slow down, to savor and taste until her body was writhing beneath him.

But Laura was a quick student. Soon Jake found himself breathing in shallow gasps as her mouth worked its own magic, her fingers following suit. She came to her knees beside him, and with a wanton need she had never felt before, she wove a tapestry of pleasure on his body with her tongue and mouth.

Jake reached for her with trembling fingers, this lover who was shaking his control with each breath, and rolled her onto her back. Pleased that she had aroused him so, she parted her legs at his gentle touch and brought his head down to hers for a long, hungry kiss.

As the kiss ended, shadows shifted outside the window as the moon escaped the clouds. Jake saw Laura's body shimmering in the bed, and he knew he needed to bury himself in her more than he needed breath to live. He had known other women intimately in his life, but never had he felt this soul-shaking need, this consuming passion for a woman.

When he finally entered her, his world was right. The need grew, but as it grew so did his sense of belonging. She was his wife and so much more. She was his soul. The thought flashed through his mind and was lost the next instant as she cried his name. Jake soothed her with his hands even as his thrusts pushed her closer to the edge.

Laura's body rose to meet his, her eyes glazed, her mouth parted. Jake knew that she needed release as much as he did. They gave to each other, sweet touches, wet kisses, the heated pleasure of one slick body caressing the other with each movement. And finally he thrust deeply into her, wanting to touch her soul as she was touching his, and the flame devouring them exploded.

Laura awoke much later to find Jake's arm flung over her as he slept. Smiling, she curled up against his warmth, reliving their lovemaking. She had abandoned her control so completely that for a moment she was afraid she might have cried out that she loved him. But, no. She remembered every precious second, and she had cried nothing but his name. *Her husband's name.* She was truly his wife now.

Laura turned her head slightly to watch him sleep. He had been so gentle, so determined to give her pleasure, that it made her heart catch. If only he loved her in return.

She had never lived her life on "if only," she reminded herself. Jake was her husband now, and that would have to be enough.

When Laura woke the next time it was morning, and Jake was gone.

She found him in the kitchen making French toast and bacon. His eyes lingered on her as she headed for the freshly brewed coffee. "Party of the Second Part," he said softly, "you look great this morning."

"Party of the First Part, I feel great," she said, smiling. She leaned against the counter to take her first sip.

"Have I told you I like that nightgown?" he asked, one eye still on her as he turned the bacon.

"Umm-hmm," she said. He was wearing his jeans and a blue denim work shirt. She could see part of his bare chest below his throat. Just thinking about how that chest had felt beneath her lips made her heart go into overdrive.

"I like it even better after I've tossed it on the floor," he told her, grinning.

She could feel heat climb inside her, but before she could answer, Molly's footsteps thumped on the stairs.

"Hey, you guys!" she called, racing into the kitchen. "I smell food! Can I eat a candy bar for breakfast?"

"No," Jake and Laura said in unison.

"Then can I have a candy bar for dessert?" Molly pressed, going to her mother and hugging her legs.

"Nice try, Mollykins," Laura said. "But no cigar."

"It's not a cigar, Mom," Molly said. "It's a chocolate bar." She laughed uproariously at her own joke, and Laura smiled at Jake over Molly's head.

"Can I wear my costume to school?" Molly asked, dancing in place and still hugging Laura's knees.

Laura sighed, but she smiled. "No, because spiders can't read, and you're the best reader I know."

"I am," Molly agreed, looking pleased. "And now I'm going to go write Jake's name for him."

"Get dressed for school," Laura reminded her, calling loudly because Molly was singing as she climbed the stairs.

"I've got to go," Jake said, pushing the spatula into her hand. "I have to meet Billy and Frank. I'll be back this afternoon."

He gave her a quick kiss on her cheek and then he was gone. Laura sighed and flipped the French toast as she heard the front door close.

"I love you," she whispered under her breath.

Chapter Twelve

Laura dropped the potato peelings into the garbage and pushed aside the curtain to look out the window. Jake and his brother Jordan were helping Molly gather black walnuts from the ground. Jordan had come by after visiting his mother and John in Pierce, Illinois, about fifty miles south of Sandford. Lost in thought, she watched a moment longer, then went back to fixing dinner.

Both of Jake's brothers, his mother and John's wife Rachel and son David had taken to visiting lately. Laura liked having them around. She'd always wanted a big family, and now she had one, albeit courtesy of a contracted marriage.

Still, something was missing.

It had been ten nights since Jake had first made love to her. He came to bed with her every night, and he made love to her. It was as passionate and heated as the first time.

But he was almost always gone when she woke up in the morning. And he never uttered the word *love*.

She had known when she married him that she would probably never hear him say it, but she hadn't known how hard it would be to continue yearning for it night after night.

The door slammed, and she turned, her smile instantaneous as her husband came inside, Molly and Jordan right behind him.

"Walnuts," he said, holding up a paper bag. "Tons of walnuts."

"I hope you're all up to cracking and picking through them," she told him, smiling nevertheless.

"*I'm* not," Jake said, depositing the bag on the table. "Molly's going to visit Beth, and I'm taking you out to dinner, remember? Just you and me."

No, she didn't remember, and the idea flustered her. They had gone out to dinner with Molly a few days ago, back to the Hamburger Haven. Now the thought of eating dinner with him alone made her pulse flutter.

"Jake, we can't just desert Jordan," she protested.

"Sure we can," he assured her. "I've been doing it since I was ten years old."

Jordan said ruefully, "when I was nine I told Mom I was going to save up my allowance so I could hire a private detective to find out where Jake was going."

Laura laughed. "And what did you find out?"

"That Mom wasn't about to let me call a detective in the yellow pages and that Jake was having just as much trouble outmaneuvering John. It turned out that he was doing mostly farm work, anyway. Or tagging along after carpenters. I mean to tell you, it was a disappointing revelation for a kid."

"Yeah," Jake agreed dryly. "When Jordan found out farming involved physical labor he quickly picked another career."

Jordan shrugged good-naturedly. "It wasn't the labor. It was the odors. Take a fertilized field in the spring, add a hog confinement building and you've got just the thing to send a guy running for the city." He tapped Molly lightly on the head with his knuckles. "You take care, kiddo. I've got to head back to St. Louis. Two big business meetings tomorrow."

"The entrepreneur takes his leave," Jake said, but there was affection in his tone.

Jordan hugged Laura and whispered in her ear, "All Jake could talk about outside was you. Big brother is smitten but good."

"Bye, Jordan!" Molly called as he headed for the door. "I'll save you some chocolate chip cookies with walnuts in them."

Laura busied herself with the potatoes again. Jordan's assessment made her feel good for the moment, anyway—if she dared believe it. And she wanted to believe it so badly. That's what scared her.

"Forget the potatoes and let's go out," Jake said at her ear, his hand coming to rest on her shoulder and caressing her neck. "What are you in the mood for tonight?"

You. She was always in the mood for him, but she didn't say it and didn't let it show in her eyes.

"Hamburger Haven," she said after a moment's consideration.

Jake laughed. "You've got to be kidding. You have your choice of anyplace, and you want to go to Hamburger Haven?"

Laura nodded. "I like the atmosphere."

Jake shrugged. "Hamburger Haven it is then."

"I'll go put on a skirt." She hurried past him before she would be too tempted to look into his eyes. She'd done that far too often lately, the result being weak knees and a rapid pulse.

Jake smiled as she started up the stairs. They both knew that there was no reason to change for a dinner at Hamburger Haven, but he liked seeing her in a skirt. And he liked taking it off her.

Every time they'd made love had been as explosive as the first. He had thought himself long past passion. It was a revelation to discover that not only was he wrong on that count, but he had never felt this kind of physical need in his life. His hunger for Laura was endless. He'd buried himself in her every night and yet felt no satiation, only a restless hunger for more.

Jake helped Molly gather up the books and toys that she assured him she'd need at Beth's house.

"By the time you eat dinner there, you won't have any time to play with all this stuff," he teased her.

"Yes, I will," Molly insisted. "Beth's mom said you and my mom are on your honeymoon. She said you want to do things together. She called it playtime." Molly grinned at him. "I'm glad I won't have to give up playtime when I get old." She danced toward the stairs. "I got to go get my best doll."

Jake smiled back. The "old" part not withstanding, Molly was right. He and Laura had been enjoying each other like a couple of kids lately.

But there had really been no honeymoon, unless he counted the feverish nights in bed together. Laura really deserved more than that. She'd had the wedding she wanted, and she was entitled to the honeymoon along with it.

"Are you comatose from hunger?" a teasing voice asked behind him, and Jake turned quickly to find Laura in the doorway.

She took his breath away, literally. She had changed into a beige wool skirt and a dark green silk blouse. Her red hair was brushed to a coppery sheen and pulled back on one side with a clip. Small gold hoop earrings caught the light when she moved closer. Her blue eyes were even larger and more luminous, the lids smudged with a smoky gray shadow. Her skin glowed, and Jake found himself swallowing hard as he stared at her.

"I picked up a few cosmetics the other day," she said hesitantly. "I hope it isn't too much."

Too much? It was magic, it was enchantment, it was a beguiling vision. Too much? No.

"You look beautiful," he said, his voice rough with desire.

She relaxed then and smiled. "It's been a long time since I . . ." She shrugged.

He knew what she had been about to say. Since she had worn makeup or dressed for a man's pleasure. He was immensely pleased that she'd done it for him.

She was standing just a few feet from him now, still hesitant. Jake closed the distance in two strides and cupped her face in his hands. "Party of the Second Part," he murmured just before his mouth closed over hers. "You are one hell of a lady."

His voice and mouth combined to make her shiver down to her toes. Jake had that power over her, to make her feel like a beautiful, desirable woman with just a word or a touch. She had bought the makeup because of him, and now she knew it was well worth the momentary guilt it had caused her.

It had been too long since she'd let herself explore the possibilities of womanhood. Too long that she'd let the rest of the world tag her with a spiteful label because of things she'd done while still a child. Laura had denied herself the pleasures of just being a woman out of a perverse sense of penitence.

But the feel of Jake's mouth on hers and his hands stroking her hair and neck chased all thoughts of penitence from her head. She felt as if she'd fought her way through an endless swirl of fog to find her way home.

And she was here now. Home in Jake's arms.

Already fire was sizzling through her veins, and she couldn't hold her hands still. She ran them through Jake's hair, loving the silky feel against her fingers.

"Is it playtime again?" Molly's voice impatiently asked behind them. "I thought we were leaving."

"We are," Jake murmured against Laura's throat. "I just want to see if your mom tastes good enough to take out."

Molly giggled, and Laura buried her face against Jake's shoulder, laughing. "Does she?" Molly wondered.

"Yeah. Real good." Jake wound his arms around her. "So good that I may eat her up instead of a hamburger."

Molly broke into laughter. "Taste me!" she cried, dancing on her sneakers.

Jake obliged, releasing Laura to bend down and kiss Molly's cheek. "Mmm," Jake said. "Very tasty."

Molly squealed and ran for the closet to get her coat. "Wait'll I tell Beth!" she called.

"Oh, great," Jake groaned. "I can just imagine what Ali will make of that."

Laura grinned. "You asked for it," she informed him with a laugh.

"So I did," he agreed softly, lifting her chin to kiss her again. He brushed his lips over hers gently and repeatedly until Laura felt as if her knees might buckle. She clutched Jake's shirt for balance. "Come on," he said, groaning as he pulled away. "Let's go to Hamburger Haven before I make you the main course."

As Esther took their orders Laura was offering silent thanks that Molly wasn't with them tonight. A few choice words from the talkative seven-year-old about her mom and Jake's "playtime" and Esther would be giving them more trouble than she already was.

"No onions," Esther decided, contradicting Jake's order. "A nice big hamburger steak with mushrooms and *no onions.*"

Esther turned to Laura who raised her brows. "Are you going to decide for me, too, Esther?"

Esther pondered the question. "Nothing better than our Italian burger," she decided. "A little mozzarella, a little tomato sauce and some mushrooms. You'll like it." She started to walk away, then added, "And we'll hold the garlic."

"I *like* garlic," Jake protested.

Esther only smiled over her shoulder at him and muttered something about St. Jude.

"I bet even St. Jude liked garlic," Jake called after her, but Esther was already disappearing behind the counter.

She poked her head around the corner long enough to announce in a stage whisper, "You probably need oysters more than garlic, anyway."

It was the first time Laura had ever seen Jake blush, and she hid her amusement with a sip of water.

"She's getting addled from talking to that concrete garden dwarf," he muttered, but he was almost smiling.

"She really cares about you," Laura said after a moment.

Jake sighed. "I suppose so. She's always been here when I needed her."

"You're a lucky man to have so many people who care about you," she said with a little envy.

Jake slowly met her eyes. "You have just as many people, Laura. You just never knew it."

Her eyes slid away, but she looked back at him when his hand reached out and covered her left hand, the one with the wedding ring. "Jake?" she asked softly.

"What is it?"

"Nothing." She sighed.

"What is it, Laura?" he persisted. "When I told you you could always ask me anything, I meant it."

She took her time forming what she would say. It was something that had nagged at her for a long time. But she wasn't sure what Jake's reaction would be.

"It's about Beverly...and Andrea," she began hesitantly. "I don't know anything about them, Jake." She gathered courage when he continued to look steadily into her eyes. "They were both a part of you—or what you are—and I want to know everything about you."

Jake snorted. "I don't like to think that Andrea was ever really a part of me, but I suppose she did have a hand in how I feel now."

Laura swallowed. "How you feel now?" she repeated.

"Damn lucky to be married to you," he said, and she felt the hand holding hers tighten. Jake took a deep breath. "Beverly was my first love. We were both young and pretty innocent. She wanted to create a good home, and she did it well. I admired her talent, her patience." He smiled tightly. "Although sometimes she was too patient. I never could get her to fight with me." He shrugged. "I guess when she died I made her into a saint in my head."

"She sounds like she was one," Laura said.

Jake studied her face but didn't comment.

"And you started drinking after the accident?" Laura prompted him.

Jake nodded. "I blamed myself for not going with her that night. I'd lost everything that mattered in my life in that one split second on the highway." For a moment his gray eyes turned bleak. "I started drinking to forget, and before long I did forget—everything except how miserable I was. That's when Andrea came along." He leaned forward and closed his eyes for a moment. When he opened them they were sharp and haunted with memory. Laura couldn't move, couldn't stop hurting for him. His pain became hers.

"It's hard to explain, but Andrea was like alcohol in another form. I used her to forget, and she used me in turn."

He stopped speaking abruptly and let go of Laura's hand as Esther returned with their food. Sharp-eyed as ever, the waitress apparently concluded that something important was under discussion, and she slipped away without comment.

Laura toyed with her food, waiting for him to speak again. She knew that she didn't really want to hear this, but she needed to hear it. She needed to understand what had happened to Jake. She needed to know what kind of women haunted his past, the same way he'd needed to know what ghosts peopled hers.

Jake made a show of eating, then slowly set down his fork and looked at Laura again. "This isn't easy for me to say, Laura. I'd never been played for a fool before."

"I'm sure it's not very pleasant, Jake."

"It leaves an ugly taste in the mouth." He took a swallow of coffee and frowned. "Andrea moved in with me and made herself right at home. I thought things were fine. But a few weeks later I found out what she really wanted." He grimaced at the memory. "I found her packing one afternoon. I was groggy from drinking too much the night before, and I didn't know what was going on. By the time I could think clearly she was gone, along with my car. The next day she still hadn't returned." He laughed without humor. "In my confused state, I called Carl and reported the car stolen." He swallowed more coffee and regarded Laura carefully. "Then came the call from Esther. Her niece is a teller at the local bank, and she told Esther that Andrea had drawn out a large sum from my savings account the day before. She had all but emptied it."

"But how could she do that?" Laura asked.

Jake smiled bitterly. "When I was, shall we say, very inebriated one night she apparently gave me papers to sign. I don't really remember. Actually I don't remember much of that time at all. The papers put all the money in a joint account and the car in her name. Since she was living with me the bank didn't think too much about it."

"She swindled you," Laura breathed quietly, her eyes wide.

"I think I was an accomplice in my own financial downfall," Jake said. "A drunk is a poor manager of his money, much less his life."

"Did you get anything back?" Laura asked.

Jake shook his head. "A good case could have been made in court that I wasn't competent when I signed the papers, but... that's not something I particularly wanted to make public, and she knew that."

"You mean she got away with it?" Laura demanded indignantly. "Jake, she's probably swindling someone else right now."

Jake smiled. "Not unless she's found a way to do it in prison."

"Prison? You mean you pressed charges, anyway?"

"I didn't have to. Carl found out where she was and notified the authorities and banks there. She made a bad mistake when she tried it again." His smile was almost satisfied. "She tried forgery the next time, and she got caught. I was still drinking then, or I would have gone to her trial."

Esther came by with the coffeepot, and Jake fell silent. Laura sat back and toyed with her food. Her appetite had fled as Jake told his story. One question kept spinning around her head, screaming for an answer.

After one experience with a disreputable woman, why had Jake married Laura? She understood the contract now—it was as much for his protection as hers, though he might not consciously realize that. It was generous in the event of a divorce, but still it would prohibit her from taking everything he had.

Everything he had. If only he knew that Laura had no interest whatsoever in his material possessions or his money. All she wanted was this man's love, and the verbal part of their contract specifically made that forbidden. Jake had provided for her financial security, but to her it was cold comfort. He had told her she wouldn't have his love, and now she could see why. It was a far more precious commodity than money.

"What are you thinking about?" he asked, and she looked up to see that Esther had left. Jake's fingers traced a pattern on the Formica tabletop and his gray eyes moved over her face with the same restlessness.

Laura chose her words carefully. "I guess I was thinking that experience has made you a cautious man." When she saw him frown she added, "And rightfully so."

Jake shifted in his seat, leaning forward. "Laura, do you think I had that contract drawn up because of my experience with Andrea?"

It was precisely what she thought, but she didn't want to argue with him.

"Jake, there's nothing wrong with caution. Especially after what happened to you."

"Laura, listen to me," he said, reaching out to capture her hands and draw them toward him. "That contract has nothing to do with Andrea."

He could see that she didn't believe him. She was nodding, but he suspected it was only to pacify him. The truth was there in her eyes.

Jake swore softly and released her hands. "The contract was to protect you," he said, but even as he spoke the words he realized that Laura was at least partially right. He was using a piece of paper to build a wall around both his bankbook and his heart.

* * *

She didn't speak on the ride home, and Jake couldn't find the right words to reassure her.

All of his good intentions were for naught, he thought later as he got ready for bed. He'd wanted to protect her, to provide some security for her and Molly, and he'd ended up hurting her.

Jake came to her bed as usual and in the dark she turned to him and buried her head against his bare shoulder. Jake stroked her hair as her lips began to slowly explore his collarbone.

He was ready to make love to her in an instant, but he was unsure. Given what she believed, whether she wanted this tonight was questionable. His hands tightened on her shoulders, and he took a deep, sustaining breath.

Laura continued to kiss and nuzzle him, her mouth moving ever lower. Jake was nearly trembling, his breathing ragged and shallow. He tried to say her name, but it came out as a gutteral moan.

She laved his belly with her tongue, then slipped lower, pulling his pajama bottoms down over his hips. Jake sat up long enough to throw them on the floor. Laura pushed him back down, wordlessly driving him out of his mind as her mouth found him and began a slow, torturous stroking.

With a wrenching groan Jake moved his hips. "I need you," he rasped out. Clutching her shoulders, he pulled her up to lie beside him. One quick motion and he stripped off the white nightgown he loved so much. He was dimly aware of a tearing sound as it gave. The next instant he was looming over her, his hands and mouth urgent.

With her own cry of hunger, Laura arched against him as he entered her swiftly.

There were no words, only a desperate communication of hands and mouths, of kisses and groans. Jake felt his own need overtaking him, but he made himself pleasure her first. When she exhaled sharply and arched, shuddering with release, he let himself follow her.

As he kissed her deeply one more time, he knew he was sated only for the moment. He never got enough of her. He threw one arm over her as he felt sleep drift over him like a tide. He couldn't imagine going to sleep without her at his side, but he didn't know how to tell her in a way that she would believe him.

Laura found sleep impossible despite her exhaustion. Despite Jake's arm draped possessively over her, she felt as though the contract were in bed with them, driving a wedge between them even as they made love.

It was a fool's agreement, she told herself.

But she had wanted Jake so badly, still wanted him. She would probably sign the damn thing all over again just to have him beside her like this.

She rolled over in his embrace and listened to his soft, even breathing. He was fast asleep.

I love you. She mouthed the words, afraid to say them out loud even when she knew he wouldn't hear.

Jake heard laughter when he came home after work. It was the day before Thanksgiving, and the next morning he and Laura were driving to his brother John's house for the big dinner.

Laura and Emma had worked feverishly on the christening gown orders, and it looked as though they were right on schedule.

Jake hung up his coat and headed for the workroom. Mingled with Laura's clear, bell-like voice and Emma's grave one were a couple of unfamiliar voices.

He cautiously poked his head into the workroom. Laura stood with her back to him, holding up a tiny Christmas tree with Victorian ribbon and lace trim. Miniature dried flowers completed the decorations. Emma sat at the worktable, smiling as she listened to the interchange between Laura and the two women opposite her.

"Oh!" one of the women exclaimed. "Your husband's home." She gave him a bright smile and introduced herself as Doris and her companion as Kathy.

"Their children are in Molly's class at school," Laura explained, turning and lightly resting her hand on Jake's arm. "They stopped by to ask if I could help with the children's class Christmas party this year."

This was what he loved about coming home to Laura, the soft touches, the warm smiles, the obvious welcome.

He chatted a moment with the women, then excused himself to go get cleaned up.

When he came back down fifteen minutes later Laura and Emma were totaling up the sale they had just made.

"Three trees, five lace collars and a christening gown!" Laura said excitedly. "This is our best month for sales yet."

Emma, who had an innate interest in money transactions, was grinning. "And they said they have friends who will probably want to order more things."

"It looks like you ladies are doing a brisk business," Jake said, pleased.

A horn honked outside, and Emma jumped up. "My ride," she said. "I'll see you Monday morning."

Laura got Emma's black coat for her and saw her out the door. When she returned to the workroom Jake was holding up a delicate piece of lace. He set it down and smiled at her.

"You've really made a go of it," he said, leaning back against the table.

Laura looked almost surprised. "Yes, I guess I have. And Emma. She's such a good worker."

"Not just the business," he said. "You're making friends here, Laura. And nobody seems to care about your past."

She just looked at him a moment as comprehension dawned. Then her smile bloomed again. "You're right," she said, coming closer and putting her arms around his neck. "You know, it's funny how happiness can sneak up on a person."

Laura brought his head down to hers and kissed him invitingly. Jake felt warmth spread throughout his body, not just from the kiss but from her admission that she was happy.

But still he wondered.

Sometimes at night he caught an unguarded look in her eyes, a sadness. And since the night he'd told her about

Andrea and she'd drawn her own conclusions concerning the contract, there had been an almost imperceptible wall between them, as gossamer as the lace he'd held a moment ago, but far stronger. Even when he held her in his arms and made love to her at night he could feel her holding something back.

It made him restless and edgy, because he wanted all of her. She was a hunger in his blood, and he was relentless in seeking satisfaction of that hunger. He lost himself in her every night, and still, when the morning light broke he felt the hunger rise again, stronger than before.

Even now.

"Where's Molly?" he asked when he raised his mouth from hers.

"She's having dinner at Beth's house tonight."

"Good," he said with a predatory smile. "I have you all to myself." The next instant he was sweeping her into his arms and striding for the stairs.

Laura didn't protest, only nuzzled her head into his shoulder. She knew how much he wanted her, because she felt the same unappeasable need. He might never love her, but this was one hold she had on Jake. And she would shamelessly use it.

Laura was tense on the ride to John's house in Pierce, but she tried not to let it show. Jake's family had made her feel more than welcome, but she was still reluctant to believe in the family closeness she'd begun to feel so much a part of.

Robert's parents had dropped in occasionally—and unexpectedly—to visit before she and Robert moved in with them. Laura always felt as if Trina were trying to catch her at something. She even imagined that once in a while she spotted Trina following her while she went about running her errands. Whether Trina's oppressive watchfulness was real or imagined, Laura had never felt comfortable around her.

But Jake's family was entirely different. From the kind and always-smiling Elizabeth to the devilish and free-spirited Jordan, they each took pains to let her know that she was accepted. It was a startling experience for a woman who was used to suspicion.

"Look at the Christmas decorations, Molly," Laura said, pointing out the lighted Santas hung above Pierce's main street on fat strings of garland.

"Where did all the water go, Mom?" Molly asked, puzzled. "In school they said everything got flooded."

"It did," Jake assured her. "But the water slowly went back into the river and into the ground. See over there?" He slowed the truck and pointed down a side street that was only a block from the river. "That dark line halfway up the house is the water line. That's how high the flood was."

"Wow." Molly was wide-eyed the rest of the drive.

"The town's come back pretty well from the flood," Jake said. "A lot of business was lost when the bridge closed for three months."

"You came down and helped during the flood, didn't you?" Laura asked, remembering some things John and Jordan had said.

"As much as I could. Something like that can make you feel pretty helpless." He glanced at her. "When the levee broke we couldn't save John's house."

"I know." She thought of the quiet stoicism John had shown when he talked about it. "Your childhood home. It must have been hard to see it go."

"But life goes on," Jake said, giving her a smile. "And sometimes it can be better."

Sometimes, she thought. And sometimes it left you aching for more.

When the truck turned off the main road, Laura realized that they were near the Mississippi River. A bald eagle was soaring high in the air above the trees, and she knew they stayed close to the water.

The gravel road stretched upward, but cedar trees blocked any view of their destination. She found herself curious about where John and Rachel lived. She knew that it was a cabin Rachel had bought when she came back to Pierce. And she knew that after the flood took John's home and he and Rachel were married, Jake had helped them enlarge the cabin. She was curious because this was her husband's work but also because John and Rachel had such a strong bond that it was clearly evident to anyone just meeting them how much they loved each other. She wanted to see where they lived as if it might tell her how they had made their marriage such a vital partnership.

The truck topped the rise, and Laura expelled her breath in a silent sigh of appreciation. The cabin was redwood with slate shingles, the construction low and rambling, designed to blend with the surrounding trees. One side was almost all glass with huge windows reaching nearly from floor to what looked like a cathedral ceiling. The porch stretched around the house, gracefully blending into a deck in front of the section with all the windows.

Laura realized that Jake had turned off the engine and was watching her.

"It's breathtaking," she said, shaking her head.

Jake grinned. "John and Rachel designed it themselves, and I did the contracting. All of us pitched in on the actual labor. Even David. I think it gave him a chance to get to know his dad better, working side by side with him." Jake glanced out the window and grinned. "Here he comes now."

The dark-haired boy racing toward them had John's familiar grin, the same grin that Laura loved seeing on Jake's face. Jake had told her that John hadn't even known he had a son until the year of the flood when Rachel came back to town.

"Hey!" David called as he peered into the truck. "Grandma says for you three to get in here and help her keep Uncle Jordan away from the turkey."

Jake laughed. "We'd better go defend our dinner then," he said. "I bet the pie's in danger, too."

The aroma of roasting turkey and a chorus of voices greeted them when they stepped inside, and Laura could feel the warmth of Jake's family as palpably as the oven heat emanating from the kitchen.

"They're starving me, Molly," Jordan complained, punching his brother on the shoulder and hugging Laura before he bent to grin at Molly. "I can't have so much as a celery stick." He eyed the cherry pie in Laura's hands. "Laura, dear, kind sister-in-law, take pity on me."

Molly giggled, and Laura laughed. "You're breaking my heart, Jordan. Do you have the strength to carry this to the kitchen?"

Jordan took the pie and headed for the dining room, but amid protests John and Jake herded him back toward the kitchen.

"You sure look nice, Aunt Laura," David said as he helped her off with her coat, and she smiled at him.

"I can see who got the charm in the family, David. Thank you."

"Mom made stuffing with raisins in it," he advised Molly in a low voice. "It's Jordan's favorite, but she promised I could sneak some in the kitchen before dinner."

"Can I have some, too?" Molly whispered.

David nodded and the two of them tiptoed to the kitchen, no doubt to see if it was tasting time yet. Laura could hear Jake in the kitchen discussing some detail of the house with John.

Laura looked around the massive family room with its redwood walls and stone fireplace that dominated one entire wall. It was a warm, inviting room with braided rugs on the hardwood floor and a blue-and-red quilt in the log cabin pattern hanging on one wall. The furniture around the fireplace was overstuffed. The pine sideboard and table were two different styles but looked just right together. It was a home, Laura thought. A real home.

She heard laughter in the kitchen and glanced that way just in time to see John swat Rachel on the bottom as he reached around her with his other hand to steal a deviled egg. Elizabeth was up to her elbows in roll dough, and David and Molly leaned on the counter beside her, watching the whole process. Jordan was attempting to sneak a sliver of pie until Elizabeth caught him.

Elizabeth saw Laura watching and smiled. "You'd better get in here, Laura, before my starving son demolishes your pie," she said. "You'd think he fasted all week."

"I've been too busy to eat a decent meal in ages," Jordan said, trying again for the pie. This time John fended him off.

Laura was irresistibly drawn to the kitchen and the charmed circle of family there. Rachel looked up and grinned at Laura, then moved aside to give her space at the counter. "Would you finish the eggs for me?" she asked. "The baby's kicking up a storm."

"Probably from starvation," Jordan noted dryly, but his eyes were merry.

John was reaching around Rachel again, this time to flatten his hand on her swollen belly. "David," he said over his shoulder to his son. "I think your brother or sister is going to be a soccer player just like you."

Laura watched them and felt their closeness. She glanced over at Jake, who was leaning against the table and emptying a jar of olives into a dish. He met her gaze but didn't smile. Laura could feel her heart constrict. *I want this*, she thought with longing so intense that it made her clutch the counter. *I want my life to be like this. I want my husband to look at me like John looks at Rachel.*

She realized with a sharp pang that what she wanted was love—Jake's love.

"You know, I forgot to give Laura the nickel tour," Jake said, straightening with a deceptive casualness. "It'll give me a chance to brag on the good carpenters in this family."

"Be sure to show her the stereo system I installed," Jordan reminded him, still trying to nab a taste of pie despite his mother's defensive efforts.

Jake stepped to Laura's side but didn't take her hand or touch her in any way. It was all Laura could do not to lean against him, hungry for any contact.

She had it bad, she told herself as she followed him through the kitchen doorway. Like a lovesick teenager.

She dutifully took in all the details Jake pointed out to her, but her mind stubbornly kept returning to her husband. They were in the master bedroom and she was admiring the view of the river from the spacious windows when she realized that Jake had fallen silent. She turned to look at him and found him studying her.

"What is it?" she asked, unsure of herself.

She fit in here so well, he thought in distraction. He had never thought that he could bring another woman here to be with his family—certainly not after Beverly died—and yet here he was. And Laura took her place with an ease and grace that belied the difficulties she must be experiencing. He thought of her handing the pie to Jordan with a sassy retort, and it made him proud to be with her.

Something else had occurred to him. Just as John and Rachel had turned this house into a home, Laura had done the same thing with their home. He remembered how cold and sterile the place had seemed when he'd seen it occupied by the previous owners. And how changed it was now. For one thing, there was her whimsical rogue's gallery of adopted portraits by the front door.

"I was thinking of those old photos you collect," he told her honestly.

"They were the only family, other than Molly, I had for a long time," she said.

She left it unspoken, but he understood. She had Jake and his family now.

He looked at her a long time in silence, then turned toward the doorway. "We'd better get back before Jordan finishes off the turkey," he said, standing aside for her to precede him.

Laura didn't know what he was thinking, and her heart pounded in her throat. She couldn't decipher the look she'd seen on his face. She didn't know what it was in her words that had caused it. But suddenly she felt even more vulnerable to him. Did he guess that she loved him? Was that what she'd seen?

After a sedate prayer of thanksgiving, dinner was boisterous, and everyone groaned when it was time to clear the table. The general consensus was that one and all had eaten too much. Jordan had polished off two pieces of Laura's cherry pie and declared it first-rate.

Laura felt Rachel's eyes on her as she helped carry plates to the kitchen. She had kept up her end of the dinner conversation, smiling and laughing with the others, but she suspected that Rachel saw the pain beneath her facade.

"So," Rachel said bluntly, "did you and Jake have a fight?" She and Laura were alone in the kitchen. The rest of the family was in the other room, the TV on, shelling walnuts for the Christmas cookies Rachel and Elizabeth planned to begin baking the following week. Rachel had shooed them all out of the kitchen, apparently intending to get Laura alone for a heart-to-heart talk.

Laura set down the pile of dishes and shook her head. "No, we didn't." She took a deep breath and let it out slowly. "I think being here, with all of you, has given him second thoughts about things. About me." She couldn't quite make herself meet Rachel's eyes.

"About you?" Rachel repeated, giving up all pretense of stacking dishes and leaning back against the counter, her arms crossed over her chest. "Believe me, Laura, Jake's not one to have second thoughts about anything. Once he makes up his mind, that's it. He wouldn't have married you if he'd had any doubts."

Rachel sounded so positive, but Laura wasn't at all sure. Jake had had no doubts at first because the marriage was based on a contract. There were no real emotional strings. But now...if he guessed how much she loved him, he might feel uncomfortable about their arrangement.

"Tell you what," Rachel said, "get your coat and go watch the river awhile, and you'll feel much better. I guarantee it. It's worked for me lots of times. John will help with the dishes."

Laura was skeptical, but she slipped out quietly so no one would hear her go. She took a deep, calming breath and then walked closer to the edge of the bluff. Someone had built a small stone wall there, no doubt a precaution to keep anyone from walking too close to the edge.

Which was precisely what she felt now—too close to the edge emotionally.

Laura hugged her arms to herself and looked down at the river surging gray-blue in the waning light. The wind gusted slightly and lifted her hair from her neck, and as she turned her head she shivered. But it wasn't with the cold. It was with the sight below, on the floodplain to the right. A bare concrete foundation sat abandoned among dead weeds. Laura knew what must have stood there once, and it made her ache inside. The house that John, Jake and Jordan had grown up in.

"We're planting that in corn next year," a voice said from behind her, and she turned to see John. Catching her surprised expression, he added, "I broke a dish and got banished from the kitchen."

Laura suspected that it was more likely that Rachel had sent him here to talk to her, but she was grateful for whatever reason brought him. "I can't imagine watching your home be destroyed by a flood," she said, shaking her head.

"I think we were all so tired by then that we couldn't really feel the horror of it," John said matter-of-factly, and Laura recognized the same stoicism she had found in Jake. "All that really mattered was that everyone was safe. The worst thing would have been to lose someone."

Laura nodded, her eyes going back to the river. It must have seemed like a vengeful beast that year.

"Has Jake talked to you about what he went through when he lost Beverly?" John asked.

Laura realized she had been right—Rachel *did* send him out here. "Yes," she said, afraid to meet his eyes. "He was devastated."

"*Was*," John said with finality, and, startled, she turned to look at his face. "It took a long time, but he recovered from that loss. Andrea was another matter altogether, though."

"The scars run deep," she agreed.

"When someone dies you grieve and eventually heal, but when someone betrays you the wounds can fester. That Jake didn't drink himself to death is a testament to his inner strength."

Laura soaked in his blunt assessment. "Are you saying he's not over what she did?"

"I'm saying he's not going to open himself easily after what she did. It doesn't mean he cares any less, only that he can't show it yet."

Laura flushed at the knowledge that John could so easily see the distance between her and Jake. But of course he would, she thought. Given the closeness of his own marriage, hers would be transparent to him.

"Rachel and I went through a tough time ourselves," he said as if reading her thoughts. "You and Jake can get through this, too. Just don't give up on him. He needs you."

Laura was startled again. *Jake* needed *her?* Jake who was so strong and stoic?

"I don't know about that," she said slowly.

"I do," John assured her gently. "The McClennon men are tough and proud, but they definitely need that one woman who makes the world turn for them. Jordan will find that out one of these days."

Laura smiled at that. She couldn't imagine free-spirited, driven Jordan discovering that he needed *one* woman.

"Come on," John said, looping an arm around her shoulder. "Time and patience will bring Jake around."

Laura hoped he was right. But she was beginning to wonder if she'd fallen in love with the toughest, proudest McClennon of all.

Chapter Thirteen

Molly had fallen asleep on the ride home that night. Jake carried her upstairs to her bedroom, then went back downstairs while Laura put pajamas on her.

Jake had hardly said anything during the car ride. After making sure that Molly was tucked in and sound asleep, Laura speculated on his quiet mood as she went back downstairs.

She had changed into a dark green nightgown and matching robe. Mentally she chastised herself for being unable to think of anything but Jake in his jeans and gray sweater. Every night he dominated her thoughts until she had him beside her in bed, and they lost themselves in a pleasure not bound by the marriage contract.

Jake was just shrugging back into his coat when she reached the foyer. Her heart sank in disappointment. "Were you going out?"

Jake hesitated, noticing the slump of her shoulders as she watched him. He brought out a gentle smile for her and took off the coat. He'd intended to drive past the new site where

Billy and Frank would begin work next week. He always liked to do a thorough job of checking things out, and now that he was progressing well on Laura's—and his, he amended—house, he needed to get back to his other jobs. But checking out the new site could wait.

"No," he said. "I guess I'll stay in tonight."

Laura put on water for tea, watching from the corner of her eye as he went back to the parlor and sat on the couch, stretching his jeans-clad legs out to rest on the coffee table. She needed to buy an ottoman, she thought. It was time the house had a few comforts that Jake would appreciate.

He'd worked so hard on the house, too. He was almost finished in the parlor, and only drop cloths and plaster chips attested to what had once been a gaping hole in the ceiling.

"I really like your family," she said later, as she sat down beside him and sipped her tea.

"They like you," Jake said. "In fact Rachel gave me a long lecture about how much they like you while you were outside with John."

Laura carefully set the cup on the table next to the couch. She knew that he must be wondering what she and John had talked about, and he certainly must wonder how much John now knew about the marriage contract.

"I think John sensed that we...aren't conventionally head over heels in love," she said, choosing her words cautiously and repeating the phrase he had once used. "He just wanted me to know that these things take time."

"To fall head over heels in love?"

She couldn't read any emotion into the lack of inflection in his voice. And she wasn't at all sure how to answer.

"No," she said softly, shaking her head. "To open up, to be honest with each other."

Jake didn't say anything for a minute, and Laura finally dared a sideways look at him. He seemed lost in thought, almost as if he were a long way away.

"I sometimes wonder," he said at last, his voice still distant, "if I've ever been completely honest with anyone."

His words stunned her, and she sat silently, wondering what he meant.

"I never told Beverly this," he said haltingly, "but I always felt there was something missing in our marriage. I suppose to outsiders we were the perfect couple, but there was no..." He shook his head as if to clear it. "I don't know what to call it—passion, I guess. We were both sensible and responsible. Nothing ever overwhelmed either of us. But by the same token we never had loud fights—I hardly remember a single disagreement—or those moments when two people laugh over something only they understand. I never said anything to Beverly about missing something. And she never said anything to me." Jake turned and looked at Laura, frowning. "I think that maybe I took the coward's way out, Laura. When I had that marriage contract drawn up, I practically guaranteed that there would be no real communion between us. It was a business arrangement, pure and simple. I guess that's all I could deal with."

Laura's heart sank. She saw the prospects of Jake ever loving her slipping into oblivion. *A business arrangement.* It was all he'd intended. And, even now, he could offer her nothing else. Except that she sensed there was an apology beneath his words. She realized that when he had talked of passion he simply meant a depth of feeling between a husband and wife.

"It's all right," she told him. "I understood then and I understand now."

Jake smiled ruefully. "That's your strength, Laura. You always understand." He reached out and lifted her chin with one finger. "You've been very patient with me."

Patient was the last word she would use to describe herself. It was only because she loved him so much that she could keep from throwing herself into his arms and begging for the love he couldn't give. If that was patience then she was more addled than she thought.

What it was was desperation. She didn't want him to find out how much she loved him—she was afraid he would end the marriage. After all, love was a breach of the rules.

"You know," Jake said, breaking into her thoughts, "we never had a honeymoon."

Laura shrugged. It seemed a small matter, given that she had Jake in her bed every night.

"I was thinking that you might want to get away," he said hesitantly. "Just for a couple of days or so. It would give you a break from the cooking and cleaning here. And I'd get a break from Billy and Frank," he added wryly.

Surprised, Laura lifted her eyes to him. "I *could* spare the time now," she said slowly. "Emma and I are caught up on orders. And Emma has a lot of work to do at home."

"I wondered where you might like to go," he said, and again she heard the hesitation in his voice. "The beach or a resort—something like that? Someplace warm?"

Laura shrugged. "I don't particularly like to be around crowds. And I like winter. Whatever you'd like."

"I have a fishing cabin down in Pierce," Jake said. "A long time ago I used to spend a lot of time there. I don't know what kind of shape it's in. I guess I could call John and have him check."

Laura felt a selfish gleam of satisfaction at the prospect of having Jake all to herself. At the same time she couldn't quell her curiosity about Jake and his first wife. Had he taken her there?

"I think the cabin would be perfect," she assured him. She couldn't resist teasing him though. "Does it come with a cook?"

Jake raised his brows, and Laura laughed. "It doesn't matter," she said. "I'll get some groceries for us to take."

"I'll take care of it," Jake told her. "I want you to just relax for a change."

Relax, she thought later as Jake was in the bathroom getting ready for bed. It was an impossible task anytime he was near her. She felt as tightly strung as a violin string, as if the slightest touch would make the tension snap and she would fly into a million pieces.

She still felt strangely unsettled after her talk with John and after Jake's confession about Beverly.

Laura paced the bedroom, listening to the water running in the bathroom. When it stopped she hurriedly sat in the rocking chair near the bed and began brushing her hair.

"Not tired yet?" Jake asked as he came into the bedroom toweling his hair. He was barefoot and wearing only dark blue pajama bottoms. It was all she could do not to stare at him.

Laura shook her head. "All keyed up, I guess."

Jake stood and watched her. Her hair gleamed like polished copper in the lamplight. He wanted to tangle his fingers in it and draw her face to his for a hard, hungry kiss, the kind that always led them to passionate abandon in bed. He couldn't believe that he still felt this earth-shattering need for her. Incredibly, it seemed to grow stronger each time he made love to her. Even now, just anticipating having Laura in his arms, his body was quickly stirring with sexual heat.

She was worried about something. He could always sense it with Laura. And it made him wonder why she felt she couldn't just confide in him.

But there was a ready enough answer for that—the contract. She didn't feel she had rights beyond what was written on paper. And that both angered and saddened him. Because that was his doing.

Jake tossed the towel onto the back of a chair and crossed the room to her. Her hands stilled when she saw him in the mirror. He thought that he had never seen a more beautiful woman. Her eyes were the brilliance of sapphires, her hair like liquid fire. He reached out and touched the silk in front of him, letting it sift through his fingers.

"What are you thinking about?" he asked. "Is it the cabin?"

Laura swallowed. It was difficult to think coherently when he was this close, much less touching her. Her body instantly ached for him to make the caress more intimate.

"It's nothing, Jake." Her voice was a throaty whisper, and even she could hear the hunger in it.

"Laura, if you're thinking about what I said about Beverly, you have no reason to worry." His fingers continued their slow exploration of her hair and the nape of her neck. Laura shivered with the force of her need for him.

"I'm not worried, Jake. All right," she admitted under the spell of his seductive fingers, "I guess I am. I'm afraid you'll have to deal with old memories when we get there. And that you'll pretend that everything's okay for my sake.''

Jake murmured something softly, a denial or an endearment she didn't know which.

"Don't even think about it, Laura," he said. "Beverly was never in the cabin. She hated the outdoors and fishing in particular.'' His hands slipped to Laura's arms, drawing her inexorably upward. When she was standing he turned her to him, his fingers working their bewitching magic on her throat. "I used to go there to be alone.''

Through the haze of desire swamping her, she dimly realized that the site of their honeymoon would be theirs alone he had never taken another woman to that place. It was a provocative thought, but even more provocative at the moment was the sensation he was creating as his fingers played over her skin.

Laura's arms wound around his neck, pulling his head down to hers. His dark hair was like silk against her fingers, making her shiver with delight. She loved his body, the texture of his hair, the hardness of his chest and back, the strength of his arms, even the rough calluses on his hands. She loved everything about him. But she willed herself not to show it.

One swift move and he'd slid the straps of her nightgown from her shoulders. Laura felt the heat inside her build as the silky material settled over her breasts, barely covering them. Jake's hands quickly followed, arousing and caressing her nipples to pebbly hardness. Laura groaned and clutched at his shoulders.

Jake's mouth followed his hands, kissing her through the fabric and making her knees shake. She murmured his name, her palms skimming his chest, her fingers lingering to explore his flat nipples.

He groaned in turn. "What you do to me..." he began but bent to suckle her nipples through her nightgown before he finished what he'd started to say. She didn't have time to think about it, because her breath was coming in short gasps as his hands slid lower.

"Come to bed, Party of the Second Part," he whispered, pulling her toward him as he walked backward. She was nearly mindless with the pleasure he was giving her, but she managed to climb into bed despite the fact that by then he had her nightgown down to her knees. Jake pulled it completely off and lay down beside her. Laura fumbled with the snap at his waist until he helped her.

Then they were touching and kissing and caressing as if they were so starved for each other that they couldn't wait any longer. It was always like this, and as Laura feverishly brushed her lips over his chest, stopping to flick one hard nipple with her tongue, she wondered if she would ever have enough of this consummate pleasure with Jake.

Never, she admitted. *She would never get enough of him whether he loved her or not.*

A week later they dropped Molly off at Ali's house and drove to the cabin. The wind was brisker, the air crisper than it had been at Thanksgiving. It was December now, and winter was taking over one cold degree at a time. Laura stared out the window at the corn fields stubbled with dried, broken stalks left behind at harvest. She had been melancholy all week, looking forward to being alone with Jake but dreading it at the same time.

She wasn't sure how much longer she could keep him from finding out that she loved him. Despite her best efforts, the words nearly slipped out each night as she lay in his arms. She wanted so badly to say them out loud, but she knew that it would be a breach of their contract. And probably the end of their marriage.

Jake turned the truck down a rutted road near the river, and Laura stirred. Outcroppings of limestone were laced with icicles where water had flowed between and over the rocks. Jake downshifted as the road angled upward and the tires sought purchase on the loose gravel.

It was a lower hill than the one leading up from the river to John and Rachel's home, but to Laura the place had the same feel. Isolated and hidden but somehow comforting.

She supposed that was a woman's view; *comforting* was probably the last adjective Jake would choose.

The cabin sat in a clearing at the top of the rise. Laura could see the churning river spread out below. The cold wind whipped up small whitecaps that were quickly swallowed by the current. From the north a tugboat moved slowly downstream, pushing several barges.

The cabin's roof sagged slightly in front, but the steps looked sturdy enough.

"I asked John to clean it up for me and stock a few things," Jake said over his shoulder as she followed him to the door. He fooled with his key ring until he came up with the right key. "John replaced the lock last year."

Laura stood inside the door, looking around as Jake deposited their suitcase on the floor and set about building a fire in the wood stove that stood on a ceramic tile inlay by the far wall.

Laura rubbed her hands together, then smoothed them down her green corduroy slacks. Idly she tucked the necklace Jake had given her back inside her wheat-colored fisherman's sweater.

Her eyes moved lovingly over Jake. His jeans were molded to his thighs, those thighs that she loved to feel pressing against her legs as they made love. His black pullover sweater made his gray eyes look even more mysterious. She could feel a familiar heat grow in her belly as she watched him.

Turning away, she forced herself to look around the cabin.

It smelled of furniture polish, window cleaner and fresh air. The rugs on the wooden floor were worn but clean. A small table sat in front of the window, a tiny vase of roses on top. Beside it was a bottle of sparkling apple cider and a card.

Jake stood up from starting the fire and stretched, frowning when he noticed the bottle and card. He read it, then grinned wryly and handed the card to Laura.

"Welcome to the honeymoon suite. 'The management' hopes you find everything to your satisfaction. By the way, we think you'll find this bed an improvement over the old one." It was signed, "John and Rachel."

Laura had avoided looking at the alcove where the bed was located, but now it was impossible to ignore. Jake was already standing by the bed, his hands on his hips, shaking his head.

"I don't believe this," he said. "The bed is new, apparently a present from John and Rachel." He smiled. "I always suspected that they were here—working a few things out—before they got back together for good."

Laura stood beside him, looking at the bed. It was an oak four-poster, small enough to fit into the alcove but just large enough for two people. The quilt on top looked new, too. Laura recognized the Ohio Star pattern done in red and green. An oak trunk sat at the foot of the bed, another quilt on top of it.

She reached out and touched the quilt, thinking again of John and Rachel and the marriage they had worked to build. It was their love for each other that made their marriage work. It didn't take a genius to recognize the way they looked at each other. What she wouldn't give to have Jake look at her like that...

Embarrassed at the direction her thoughts had gone, Laura moved away, not looking at Jake's face. "I ought to check the refrigerator," she murmured, clearing her throat.

She didn't realize that she was staring vacantly at the contents of the refrigerator until Jake put a hand on her shoulder.

"Anything interesting?"

Laura made herself focus on what was in front of her. "A container of take-out chicken, some salads, cheese..." Her voice trailed off as Jake began slowly rubbing her shoulder. She straightened and closed the door.

"I'll unpack our clothes," she said, edging away.

Jake caught her arm and reached out with his other hand to turn her face toward him. "What's wrong, Laura?" he asked softly. "Why are you so nervous?"

"I'm not," she said a little too quickly. The truth was, she was aching with the need to have Jake hold her. But even more, she needed to hear him tell her what she meant to him. And she was perilously close to coming right out and asking.

Jake sighed. "I think I know what we both need."

Laura stiffened, suddenly feeling even more skittish.

"Let's take a walk," he said. "It's been a while since I've poked around out here."

She could feel some of the stress ebbing away as they stepped off the porch and started down the hill on the opposite side of the cabin. The wind had quieted, but Laura pulled up her collar to keep her ears warm. She stuffed her hands into her coat pockets and matched her stride to Jake's.

"Do you own all this land?" she asked suddenly. She didn't see another house anywhere around.

Jake shook his head. "Most of it is part of a farm. I just own the cabin and about six acres." He stopped walking and shoved his hands into his pockets. He looked distracted, and Laura followed his gaze. All she could see was a large cedar tree standing a little apart from the edge of a stand of trees.

He was hesitating, and Laura didn't know why.

"What is it, Jake?"

Gently he took her hand and led her toward the tree. He stopped in front of it, and she looked at him, puzzled.

"Right there," he said, pointing.

She looked at the tree, and then she saw it. Jake's initials carved into the bark. They were little more than a faint scar now, and she had to look closely to make out the *JAM*.

"I inherited my father's middle name," he said as if hearing her unasked question. "Aaron. I used to hate it. I also inherited something else I hated, his alcoholism."

Laura went still, hearing the tension in his voice and knowing how hard this was for him to talk about.

"We never saw my father drink at home. He used to come here to this cabin to do it. He was a big, muscular man like all the McClennons. And, like them, he needed solitude. You would think that farming would be solitary enough, but I guess he wasn't alone enough even then."

"Did he come home drunk?" she asked tentatively, thinking how hard that must have been on Elizabeth and the boys.

Jake shook his head. "Sick, yes, but not drunk. Sometimes he was gone for days at a time. My mother would say that he was out hunting or fishing. It's a funny thing." His smile was more melancholy than humorous. "I don't think my brothers ever really knew the extent of his problem. My parents pretty much kept it from us. But I'm the oldest. I guess I saw things and heard things that put it all together for me. And one time he took me with him to fish. And he got drunk then."

Jake raised his head and looked hard at his initials. "That's the day I carved these on this tree. It was like a promise to myself that I'd never be like him." His laugh was dry. "Some promise."

Laura laid her hand on his arm, feeling the tension running through him like an electric current. "Jake, you beat your drinking. That was keeping the promise."

Jake looked at her then, his gray eyes traveling her face, his expression softening as he did. "Maybe I did," he whispered. "But not without paying a price."

Laura could guess at the price. A feeling of profound isolation. The sense that he was somehow tainted for being like his father. And the belief that he could never love another person fully, because he didn't have enough to give.

It explained the sadness she'd sensed in him from the beginning. And the lack of true intimacy he'd admitted to in his first marriage. And the reason he couldn't love her.

Laura felt pain wash over her like scalding water. She hurt for Jake, and she hurt for herself, for what he couldn't give her. But she understood him all too well. Because she'd felt the same things. She'd believed that she didn't measure up to anyone else's standards, that she could never be good enough.

But she had healed. And she desperately wanted Jake to heal, too.

"How did the cabin come to be yours?" Laura asked, feeling herself very near to tears.

"My father gave it to me." Jake expelled a long breath. "He was sick in the last years and he stopped drinking. Actually, I think he knew he was dying. John ran the farm after Dad's death. My heart just wasn't in it. That's why I took up contracting and eventually restoration."

Laura could understand that. It was part of the reason she sewed christening gowns. She wanted to make something that endured, something that was treasured. She knew that Jake looked at old houses the same way.

"I've never brought anyone else to the cabin," Jake told her. "I used it when I needed to be alone. I guess I was more like my father than I ever wanted to admit."

Jake was still holding her hand, and Laura realized that he had needed the physical contact to tell her all of this. She also felt an incredible pride that he'd told her things she was sure he'd never said to anyone else. It gave her hope.

Jake smiled at her suddenly. "I think I like having you here much better than coming to the cabin alone," he said. Laura's heart began to pound as he searched her eyes. She was afraid her emotions were becoming far too easy for him to read. It was becoming almost impossible to hide her love for him.

They both looked up as something cold and wet dusted their faces.

"Snow," Laura said as if she'd never seen it before. "It's snowing, Jake."

"My mother used to say that whatever day we had the first snow, that was the number of snows we'd get that winter." He smiled at her again. "Are you superstitious?"

Laura shook her head. "No. Too bad, too. This is only the seventh."

Jake laughed. "Seven snows. We'll see." He hooked an arm around her shoulder. "Come on. Let's go see what the muskrats have done to the pond."

They were chilled and damp when they got back to the cabin. The snow was falling faster now, and Laura warmed her hands by the wood stove while she watched out the window.

She turned slightly when she felt Jake's hands on her shoulders. "You're worried again," he told her, dropping a light kiss onto the top of her head. It was the kind of kiss she treasured, soft and natural, the kind a husband gives his wife.

"Only about getting snowed in," she lied.

"That wouldn't be so bad," he said. "At least until the food John and Rachel left us runs out." He turned her to him and studied her face. "It's more than that." Holding up his index finger, he said, "Wait right here. I have an idea."

Laura watched curiously as he rummaged in a kitchen drawer.

He returned with two pieces of paper and a pencil. "Here," he said, guiding her to one of the chairs at the small table by the window. He placed a sheet of paper in front of her, then sat down in the opposite chair.

"This is something my mother used to have us boys do when one of us was worried about something, but we didn't want to talk about it." He held up the pencil and raised his brows. "Here's how it works. You simply write down what it is that's worrying you. My mom always said it helps to put it in the form of a wish." He wrote something quickly, but Laura couldn't read it from her position. "Then," he said, "you wad up the paper. And, there we have it." He held up the crumpled paper with a flourish and pushed the pencil across the table to her.

Laura looked at him skeptically. "And this works?"

Jake grinned. "Most certainly."

She wasn't about to write down what was really worrying her, not when there was a good chance that Jake would see the paper.

Noting her hesitation, Jake said, "Did I mention that we then burn the paper? The worry goes up in smoke, quite literally. It's a surefire way to find a solution."

Still skeptical, Laura decided to go along with this. She cradled her left arm around her paper, feeling like a kid taking a school test. She tried to transfer the words in her head onto the paper, but she couldn't seem to get started.

The pencil made aimless passes at the sheet as she shifted restlessly.

Jake reached across and touched her arm. When she looked up he said, "Remember, phrase it as a wish."

As he removed his hand she took a deep breath and stared at the paper again. From the corner of her eye she saw Jake push back his chair and turn toward the window.

She hesitated a moment longer, then wrote the words that came straight from her heart. "I wish my husband loved me."

Laura crumpled the paper, and Jake turned from the window. "Now what?" she asked.

"Now we send our worries up in smoke," he said. He opened the door of the iron wood stove and tossed his crumpled paper inside. Relieved that she wouldn't have to worry about Jake finding her paper and reading it, she tossed hers in after his.

"Now what?" she asked, intrigued.

"We read the smoke," he said, smiling at the skepticism firmly back on her face.

Jake closed the glass door and stood, grabbing Laura's hand and pulling her toward the door.

"Can't we read the smoke from in here?" she demanded.

Jake laughed. "Come on. It'll just take a minute."

She shivered as they stepped off the porch onto the hard ground with its dusting of snow. Jake turned her so she was facing the chimney at the side of the cabin and wrapped his arms around her from behind. Snow continued to fall, silently and thickly, leaving melting flakes on her face and hair.

Laura warmed instantly, letting her body relax back against Jake. She stared up at the smoke lazily curling toward the gray sky and was struck by how close it was in color to Jake's eyes. And just as unreadable, she thought wryly.

"Getting any messages?" she asked him.

Jake nuzzled her ear and chuckled. "I see a tall, dark man in your life," he said in a thick accent. "He wants your body."

Laura laughed despite her worry. "Lucky me." She turned her head to look up at him. "Did your mother really read the smoke when you were a boy?"

"Absolutely," Jake said, smiling down at her. "She came up with a good solution to what was worrying me every time. I didn't figure out until I was older how she did it."

"And how *did* she do it?"

"She'd have me write my problem on a thick pad of paper. Then, when I was busy wadding up the paper and watching it burn, she'd read the impression my pencil had made on the next sheet."

Laura flushed, glad she'd had only a single sheet of paper. "A clever woman, your mother," she said. She shivered as Jake traced a pattern on her jaw with his lips.

"Let's go inside," he said. "You're cold."

But she wasn't at all cold now. She could feel a sweet fire racing through her veins as he pressed her more tightly against his chest. She tilted her face up, murmuring his name.

"What is it, Laura?" he whispered, his eyes edging into a darker shade of pewter. "What's worrying you?"

She found the snow and his dark eyes mesmerizing. She was tempted to tell him the truth and get it over with. *I love you.*

But the one bond she had to hold him was the contract. If she breached that, the marriage could end.

When she didn't answer, Jake studied her a moment longer, then lowered his head and kissed her, making no attempt to disguise the hunger that was consuming him. Laura pressed herself more tightly against him, a low throaty groan escaping her. Her hands roamed his chest and finally clutched his shoulders.

"Did you know," she managed to say teasingly when he raised his head, "that there's a tall, dark man who wants my body?"

"Then you'd better not keep him waiting," Jake said, picking her up and striding toward the door.

Laura twined her arms around his neck, thinking as he carried her over the threshold that this was the one sure way he could make her worries go up in smoke.

Chapter Fourteen

Laura woke and stretched slowly Sunday morning, feeling a stab of disappointment when she realized that today was her last day at the cabin with Jake. She turned so that she was facing him, snuggling under the arm he'd thrown over her in the night.

She'd grown to love him even more during their make-shift honeymoon, if that was possible. They had walked for hours each day through the snow, talking quietly or just keeping a companionable silence. He had talked about his father, his brothers and his hopes for the future.

He had told her how much he loved the house she had bought, and they talked about the restoration they would do to bring it back to its former glory.

Laura was beginning to believe in the future, something she had never dared hope for. Life was better than she had ever thought possible. If Jake could love her...

Her heart began to race as she looked up and saw Jake watching her.

"Good morning," he said huskily. "How did you sleep?"

"A little too well," she said ruefully. "I don't think I've felt this rested in years. This has been wonderful, Jake."

His answer was to lower his head and nibble gently on her neck. Laura sighed and pressed her body against his. They had spent as much time in bed as out of it during the weekend, leaving it only to eat the food John and Rachel had left for them or to take a long walk. At night they stoked the fire, then crawled under the covers, reaching for each other immediately. Laura could never remember being so happy.

"We have to go home today," she murmured, even as she turned in his arms and kissed his chest.

"We could stay longer if you want." His hands were caressing her through her nightgown, making her squirm against him in rising desire. She felt as if she went up in flames every time he touched her.

"We should get back," she said as her hands roamed lower, eliciting a groan from him. "Frank and Billy will come looking for us."

But neither seemed inclined to stop what they were doing at the moment. Breathing quickened, heartbeats collided and bodies shuddered as their caresses grew more intimate.

Afterward, Laura lay in his arms, her pulse slowly returning to normal, her thoughts drifting.

"What do you want for Christmas?" she asked idly.

He was silent for so long that she finally turned her head to look into his face.

His gray eyes were solemn as she reached up to touch his cheek. "What is it?" she whispered.

"I want you to be happy," he said, watching her face.

"I am," she told him. "I'm very happy."

"Are you sure?" he asked, and she could hear the hesitation in his voice. "Is there anything you need?"

She couldn't tell him what it was she needed so badly. He'd already told her that what she wanted was impossible.

"I have more than enough," she said instead, trying to smile. "More than I ever expected." Firmly she pushed her aching need back into a corner of her heart.

"Party of the Second Part," he said wryly, "you're lying. But I'll leave that to another day."

Her heart had skidded to a halt, then painfully started again. She watched as Jake slid from the covers, overtly admiring his naked body as he reached for his clothes. It was becoming more and more difficult for her to hide the truth from him. She knew that it wouldn't be long before he guessed how she felt about him. Whether he would accept her love or not was what drove her to the brink of despair every time she thought of the contract.

"Let's go Christmas shopping on the way home," he said, zipping his jeans. "Come on, Laurie, up and at 'em." He punctuated the command with a playful smack to her bottom.

Laura laughed and kicked off the covers, diving for her clothes on the chair. Her face was flushed, but it was from the nickname he'd used. Jake had called Molly by a nickname before, but never Laura. She was still grinning as she washed her face and brushed her hair.

As they walked to his truck later in the morning, having brought the remaining food with them and closed up the cabin, Jake put his arm around Laura's shoulders. She glanced back at the cabin through the frost on the truck window and sighed.

"Do you think we could come back sometime?" she asked wistfully.

Jake paused with the key in the ignition. "Do you mean that?" he asked.

"Yes, of course." Looking into his face, she realized that he truly had never shared this place with anyone else and that it was incredible to him that she liked it as much as he did.

Jake smiled. "Then we'll come here every chance we get."

Laura was in an incredibly good mood as they drove back toward town, so good that she managed to coax Jake into singing a chorus of "Santa Claus is Coming to Town" with her.

A mud-spattered white van had been behind them from the moment they'd turned onto the main highway into town, and Jake idly wondered where the guy behind the wheel was headed. Probably out to visit his mother, he thought, dismissing his initial unease as the van passed them when they pulled into the parking lot of the strip mall.

His gray eyes were alight with pleasure as he helped her out of the truck. They picked their way over the hard clumps of snow shoveled from the sidewalk and stepped inside the warmth of the department store. Most of the town's shops didn't open until noon on Sunday, but this was the Christmas season, after all, and already business was brisk.

"Why don't we look at these dresses?" Jake suggested, and Laura raised her brows.

"Is this a recent interest of yours?" she teased him.

"Very recent," he said, "and if you give me any more trouble you're going to find coal in your stocking."

She grinned back, having every intention of giving him more trouble. But then she saw the black cocktail dress he'd hooked from the rack. He held it up with one finger, his dark brows drawn up in speculation.

Jake watched her eyes darken in pleasure as she looked at the dress. He could picture her in it, the thin straps showing off her slender shoulders, the shiny fabric clinging to her breasts and hips. Her skin would look milky next to the black, her hair a glorious contrast of silky heat.

"Try it on," he urged her, dangling the dress just inches from her. "I want to see how you look in it." He already knew how she'd look, and he was anticipating that, his belly tightening with slow heat.

Laura gave him a soft, teasing smile. "All right," she said in a husky voice.

He watched her disappear into the dressing room, marveling at the change in her in the short time they'd been married. She had shunned makeup and sexy dresses when he first met her. Not that she'd really needed them to look pretty. But now she was like a flower that had finally opened to reveal a stunning beauty. Sometimes it took his breath away to see her walk into a room. He had to constantly remind himself that she was his wife, that he had a right to look at her like a starved man, a right to take her to bed and make love to her until they were both exhausted.

But it was only a piece of paper that gave him that right, he always reminded himself. There were no other ties to hold her to him or him to her. No emotional strings. He was giving her all he was capable of giving, and it sometimes saddened him that she might at some point find another man capable of giving her more. When that thought crossed his mind his heart would contract painfully.

When Laura emerged from the changing rooms all thoughts left Jake's head. She was a vision, her hair tumbling around her neck and bare shoulders, her eyes a deep, smoky blue with all the beguiling invitation of a temptress. He had been right about the dress clinging to her breasts and hips, and the sight left him staring and speechless.

"What do you think of it?" she asked softly.

"I think," he said, "that I'll probably never let you leave the house wearing that dress." It was a chauvinistic statement and one that he sincerely meant.

Laura smiled, her eyes meeting his with unspoken messages. She glanced over his shoulder and suddenly froze, her smile sliding away.

Jake turned to see what had chilled her so quickly.

Instinctively he stepped in front of Laura as if to protect her. Trina stood watching them from several feet away, her arms crossed over her winter coat, her expression grim and filled with disapproval. After so long a time without a word from her, her sudden appearance was even more of a shock.

Behind her Jake could see her husband—or at least a portly man he assumed was her husband. It was obvious from his resigned stance that his wife made the decisions in the marriage. And no doubt without consulting him.

It always irritated Jake when he ran into someone like Trina, someone who took it upon herself or himself to pass judgment on the rest of the world. And it was judgment that Trina was most assuredly thinking about at the moment.

To his surprise, Trina turned without a word and stalked away. Her husband stood a moment, unsure of himself, then nodded uncomfortably to Jake and Laura and moved on.

"What do you suppose she was doing?" Laura asked in a quiet voice next to him.

Jake automatically put his arm around her shoulders. "I don't know," he said. "Maybe it was just a chance meeting."

Laura shivered. "Not where Trina's involved. That woman leaves nothing to chance." Especially where her granddaughter was concerned.

Trina's appearance threw a specter over their shopping trip, and Laura and Jake decided to go to Ali's house to pick up Molly after they'd bought the black dress. Laura was uneasy, remembering the last time Trina had contacted Molly at Ali's house. She grew more withdrawn the closer the truck got to the place.

Jake reached over and clasped her hand. "Whatever it is this time, we'll deal with it," he told her with quiet authority.

She believed him. But still, her heart lurched when Ali opened the door with worry in her eyes. Molly was standing behind her, her finger stuck in her mouth, a habit she had broken when she was three years old.

Laura knelt down to hug her daughter, her eyes seeking Ali's over Molly's head.

Ali took a deep breath and nodded. "She was here," she said almost inaudibly.

Over coffee, Molly on Laura's lap, Ali told them that Trina had knocked on the door, her husband in tow, and demanded to see Molly. When Ali refused, Trina began shouting, and Molly heard her. She came to the door, and Trina told her to start packing, that Molly was coming to live with her.

"Trina said that it wouldn't be much longer that she, quote, 'Had to put up with her sleazy, so-called daughter-in-law and her drunken husband.'" Ali was nearly shaking with her anger. She shot an apologetic glance at Jake.

"I shouldn't even have repeated what she said," she said, clasping her hands on the table, "but she just makes me so mad."

Laura met Jake's eyes over the table. So the marriage hadn't deterred Trina from her original objective—to obtain custody of Molly. What now?

Laura saw the answer in Jake's steely gaze. His gray eyes never wavered. *We fight.*

"I'll call Rowen in the morning," he said as if in answer to a question he'd felt more than heard.

Laura felt suddenly weary, as if a huge weight had descended once again onto her shoulders. This wasn't fair, she thought. It wasn't fair to Molly who was so scared of losing her mother that she was becoming a withdrawn, insecure child again under this latest threat. It wasn't fair to Laura who had worked so hard to establish a new life and earn a little happiness. And it wasn't fair to Jake who had taken on her burdens without asking for anything in return. This would tax him emotionally, socially and possibly financially.

She thought again of the marriage contract. He was the one giving everything. And the only thing she had to give him in return was something he didn't want, her love.

It had been an impossible arrangement from the beginning, but she'd been too besotted with the man to see it.

Neither spoke on the ride home, and Molly sat silently between them, her finger still stuck in her mouth.

When they were inside their own home, Jake turned up the heat and carried their suitcase upstairs while Laura sat with Molly on the parlor couch and tried to comfort her.

But Molly wouldn't talk about Trina or anything else for that matter. She leaned against Laura and stared at the opposite wall. This was breaking Laura's heart, but she had to do something. Talking obviously wasn't working, so she held Molly, put her arm around her and pressed her tightly against her side.

Jake came back into the room, took one look at them and ran his hand through his hair, visibly angry. "Do you need anything?" he asked Laura.

She shook her head, dredging up a smile of gratitude.

"Is Grandma going to make you go away from Mom, too?" Molly asked him around the finger in her mouth.

Jake's jaw clenched before he answered. "No, honey. Your grandmother can never do that. And she's not going to take you away, either." He looked at Laura and started for the kitchen. "I'm going to call Rowen now."

"Jake, it's Sunday," Laura protested.

She couldn't hear what he answered because he was well on his way to the kitchen by then.

He didn't tell her what Rowen had said until much later that night after Molly was asleep. Still withdrawn, Molly had spent the afternoon and evening in a silent vigil at the window, her eyes fixed on something in the distance only she could see. Laura was exhausted and restless by the time she had assured herself that her daughter was asleep.

Laura was already in bed waiting when Jake finally slid under the covers. He didn't reach for her immediately, and Laura felt her anxiety grow. Had Trina finally succeeded in driving a wedge between them?

Laura waited for what seemed an eternity, then hesitantly reached out and touched his shoulder. His arm came out and caught her to him, so quickly that it took away her breath.

He didn't have to tell her how much he needed her. It was there in his touch, his hungry kiss, his shaky breath.

They found respite from their worry in each other's arms, and when they lay quietly together afterward Jake told her what Rowen had said.

"Trina's lawyer is from out of town, and he's already been following us and asking questions. That's apparently how Trina's been able to find out when Molly's at Ali's house." What Jake didn't tell her was that he was pretty sure the lawyer drove a white van. "I doubt if the lawyer is too experienced if he can't afford to hire someone to do his spying for him. Rowen thinks he and Trina must be trying to build a case of child neglect."

"Neglect?" Laura said the word in utter disbelief.

"I know. It doesn't seem at all possible. But, remember, the lawyer's not from around here, and Trina's living in her own little deluded world. She's not going to get off our backs until we do something, Laurie."

Laura went weak inside. He'd said *we* and he'd called her Laurie again. She hadn't realized until this moment how isolated and alone she'd felt since they'd seen Trina in the store. But Jake saw this as their problem, not hers alone.

"What's the matter?" he asked as she took a shaky, audible breath in her relief. He pulled her more closely against his bare chest.

"I was afraid . . ." She didn't know how to tell him about her doubts. "I'm sorry for dragging you into all of this."

"You didn't drag me into anything," he said emphatically. "This is precisely why we got married, to keep Trina from—" He stopped abruptly, realizing what he'd said and how callous it must sound. "Laura, I didn't mean—"

She stopped him by placing two fingers against his lips. "It's all right, Jake," she said in a resigned voice. "I understand. I accepted that when we got married." But though she said the words, she knew that they weren't true. If she were honest she'd admit that she'd never really accepted that as the basis for their marriage. She had cared about Jake from the beginning and had deluded herself into believing otherwise because of the contract. It was too late now.

"What are we going to do?" she asked, marshaling more steadiness than she felt into her voice.

She felt Jake's chest rise and fall as he sighed heavily, apparently unwilling to continue any discussion of why they got married.

"Rowen is a firm believer in settling things outside of court whenever possible. Especially in this case where Molly would be traumatized by having to watch her grandmother publicly battle her mother over who gets custody."

Traumatized was an apt word, Laura thought bitterly. As anxious and worried as she was, she realized that Molly was feeling those emotions on an even more frightening level. And she had only a child's experience in coping with them.

"Does Rowen suggest that we meet with Trina and try to settle this?"

"Yes, but not the way you think."

"What does he have in mind?" she asked warily. "I have to be honest. I'm not going to make concessions to Trina. Not where Molly is concerned." And she couldn't imagine

Trina Halstead actually negotiating. The woman wanted her own way with no room for compromise.

"No concessions," Jake assured her. "Rowen suggests that we throw a little Christmas party. Invite all our friends. Rowen included," he added dryly. "Then invite Trina and her husband. And make sure that everyone else is here before Trina arrives."

Laura was beginning to understand. "Present a united front, so to speak?"

She felt Jake nod, his chin moving against her hair. "Trina may have someone checking up on us, but she can only know bits and pieces of what your life is like. She obviously still thinks you're alone with few friends and no means of emotional support. I'm sure she thinks she can frighten you into giving up. We need to show her otherwise."

"What about Molly?" Laura asked, maternal instinct making her worry about what effect this would have on her daughter. "What if things get ugly at the party and Molly's there?"

Jake's arm tightened around her. "We're a family, Laura. It's important that Molly know that, too. If we send her away she won't understand."

He was right, of course. Molly was the center of all this contention. It wasn't fair to her to keep her completely apart from it. She had already faced Trina's bitterness without her mother present. It was time she knew that her parents were there for her.

Parents. She didn't even know when she had begun to think of Jake as Molly's father. He was such an integral part of both their lives. And all because of a piece of paper he'd signed.

"All right," Laura said softly. "I'll start planning a party. When should we have it?"

"The sooner the better. How about this Friday night?"

It wasn't much time to prepare, but Laura recognized the dangers of procrastinating. Trina could file a custody petition at any time now. Then things would really get messy.

"Friday night," she agreed. She didn't want to leave the security of his arms. Here she felt warm and protected, a luxury she hadn't known until she'd married Jake. So she stayed where she was, snuggled against him, thinking about the party as if it were a test of fire.

When she woke in the morning just before dawn, she was still in Jake's arms. She had turned during the night so that his chest was against her back. Now he had one leg and one arm thrown over her and his face nestled against her neck. His breath was warm and even.

She could stay like this forever, she thought in drowsy contentment. Laura was just drifting off to sleep again when she heard a noise down the hall. It sounded like crying.

She slid out from under Jake's arm and leg and pulled on her robe, padding silently out the bedroom door.

The whimpering sounds continued, and now she was sure it was Molly. She stopped at her bedroom door, trying to adjust her eyes to the dim glow of the night-light. Everything was shadows as she moved quietly toward the bed.

"Molly?" she whispered. "What's wrong, honey?"

There was no answer, and she reached out to touch the covers on the bed only to find them empty. "Molly?" she said again.

Laura could make out shapes in the room now, and she quickly scanned everything. "Molly, where are you?" she asked, beginning to feel the first bubbles of panic. But she forced herself to remain calm for her daughter's sake.

Another sniffle seemed to come from somewhere near the bed. Laura followed the sound and knelt. "Molly, are you under there?" She stretched out her hand, feeling around beneath the bedskirt until she found Molly shivering in her pajamas.

"Come out of there, sweetie," Laura coaxed her, stroking her shoulder and hair. "You're cold."

"I'm afraid," Molly whispered in a trembling voice, but she scooted closer to her mother.

"Did you have a nightmare?"

Laura felt Molly nod under her hand. "Someone came to take me away," she said, her voice breaking.

"So you hid from them," Laura concluded, remembering how Molly used to hide when she was younger whenever she had a nightmare. "You should have come and gotten me, honey."

"They told me I couldn't see you again," Molly whimpered. "Promise me you won't leave me."

Laura promised her around the lump in her throat. She gathered her daughter to her, pulling her gently from under the bed, and rocked her back and forth.

"Is she all right?" Jake's voice asked from behind her, and Laura turned her head to see his dark silhouette filling the doorway. She felt immeasurably soothed herself by his presence.

"She had a nightmare," Laura said. She didn't have to elaborate. She knew by the way Jake strode over to the bed and by the edge in his voice as he spoke again that he knew exactly what had prompted the nightmare.

"Here, pumpkin," he said, easily taking Molly from Laura's arms and holding her until Laura was seated on the bed. He put Molly back in Laura's lap, but as he sat down on the bed beside her Molly leaned over to put her arm around his neck.

Jake was nearly bumping noses with Laura in the awkward position, but he felt a warmth spread through him as he realized that Molly wanted his comforting, too.

He managed to reach behind his back and locate an extra blanket. Pulling it loose, he brought it around and settled it over Molly. "Better?" he asked softly.

She nodded against his neck, apparently still reluctant to give up her grip on both him and Laura.

Molly finally raised her head and leaned back, bracing one hand against Jake's chest. "Mom promised me she wouldn't never, ever leave me." She was regarding Jake solemnly, hopefully.

He smiled at her and said, "And I promise to never, ever leave you, either."

That matter resolved, she settled back against his shoulder. A second later she giggled lightly. "You got hair and it tickles my hand," she said. "How come you don't got pajamas on top?"

"Because I've got hair to keep me warm," he said teasingly, making her giggle again.

"I think you'd better get back under the covers," Laura told Molly. "It's going to be time to get up soon."

Molly sighed. "Do I have to?"

Laura considered. "Not if you want to help me fix breakfast."

"I can fix breakfast," Jake offered. "Then you two ladies can take your time getting dressed."

That made Molly giggle again, and Laura smiled at Jake. The sky was lightening up enough outside to make out his features. They were rough and impossibly handsome. She let her eyes wander over him a little longer before she abruptly looked away, afraid he might be able to read her expression in the growing light.

When Laura and Molly came downstairs, full of compliments for his bacon and eggs, Jake let himself watch Laura covertly as she poured the orange juice. How was it possible that a woman could become more beautiful every day?

Her skin glowed, her hair gleamed, and her eyes seemed to deepen into sapphires whenever they lingered on him. She was wearing blue corduroy slacks and a dark blue pullover sweater that traced her curves. He was amused to see a tiny gold earring at each ear.

His Laura was quite a woman.

His. It surprised him that he'd begun to think of her like that, as his. Not as a possession by right of the contract but as his woman, the one who belonged at his side, tucked against his heart the way they had slept last night.

He wanted to stay with her and Molly, but he had to meet Billy and Frank early this morning. They were framing up an addition to an older home, and he was needed. They had to start early to get as much done as possible.

"I've got to go," he said, glancing at the kitchen clock and grabbing his coat from a hook by the back door. "See you tonight." He stopped to press a soft kiss on her mouth while he ruffled Molly's hair.

Jake could feel how much Laura wanted him to stay, though she would never say it. He silently cursed the timing that necessitated his absence today.

"Want to come along?" he asked her.

Laura shook her head. "I need to get some things done around here. Emma's coming back tomorrow." She brought his head back down to hers when he would have moved away, kissed him and murmured, "Thank you, Jake."

He was smiling all the way to the truck and halfway to the job site. But when he was about to pull into the driveway he caught sight of a white van coming in the opposite direction, and his mood soured.

Let Trina and her spies do what they wanted, he thought malevolently. There was no way he was letting that woman hurt Molly or Laura.

Frank and Billy arrived in separate trucks a short time later while Jake was still unloading tools. "I haven't had any coffee yet," Frank grumbled. "Don't say nothin' to me until I do." With that he sat on the open tailgate of his truck and unscrewed his thermos flask. He took three long gulps, then wiped his mouth with the back of his hand.

"I take it you didn't have breakfast with Esther this morning," Jake guessed, amused.

"Oh, I had breakfast with her all right," Frank grumbled. "The dang woman couldn't get an order right if her life depended on it. And, as for coffee—" Frank snorted "—she totally forgot how to make the stuff. She might as well of been pourin' crankcase oil."

Billy sighed and rolled his eyes. "Burned the toast, too. Like charcoal."

"And what had her so upset?" Jake asked.

"Some idiot in there asking a lot of questions about you and how you used to drink," Billy answered immediately, coming to a halt only at the jolt of Frank's elbow in his ribs.

"Ah, jeez, Jake," Billy said apologetically. "I didn't mean nothin' by that."

Jake waved away his apology. "I know that, Billy. Who was doing the asking?"

"I think he's some lawyer for Laura's ex-mother-in-law," Frank said, still glaring at Billy. "Esther nearly poured a pot of coffee in his lap. And then she chased him out of there. If she hadn't, someone else woulda. She weren't worth a plugged nickel as far as work goes after that. She finally went out back to commune with that concrete elf of hers."

Jake smiled grimly. Knowing Esther, she would still be upset. And word would spread quickly. By noon everyone in town would know that Trina had hired someone to dig up dirt on Jake.

"So what are you goin' to do about it?" Billy asked, his brow furrowed. Billy didn't often worry, but when he did, he did a thorough job of it.

"I'm going to throw a party," Jake said, still smiling.

"You're what?" Frank asked.

"Laura and I are having a party Friday night," Jake said. "You're all invited—and so are Trina and her husband."

"Oh, man," Frank said, wide-eyed. "This is going to be a showdown, isn't it? You and Laura against Trina Halstead."

"Not quite that dramatic, I hope," Jake said. "We aren't going to gun her down, Frank. Just let her see what Laura's and Molly's lives are like now. How many friends Laura has."

Frank nodded slowly. "So she'll realize how flimsy her case really is."

"Exactly," Jake said, reaching into his truck bed to pick up a sawhorse. "It's an old trick I learned from my father. If someone wants to buy only one horse from a team you show him how well the whole team works together. Chances are, he won't break up the set."

It was a huge leap, comparing a team of horses and a family, but Jake knew the concept was one that Frank would understand.

"Yeah, I see," Frank said slowly. "Like a toolbox. Someone ain't gonna take just the hammer when they see how nice everything is in there together."

"Well, *I* don't see it at all," Billy interrupted, frowning. "What's a horse or a toolbox got to do with a party? Is it one of them costume parties or something, Jake?"

Jake grinned and headed for the work site a few yards away, depositing the sawhorse there. Billy was following behind him with the heavy table saw cradled in both his hands.

"Jake, are we supposed to dress up for this party?" he asked worriedly. "Because, if we are, I ain't got anything that—"

"Billy, watch where you're going!" Frank shouted, but the warning came too late.

Billy tripped over the dangling cord from the saw and stumbled forward just as Jake turned around. The saw slipped out of his hands, and before Jake could move it had landed on his foot.

Jake swore loudly and with great pain. Frank hurriedly bent and lifted the saw while Billy stood helplessly, wringing his hands and moaning. "Oh, God, Jake, I'm sorry. Does it hurt?"

Jake let loose with another oath which pretty much answered the question.

"Do you want to sit down, Jake?" Billy asked soliciously. His face was gray, and his lips twitched nervously.

Frank moved in to take over before Jake could utter anything else. Shoving the sawhorse behind Jake, he told him to sit and then he carefully began taking off Jake's work boot.

After Jake howled in pain again, even Frank's face turned gray.

"To the hospital, son," he said, shaking his head.

With both Billy and Frank supporting him, Jake hopped to Frank's truck, then endured the bumpy ride to the hospital, sandwiched between the two men.

And all he could think about over the pain was Laura.

There were things he wanted to do for her yet before Christmas, and now with a broken foot . . .

And then there was the party. She was going to have to do
almost all of the preparation by herself. He would be little
help, if any. He cursed under his breath again.

"Jake, would it help if I sing?" Billy asked hesitantly.

"Sing?" Jake repeated, thinking he must not have heard
correctly. "You want to sing?"

"I don't *want* to, Jake, but if it would take your mind off
your foot—"

"Hell, no, Billy, I don't want you to sing!" Jake managed to get out from between clenched teeth. "Why on earth
would you think I did?"

"Because," Billy said nervously, "you look like you're
going to poke me in the eye, and I thought you might not if
I was to start singing."

It made no sense at all to Jake, and he began to wonder
if a broken foot could cause a man to lose his mind.

"Billy," he said with more calmness than he felt, "I don't
want you to sing, and I'm not going to poke you in the eye.
Is that clear?" He turned his head to glare at Billy, softening when he saw Billy's trembling lip.

"Are you sure, Jake? Do you still want me to come to
your party?"

"I'm sure, Billy," Jake repeated patiently. "And I want
you to come to the party."

"You ain't gonna drop something on my foot if I come,
are you?"

Jake was sorely tempted, but before he could answer
Frank interrupted.

"He ain't gonna drop nothin' on your foot, but if you
don't stop pesterin' him he's liable to choke you."

That quieted Billy, and a short time later they pulled up
in front of the hospital.

Before a nurse shuttled Jake away in a wheelchair, he told
Frank to call Laura. "But don't scare her," he warned.

She was scared. Jake could hear it in the slight tremor in
her voice that came from the other side of the door. He
cursed inwardly and pulled the hospital gown down over his

legs as far as he could. It was beyond him why they had to cut off his pants to treat his broken foot. But an efficient, no-nonsense nurse had done just that, and now he sat perched on an examining table, bare legs stretched out in front of him, a paper-thin gown barely covering half his thighs.

The door opened, and a far-too-cheerful nurse chirped, "Here's someone I bet you're glad to see." She beamed as a hesitant Laura came inside, then added before exiting again, "The doctor should be back any minute with your X rays."

Laura looked perilously close to crying. "Jake," she said, standing in the middle of the room as if she'd just been beamed there by aliens, "are you okay?"

"Not until you come here and kiss me, Laurie," he told her, holding out one arm.

She came immediately, her voice choking as she said, "Oh, honey, it must hurt so much."

It did, but he truly didn't mind at the moment because Laura was hugging him fiercely, her arms locked tight around his neck. Her mouth blindly sought his, pressing one fervent kiss after another on him. It was the best painkiller he knew.

The door popped open, and a doctor came in with an X ray, smiling genially. "Well, it looks broken all right."

"The problem with this hospital," Jake growled, "is that everyone is too damn cheerful." But his crabbiness didn't go more than skin-deep. He kept fighting the urge to smile because Laura had called him "honey."

"Should I go tell Frank and Billy that you're all right?" Laura asked as the doctor sat down to examine Jake's foot again. "They're really worried. Frank said Billy's on his seventh cup of coffee."

"Ah, good grief," Jake said. "He won't sleep for two weeks. Yeah, go tell them I'm fine." He clutched Laura's hand as she started to leave. "Then come right back."

Laura nodded and squeezed his hand. She stopped at the door and took one last look at him, trying to smile. He could see that she was fingering the gold key at her throat, probably without even realizing it.

Jake could feel a warmth in his chest that had nothing to do with his broken foot.

Chapter Fifteen

"Do you think Molly would like this dollhouse?" Jake said from the kitchen table. He held up the catalog as Laura peered over his shoulder.

"She'd love it," Laura said, "but it's awfully expensive."

Jake only snorted, his usual reaction lately when she commented that something he intended to buy as a Christmas present was expensive.

Since he had broken his foot on Monday he'd been pretty much laid up at home. He could hobble around on crutches, but he'd done that only one day. That was Wednesday when he had to supervise Billy and Frank as they framed the room addition on the site where Jake had broken his foot. Or, as he preferred to think, Billy had broken it for him.

Even that day he'd had to supervise from a chair with his foot propped up on a sawhorse. It was still painful, and he was under orders to keep it elevated as much as possible.

But that didn't stop him from Christmas shopping at home from catalogs.

"Was Christmas a big deal at your house?" she asked, amused at how seriously he was taking this task.

"Oh, yes," he assured her as he wrote down the doll-house item number so he could phone in the order. "But we never had much money, so presents weren't a large part of it. Mom made cookies and breads and we boys all helped her decorate the tree. Usually we got some new underwear and a pair of pants for Christmas. Which," he said, turning to look at her as she cleared the lunch dishes, "is why I'm *really* enjoying shopping for toys."

Laura smiled. Jake had already written checks for several local charities and had even let Ali talk him into playing Santa Claus for the downtown merchants on weekends. "We can paint your cast black like a boot and prop your foot up on a wrapped box," Ali had assured him enthusiastically. And Jake had agreed.

He was truly enjoying Christmas this year, and it made her curious. Did having a child around change things so much for him?

"I was wondering," she began hesitantly, scanning his face. "Did you and your wife have a big Christmas?"

"*You're* my wife," he said immediately, catching her arm and pulling her close to him. "As for the past, no, it was quiet. Beverly's family wanted us to celebrate at their house. Things were a little more...reserved there."

She read between the lines enough to guess that Beverly' parents had been less demonstrative than Jake would have preferred.

"What about you?" he asked. "What were Christmases like for you?"

"Not much," she said honestly. "My parents did most of their celebrating with friends. I got the usual complement of dolls and other presents, but I spent most of the time playing by myself." She didn't mean to whine about it, and she added, "They weren't bad Christmases, by any means."

No, that came later, Jake thought grimly. And if he knew Laura, she wasn't going to complain.

"Well, I never cared for Christmas since I grew up," Jake said, sighing. "It seemed like a holiday specifically designed to make the loners feel even more alone."

Laura nodded, absently stroking his shoulder. Yes, a man who didn't love anyone would certainly feel lonely at Christmas. She'd felt that way herself before she had Molly.

And it was obvious that Jake still felt that way. Her heart contracted when she realized that she was going to have to tell him very soon that she had fallen in love with him. And then would come the inevitable parting. Unless Jake wanted to continue to live together. But she would find that the worst misery of all, loving him, being with him, and knowing he could never return her feelings.

No, it would have to be a clean break.

Restless, she moved back to the counter.

"Is Ali coming to the party tonight?" she asked. She had deliberately put the party out of her mind except for the cooking. She didn't want to think of the few people who would come just to make a show of support for her. Jake had done the inviting, and she had kept out of it. She'd had enough disappointments in her dealings with people. The numerous turndowns she expected were more than she wanted to handle. Ali was the only one she knew she could count on.

"She's coming, and she said to tell you she'll bring plenty of cookies."

They wouldn't need them, Laura thought despondently. She'd made a chocolate sheet cake and a cherry pie herself, and she was sure that would be more than enough. But it was no use worrying about things that wouldn't change.

Trina would be there for sure. Jake had called her, and Laura had heard the satisfaction in his voice when she said she would come. He told Laura after he hung up that Trina sounded surprised . . . and a little gloating. Laura supposed that Trina imagined that her legal threats had scared Jake and Laura enough to make them conciliatory.

Trina would be in for a surprise if that was what she really thought, but Laura was afraid that tonight would accomplish nothing other than to show just how alone Laura and Molly really were.

People began arriving just before seven that evening, and Laura felt a little overwhelmed as they came into the house one by one and complimented her and Jake on what they'd done with it. There were warm hugs and small gifts of cookies and fruitcake.

Molly took Ali's daughter Beth up to her bedroom to play. Ali followed Laura into the kitchen with the plate of cookies she'd brought.

"Is she coming?" Ali asked as soon as they were alone.

Laura nodded, nervously fingering the tiny key on the chain at her neck. "Jake said she sounded as if she thought we were caving in to her."

"Then she's in for quite a surprise," Ali said without humor. "She's about to get a look at what she's up against."

Laura cocked one eyebrow skeptically. "Ali, I think you're overestimating this get-together."

Ali just smiled and shook her head. "No, Laura, you're underestimating yourself."

And maybe Ali was right, Laura thought as she greeted yet another person at the door. She glanced at Jake, who had taken a chair right next to the door so he could rise and greet everyone as they came in. He winked at her, and she couldn't help smiling back despite her worry.

Everything in the house was ready for Christmas. She and Molly had decorated the tree in the parlor under Jake's watchful eye. They'd arranged evergreen boughs and pine cones on the mantels and around the old photographs by the front door. The lights were low, and candles gleamed on the tables among the miniature Victorian Christmas trees and lace sachet angels. A second small Christmas tree sat in one corner of the foyer, decorated with candy canes, ribbons and sugar cookies.

Jake must have invited everyone he knew plus most of he customers, Laura thought in wonder. Even Emma and he mother came in, smiling shyly, and shaking Jake's hand.

Laura thought she couldn't be surprised anymore, when she opened the door to the next knock and found Jake's two brothers, his mother and John's wife, Rachel, on her doorstep. She tried not to cry as she hugged each one in turn.

It had never occurred to her that Jake's family would come, and she realized now what a difference it made in how she felt. She was stronger, more confident and secure. She had never had a family stand up for her before, and she was moved to tears.

"Are you all right?" Rachel asked gently as she held Laura away from her.

Laura nodded, too overcome to speak for the moment.

"This has been difficult for her," Elizabeth said, putting an arm around Laura's shoulders. "Heaven knows, I don't think I could have taken it as well as Laura."

"Do you know how much this means to me?" Laura managed to ask when she could control her voice. "No one ever...I mean, it's so...wonderful." It was an inadequate word to describe what she felt, but it was the best she could do at the moment.

"Oh, honey, I know," Elizabeth said soothingly, tightening her hug. "Don't you worry about a thing. It's all going to be just fine."

"And I'd stake St. Jude's reputation on that," Esther said as she came through the door.

Laura laughed and hugged her, too. "All right. You've all bolstered my confidence several notches. Now go have fun." She shooed them into the room to help themselves to cookies and eggnog and join in the growing volume of conversation.

Jake caught her hand before she could leave, and she mustered a smile for him. She was going to have to tell him the truth after tonight. She was in love with him. She had all but told him when she walked into the hospital room and saw him on the examining table. And even though she hadn't said the words, her face must have spoken volumes. Jake would have seen it if he hadn't been in pain.

No, she would tell him when the party was over. And in the meantime she would try to figure out what she and Molly would do when he was gone.

"Go mingle with your guests," Jake whispered. "I'll stay here."

"As if you could go anywhere else," she teased him gently, her heart breaking as her own double meaning sank in.

Jake grinned. "I'll show you the places I can go when we're alone," he said in a low voice that made the heat climb her neck.

Laura squeezed his hand and moved away as Rowen called her name from the couch in the parlor. "You come tell me how Jake *really* broke his foot," Rowen urged her. "I want to hear the true story."

Laura couldn't help smiling, but her smile froze when the door opened, and she glanced behind her to see Corky Fife Beachem standing in the foyer, shaking Jake's hand. Jake took Corky's fur coat and raised one brow before hanging it on the hall tree with the others. He turned, caught Laura's eye and grinned.

"Good Lord," she murmured under her breath. Rowen chuckled.

Corky took a quick regal assessment of the room before she saw Laura, who had recovered enough to move forward to greet her.

"You and Jake have done wonders with this house," Corky said, extending her hand for a brisk handshake. She looked around and nodded again. "Yes, very nice."

"I'm glad you could come tonight," Laura said, still feeling as though she would wake up any minute to discover the house silent and none of these people—especially Corky Beachem!—here.

Corky offered a small smile. "I think you're making... a splendid addition to the business community."

When Corky had moved on to speak to someone else, Laura nearly collapsed onto the couch next to Rowen.

"Did she really say what I thought she said?" Laura asked.

Rowen laughed. "That is as close to an apology as you'll get from Corky Beachem."

"But, why—" Laura began, still bewildered.

"I imagine part of it has to do with the fact that Trina and her lawyer have been irritating a lot of folks around here with their questions. They're outsiders, and we don't take kindly to an outsider harassing one of our own."

"But I'm an outsider," Laura protested.

Rowen shook his head. "Not anymore. You grew up here, you've moved back to run a business, and you're married to Jake. You no longer qualify as an outsider, my dear." Rowen smiled. "And then, there's something else to consider. Corky's daughter bought one of your christening gowns for her first child, due in three months. It will be Corky's first grandchild. Laura, you are now officially an institution around here, at least in Corky Beachem's eyes."

"God help me," Laura muttered, and Rowen roared with laughter.

"And let me add," Rowen said, wiping his eyes with his handkerchief, "that you look smashing tonight."

Laura smiled. Jake had insisted that she wear the black cocktail dress he was so fond of.

The mention of the christening gown reminded Laura of something else she needed to do, and she excused herself to go find Rachel. She had intended to wait until Christmas, but she knew that she and Jake wouldn't be together then. Once she confessed to Jake that she had fallen in love with him, she was prepared to take Molly and stay in a motel until he moved his things. She had even prepared herself to offer to sell the house so he could recoup the money he had invested in repairs.

Her heart felt like lead every time she thought of going on without Jake.

Finding Rachel in the kitchen talking about candy making with Emma, Laura apologized for interrupting and asked to see Rachel in the workroom.

"You look worried," Rachel said as soon as they were alone. She reached out to squeeze Laura's shoulder. "Are you all right?"

No, she wasn't. Her heart was breaking every time she thought about her impending talk with Jake. But that wasn't what she needed to do right now.

"I have something for you," Laura said, picking up the wrapped box on the table and handing it to Rachel.

Glancing at her quizzically, Rachel opened the box. She gave a muffled gasp as she drew out the christening gown, then hugged Laura long and hard.

"It's exquisite!" Rachel cried. "Oh, Laura, what a wonderful present. Elizabeth will be thrilled when she sees it. I can't tell you how it feels to have something this beautiful to give my children and then their children."

They hugged again, but Laura tensed when she heard the front door open again and then silence.

"I'd better get out there," she said reluctantly, giving Rachel a weary smile before she moved away.

"Remember, Laura," Rachel said with quiet determination behind her, "we're all here for you."

But Laura felt as if she were drifting into a bad dream instead of waking from one. Trina stood stiffly and grimly in the foyer, her husband Melvin behind her.

This was all so futile, Laura thought as she moved forward. Even if Trina backed down tonight, once Laura and Jake separated she would be at it again. The only thing Laura could foresee was moving herself and Molly farther away from here.

Poor Molly, she thought in despair. Her heart would break when Jake left.

Jake was offering to hang up their coats, but Trina was refusing, drawing herself up to her full height, which wasn't all that imposing next to Jake.

Behind her, Melvin shuffled uneasily from one foot to the other. It was obvious that he would rather be anywhere else than here.

"Come on in," Jake said, his eyes catching Laura's. She could see the reassuring smile there, though Trina would not notice it.

"I'm going to say what I came to say and then leave," Trina said coolly. She looked across the room at Laura and cocked her head slightly to the side. "I'm sure you'd rather I do it in private, so if there's a quiet room—"

"Right here will be fine," Jake said, his amiable expression not slipping even a bit.

The house was slowly growing quiet, and people began to trickle in from other rooms. Laura stood where she was, in front of the staircase, facing Trina across the expanse of the foyer. In distraction she thought what a beautiful job Jake had done on the restoration.

Trina was beginning to look a little uneasy, but she didn't back down.

"All right," she said shortly. "If you want to make this public, it's fine with me." She looked at the faces watching her curiously and said, "This woman isn't fit to raise my granddaughter. She spent time in jail, for God's sake. And, as for this man she married, he's a drunk. And even he didn't trust her. He made her sign a prenuptial agreement. It's all going to come out in court."

Oh, God, Laura thought. *She knows about the contract.* She could feel the room pressing in upon her.

"And how would you know about a prenuptial agreement?" Rowen asked sharply from the parlor doorway.

"*My* lawyer has his sources," Trina said triumphantly. "One of your secretaries is loose-lipped."

"Ex-secretary," Rowen amended dryly. "And as for that agreement, Jake wanted to protect Laura financially if the marriage should fail. The whole thing is to her advantage only. And Laura fought like the devil to keep from signing it." Rowen crossed his arms. "What kind of fool lawyer would take a hopeless case like yours?" His voice was low and casual, but his disgust was unmistakable.

"You may think it's hopeless," Trina said sharply, "but just how many of you would trust this woman with your children? How many of you would stand up for her in a court of law?" Her eyes scanned the room. Almost everyone who had come to the party had moved into the parlor doorway to listen. "I'll wager not a one," she snorted.

His eyes never leaving Laura's, Jake moved slowly toward her, limping on his crutches. She could almost hear what he was willing her to believe. *It's all right. I'm here.*

He took her hand and stood beside her, facing Trina. Laura's hands were shaking, but she grasped Jake's hand firmly.

And then Rachel and John came to stand beside her, John looping his arm around Laura's shoulders. Then Elizabeth joined them, smiling at Laura. Jordan followed. Then Rowen. And Carl. And Frank and Billy with Billy's wife, Myra. Emma and her mother. Ali. Esther. Molly's teacher. The minister who had married Laura and Jake. Mothers and fathers of Molly's classmates. One by one they came to stand with Laura, to touch her shoulder or smile and then move behind her in united support.

They all took a place behind Laura until the only person left in the parlor doorway was Corky Fife Beachem. Trina inclined her head toward Corky, an open invitation—a plea to come to the other side.

But Corky cleared her throat nervously, then joined the group with Laura.

"It looks unanimous," Jake said quietly. "And if you still want to take this to court, I'll spend my last dime defending Laura and Molly from you if necessary."

"You won't need any money, son," Rowen said briskly. "I'll do it for free."

Trina pressed her lips together. "You may have fooled all these people, but you don't fool me," she snapped at Laura. "You can't tell me you live with this man for anything more than money."

Laura took a deep breath. "I live with Jake McClennon because I love him with all my heart. And I will swear that on a stack of Bibles if it comes to that. You're Molly's grandmother, and I want you to be able to see her anytime you want, Trina. But, until you understand that I am Molly's mother, not you, then you are not welcome in this house."

Trina stared at the group facing her, and her shoulders sagged. She looked from one person to another, but with each glance her eyes lost more luster.

The battle was over.

"Come on, Melvin," she said, turning to her husband. "Let's go home."

Melvin followed her out the door, then turned back to look at Laura. For a brief moment their eyes met, and then he smiled.

The door closed, and they were gone.

It was as if everyone let their breath out at once. And then they all began talking.

Laura closed her eyes for a moment, letting their voices wash over her. Each had some word of support or encouragement for her, and though she heard them and responded quietly, she never let go of Jake's hand.

The party continued, and Laura was drawn into conversations with her friends and family. When she looked around later she saw Jake across the room talking to Rowen. He caught her glance and started to move toward her, but she quickly slipped away, pretending she hadn't seen his movement.

It was after midnight when the last guest left. Molly had gone to bed a long time before, right after Ali took Beth home. Now Laura moved restlessly through the house, aimlessly picking up dirty dishes and carrying them to the kitchen.

"I'll help you do the dishes tomorrow," Jake said, coming up behind her.

Not daring to look at him, Laura shook her head. "I'm still tense. I think I'll stay up awhile and work on these. You go ahead to bed."

She could feel him hesitate behind her, assessing her state of mind. And she could sense the question he wasn't asking. Had she meant what she said to Trina about loving him?

"All right," he said at last. "Come to bed when you feel like it. We can talk tomorrow."

Tomorrow.

She listened to him going upstairs and then running water in the bathroom. She knew she was postponing the inevitable, but she didn't want to face it just yet. Not tonight. Not when she still wanted to savor those feelings of finally belonging.

It was ironic. Tonight she had realized that she had everything she had ever wanted—a good man who stood beside her, friends who rallied around her, a place that was hers.

But it was so fleeting. Tomorrow she would have to give it all up. Because she had broken the contract.

Sighing heavily, she turned from the sink, leaving the dirty dishes stacked there, and started up the stairs.

Laura knew that Jake was already in bed. If she slipped in quietly, he wouldn't say anything. He might even be asleep already.

She turned off the last light as she topped the stairs and tiptoed into the bedroom, feeling her way along the dresser top. Suppressing another sigh, she lifted her hair and unclipped the necklace she always wore. Fingering the key for a moment, she set it down on the dresser, knowing that she would never wear it again. Not when everything it stood for would be gone tomorrow.

She slipped one strap from her shoulder, then leaned her hands on the dresser, too weary and sad to move.

"I want to take you out somewhere nice tomorrow night," Jake's voice said from the dark, and Laura jumped. "I want to see you in that dress again."

She tried to marshal a smile but failed miserably as she turned and located him in the chair beside the bed, a shadowy silhouette in the dark.

"About tomorrow night," she began before she lost her courage. If she didn't tell him right now that she would be leaving tomorrow, she didn't think she would be able to face him in the morning. He knew that she loved him; her pride wouldn't let him be the one to leave first.

"Come over here and tell me about tomorrow night," he said quietly, and she saw his arm extend toward her.

Slowly she walked toward him, but she stopped two feet away. "Jake, I need to tell you something."

"Come sit on my lap and tell me," he coaxed her.

"Jake, I—"

But he leaned forward and pulled her to him, turning her until she was off balance and tumbling into his lap. With a satisfied grunt, Jake lifted her legs over the side of the chair.

Curled up intimately against him, she resisted the urge to put her arms around his neck though she wanted to do so badly. The fabric of his pajama bottoms was thin, and she could feel the solidity of his thighs beneath her. Her hand fluttered to his chest, and coherent thought nearly fled when she touched hard, bare flesh. How could she live the rest of her life without him?

"Jake," she said, forcing herself to go through with her confession. She felt as if she would burst into tears at any moment. "I want to thank you for what you did for me tonight."

"I don't deserve the credit," he told her gently, his hand stroking her hair. "All of those people are your friends and family, too. They did what anyone who knows you would do."

"I have to tell you something," she persisted, going very still.

"What is it?" he murmured.

Laura took a deep breath, feeling an incredible ache begin deep in her heart. "I meant what I said to Trina tonight." When he didn't answer, she squeezed her eyes shut and went on. "Jake, I fell in love with you. The contract . . . is broken."

The hand on her hair stopped.

"I know," he whispered.

"You do?" She briefly wondered if it was possible to die of a broken heart.

"Yes, honey. I knew the contract was broken when I saw you come into the hospital room."

"Why didn't you say anything, Jake?" she asked miserably.

"Because, sweetheart," he said, cradling her head against his shoulder, "I was the one who broke it. I knew the minute I looked at your face that I was in love with you. And when you called me 'honey' I knew that I was never going to let you leave my life. I'd only been fooling myself with that contract."

"You love me?" she repeated, too stunned to believe what she was hearing. "Jake, do you mean it?" Beneath her cheek she could feel his heartbeat, as strong and fast as her own.

"Laurie, I've never meant anything more in my life."

"Jake, I—" But she couldn't say anything more at the moment as tears of happiness choked her throat.

When she lifted her head she could see him smiling at her, his own happiness evident in his eyes. The loneliness, the haunted memories were all gone.

"Party of the Second Part," he murmured huskily, lowering his head to hers, "what do you say we tear up that contract tomorrow and then go celebrate?"

"I'd tear it up now if we could," she told him with heartfelt sincerity.

Jake laughed, his mouth nuzzling her neck. "Right now I have another kind of celebration in mind." His mouth traced a path of fire to her shoulder. He slipped her other strap down. "Right now I need to show the woman I love how much she means to me."

Shivering with pleasure, Laura pressed herself tightly against him, finally letting go of the pain and heartbreak of the past.

She was home at last.

*   *   *   *   *

Silhouette®

SPECIAL EDITION™

COMING NEXT MONTH

#1015 SISTERS—Penny Richards
That Special Woman!

Cash Benedict's return meant seeing the woman he'd always wanted but felt he had no right to love. Skye Herder had never forgotten Cash, and now he was about to find out that Skye wasn't the only person he left behind all those years ago....

#1016 THE RANCHER AND HIS UNEXPECTED DAUGHTER—Sherryl Woods
And Baby Makes Three

Harlan Adams was used to getting his way, but feisty Janet Runningbear and her equally spunky daughter weren't making it easy for him. Janet sent Harlan's heart into a tailspin, until he was sure of only one thing—he wanted her as his wife!

#1017 BUCHANAN'S BABY—Pamela Toth
Buckles & Broncos

Not only had Donovan Buchanan been reunited with Bobbie McBride after five years, but he'd just discovered he was the father of her four-year-old daughter! Now that he'd found her, the handsome cowboy was determined to be the best father he could be—as well as future husband to his lost love.

#1018 FOR LOVE OF HER CHILD—Tracy Sinclair

Erica Barclay always put the needs of her son first. But when she fell for Michael Smith, she was torn between passion and her child. Could she still protect her son and listen to the needs of her own heart?

#1019 THE REFORMER—Diana Whitney
The Blackthorn Brotherhood

Strong, loving Letitia Cervantes was just the kind of woman Larkin McKay had been waiting for all his life. And when her son's rebellious spirit called out to the father in him, he wanted to bring them together into a ready-made family.

#1020 PLAYING DADDY—Lorraine Carroll

Cable McRay wasn't interested in taking on fatherhood and marriage. But Sara Nelson made those thoughts near impossible, and her son was proving irresistible—and Cable was soon playing daddy....

As seen on TV!
Free Gift Offer

With a Free Gift proof-of-purchase from any Silhouette® book,
you can receive a beautiful cubic zirconia pendant.

This gorgeous marquise-shaped stone is a genuine cubic
zirconia—accented by an 18" gold tone necklace.

(Approximate retail value $19.95)

Send for yours today...
compliments of ▼ *Silhouette*®

TM

To receive your free gift, a cubic zirconia pendant, send us one original proof-of-purchase, photocopies not accepted, from the back of any Silhouette Romance™, Silhouette Desire®, Silhouette Special Edition®, Silhouette Intimate Moments® or Silhouette Shadows™ title available in February, March or April at your favorite retail outlet, together with the Free Gift Certificate, plus a check or money order for $1.75 U.S./$2.25 CAN. (do not send cash) to cover postage and handling, payable to Silhouette Free Gift Offer. We will send you the specified gift. Allow 6 to 8 weeks for delivery. Offer good until April 30, 1996 or while quantities last. Offer valid in the U.S. and Canada only.

Free Gift Certificate

Name: _____

Address: _____

City: _____ State/Province: _____ Zip/Postal Code: _____

Mail this certificate, one proof-of-purchase and a check or money order for postage and handling to: SILHOUETTE FREE GIFT OFFER 1996. In the U.S.: 3010 Walden Avenue, P.O. Box 9057, Buffalo NY 14269-9057. In Canada: P.O. Box 622, Fort Erie,

---

FREE GIFT OFFER
ONE PROOF-OF-PURCHASE
079-KBZ-R

To collect your fabulous FREE GIFT, a cubic zirconia pendant, you must include this original proof-of-purchase for each gift with the properly completed Free Gift Certificate.

079-KBZ-R

the exciting series by
NEW YORK TIMES BESTSELLING AUTHOR

Nora Roberts

The MacKade Brothers are back—looking for trouble,
and always finding it. Coming this March,
Silhouette Intimate Moments presents

THE HEART OF DEVIN MACKADE

(Intimate Moments #697)

If you liked THE RETURN OF RAFE MACKADE (Silhouette
Intimate Moments #631) and THE PRIDE OF JARED MACK-
ADE (Silhouette Special Edition #1000), you'll love Devin's
story! Then be on the lookout for the final book in the series,
THE FALL OF SHANE MACKADE (Silhouette Special Edition
#1022), coming in April from Silhouette Special Edition.

 These sexy, trouble-loving
men heading out to you in
alternating books from
Silhouette Intimate Moments and
Silhouette Special Edition. Watch out for them!

You're About to Become a

Privileged Woman

Reap the rewards of fabulous free gifts and benefits with proofs-of-purchase from Silhouette and Harlequin books

Pages & Privileges™

It's our way of thanking you for buying our books at your favorite retail stores.

PROOF OF PURCHASE
SSE-PP100
Offer expires October 31, 1996

Pages & Privileges ™

**Harlequin and Silhouette—
the most privileged readers in the world!**

For more information about Harlequin and Silhouette's PAGES & PRIVILEGES program call the Pages & Privileges Benefits Desk: 1-503-794-2499

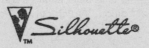

Silhouette®

SSE-PP100